FIC

D0115983

Cancelled

After All

After All

a hanover falls novel

award-winning author

Deborah Raney

HOWARD BOOKS

A DIVISION OF SIMON & SCHUSTER, INC.

New York Nashville London Toronto Sydney New Delhi

49,998

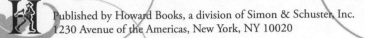 Published by Howard Books, a division of Simon & Schuster, Inc.
1230 Avenue of the Americas, New York, NY 10020

First Howard Books trade paperback edition May 2012

HOWARD and colophon are registered trademarks of Simon & Schuster, Inc.

Designed by Stephanie D. Walker

Manufactured in the United States of America

ISBN 978-1-62090-100-7

For Brynn Jordyn

Acknowledgments

$\mathcal{M}$y sincerest gratitude to the following people for their part in bringing this story to life:

For help with research, ideas, proofreading, and "author support," I am deeply grateful to Kenny and Courtney Ast, Ryan and Tobi Layton, Mary Rintoul, Terry Stucky, Max and Winifred Teeter, Courtney Walsh, the writers of ACFW, and especially the Stark-KS crew (Debbie, Julane, Mary, Sara, Susan) and the Kansas 8 (you know who you are!), who are the best brainstormers on the planet.

To my critique partner and dear friend, Tamera Alexander, thank you for everything you add to my life. You are truly a gem. And more fun than a barrel of monkeys! (I know, I know: *cliché*.) Thanks, especially, for untangling the plot in this story.

To Steve Laube, my agent, going on a decade now: you're still the best!

Deep appreciation to my amazing editors at Howard/Simon & Schuster, and especially to Holly Halverson.

To our precious children, our growing "quiver" of grandchildren, and the amazing extended family God has given us: you all are the joy of my life.

To my husband, Ken: May this new season of our lives together be as blessed as all the others have been.

A special thank-you to the selfless directors and volunteers who keep homeless shelters all across our nation up and running, providing a much-needed service—and often a first introduction to Jesus—for those enduring difficult times.

God is our refuge and strength,
an ever-present help in trouble.
Therefore we will not fear,
though the earth give way
and the mountains fall into the heart of the sea,
though its waters roar and foam
and the mountains quake with their surging.

The LORD Almighty is with us;
the God of Jacob is our fortress.

—Psalm 46:1–3, 7

If she let herself look into the sorrowful eyes of her sons, she would completely fall apart.

1

Tuesday, November 6

Susan Marlowe's three-inch heels sank into the thawing sod. The mournful keen of bagpipes wrapped around her, threatening to drag her under.

She shook the haunting notes from her head. The music wasn't real, but a memory left over from yesterday when a parade of fire trucks had borne the bodies of her husband and four other fallen firefighters down the streets of Hanover Falls, Missouri.

But David had not been buried in the Hanover Falls Cemetery with the others. Instead, as his will had long specified, they'd brought his body here, to Springfield, where he could be laid to rest in the city of his birth, beside his parents' graves.

With each step, a new layer of mud collected on her spikes. Stupid choice . . . to wear these shoes. She could barely walk, and the shoes would be ruined. But David had always loved her in heels. Said they made her legs look sexy.

She bit back a sad smile at the thought. It wouldn't do for the crowd who'd gathered to see her smiling and misunderstand. Or for David Jr. and Daniel, the two strong sons who walked beside her, both called home from college for this somber occasion. Sometimes when she looked at her boys—men now—she had trouble believing she was the mother of grown sons. Most times she didn't feel much older than they were now—though today she felt every one of her forty-two years.

The contingent at the grave was mostly made up of strangers wanting to claim the hometown hero who'd been in national news headlines ever since the tragic fire at Hanover Falls's homeless shelter five days ago. There were TV cameras here, too. Not the national stations that had been at the service in the Falls yesterday. These video cameras, riding the shoulders of photographers at the fringes of the crowd, bore the logos of at least two Springfield stations.

Davy and Danny caught her elbows on either side and followed behind the funeral director and the pastor to the row of folding chairs placed beside the casket. If she let herself look into the sorrowful eyes of her sons, she would completely fall apart. They were taking it hard, but today they'd been strong for her, and for each other.

The funeral tent snapped in the breeze, drowning out the words of the pastor who stood beneath its shadow. The man's gestures drew the crowd under the tent—as many as could squeeze onto the gaudy green AstroTurf carpet. She felt the crush of bodies behind them, blocking the wind, but blocking the sun's warmth, too.

The next twenty minutes passed in a blur. The pastor's voice droned on and she recognized snippets of the Psalms and the poem that was read. David would have declared it "sappy." Her mind raced with regrets. That she hadn't taken more care planning this memorial service. That she hadn't spent more time alone with her sons, letting them talk about how they were feeling.

But more than that. So much regret. She and David still loved each other, yet somehow in the last few months—or was it years now?—they'd let themselves get too busy for each other. He'd been pulling longer shifts since his promotion, and with the boys away at college, she'd poured herself into getting the homeless shelter up and running. She couldn't put her finger on the moment things had started to slide, but something hadn't been quite right between her and David for some time.

Still, they'd had slumps in their marriage before. If David had lived, she felt certain they would have eventually found their way back into each other's hearts. There was some comfort in that. But now she must live with regret, too. That she hadn't made the first move toward him. That she'd let other things take precedence over the most important relationship in her life. That she'd become so caught up in her passion for the shelter that she'd forgotten her passion for David.

She ransacked her brain for a remembrance of better times. Why could she only find arguments and misunderstandings in the catalog of memories accumulated over twenty-four years of marriage? There'd been love there, too. Once upon a time.

Daniel tugged at her sleeve. The brief service was over. David's life, summed up in twenty minutes. A driver from the funeral home waited outside the tent to escort them back to the limousine. Head down, she rose and gripped her sons' arms, wishing her boys could carry her across the barren winter lawn.

She felt the eyes of a hundred strangers follow their path back to the waiting car. Movement to her left made her look up. A woman stood apart from the crowd, half hidden by the gnarled trunk of an ancient cedar. Tall and slender, she wore a dressy black coat, and, like Susan, she had on black stockings and heels. A soft red scarf was wound around her head and neck, but dark hair escaped it, cascading in waves to her shoulders. She was weeping.

Strange. Susan didn't know the woman, but then, with all the media in attendance, she didn't know many of the people here. Still, the reporters weren't dressed in typical funeral garb, and though they wore somber expressions, they weren't crying.

Maybe the woman wasn't here for David's service. Maybe she was visiting a loved one buried in the cemetery. Still, it seemed odd she'd be dressed to the nines for a private visit. She stood apart from the other mourners but she watched them, as if she belonged with them.

The stranger looked up and for the briefest moment, their eyes met. Then the woman looked away quickly, as if she'd been caught staring.

"Mom?"

At the sound of Davy's voice, Susan turned back and continued on to the car.

Against the biting wind, she pulled the collar of her coat around her throat, but the image of that woman's face haunted her.

⁂

*A*ndrea Morley tucked a wayward curl underneath her scarf and blotted a tear with the fingertip of the thin leather dress glove sheathing her hand. It was a wonder her tears didn't freeze on her face.

The wind blew bitter cold across the cemetery. As she'd watched the family and friends huddled beneath the funeral tent, she'd envied the warmth they took from each other. That they had the right to comfort each other.

Oh, God. If you're there . . . forgive me.

She swallowed another swell of tears and winced at the bitter taste that filled her throat. What must it be like to be free to cry over the casket, to speak openly of precious shared memories? She dropped her head. She would never know. And it did no good to stand here and wonder.

She never should have come in the first place. She'd been foolish to take such a risk. As if she hadn't already risked enough—

"Comfort those who weep, Lord God. Grant your mercies . . ." The pastor pronounced a closing prayer over the family.

Andrea gave a little gasp. She should leave before anyone saw her.

But she couldn't seem to make her feet move. Walking away would be the end. Would force her to admit that he was gone and that what they'd shared was over. And she had no one to blame but herself.

The scent of woodsmoke drifted up from the valley, and with it a memory so strong she wasn't sure her legs would hold her against its assault. She reached for the sturdy trunk of a nearby tree and let the images come. They warmed her like sunshine on a frigid day. . . .

She'd been sitting with him in his truck after work one night. She'd brought him coffee from Java Joint and they'd sat in the parking lot behind the firehouse, talking and laughing.

She couldn't even remember now what they were talking about, but something had changed in their friendship that day. She knew the exact moment it had happened. She'd been griping about something, and he'd reached across the seat and patted her arm jokingly. "Poor baby . . ."

She'd giggled, but the laughter caught in her throat when she saw the look in his eyes. She thought he was going to kiss her—*hoped* he would. But he didn't. Not that night. Yet his hand lingered on her arm, and his fingers stroked slow circles on the inside of her wrist, while his eyes—those gorgeous green eyes that crinkled when he smiled—said things she understood as clearly as if he'd written her a letter.

Oh, how she wished she possessed such a letter from him. In paper and ink. But she didn't, and now she never would. Almost two years they'd been together . . . and she had nothing, *nothing* to show for it.

A murmur of voices dragged her back to the present. The service was over and the crowd was heading her way. She had to get out of here. A claw of fear gripped her heart.

She never should have come. She had no right.

. . . she did not want to have to call the police.

2

Eighteen months later, Friday, May 8

Susan stacked clean mugs in the cupboard above the snack counter in the shelter's commons area and dumped the dregs of this morning's coffee into the sink. The aroma, stale as it was, revived her a little.

It was after eight o'clock. Almost dark, and the first-shift volunteers still hadn't shown up. She blew out a sigh. She always sent out e-mail reminders to the shelter volunteers at the beginning of each week but made it a point never to call anyone who didn't show. They didn't owe her anything, and it was their own time they were sacrificing. That was just one downside to running a homeless shelter that depended almost solely on volunteer staff.

"You're still here?" Charlie Branson rolled his wheelchair out of the men's sleeping quarters and gave her a look intended to make her feel guilty.

"We're shorthanded tonight."

Charlie was technically a resident of the shelter, a disabled Vietnam vet who'd been relocated to a shelter in Springfield after the original Grove Street shelter burned down. But once it was up and running at this new location, Susan had persuaded Charlie to return to the Falls and offered him room and board in exchange for some light housekeeping duties and an unofficial title of assistant manager. He took the title very seriously, and the other clients respected his authority.

The shelter operated as overnight only, which served to keep the population to a manageable level. What David had called the "chronically homeless" usually migrated on to Springfield where there were full-time shelters. Here in the Falls, local churches took turns serving a light dinner each evening and provided breakfast fixings for anyone who got out of bed in time. But the shelter was vacated at eight sharp every morning and they locked the facility during the day until Susan or Charlie opened the doors again at five p.m.

Charlie worked at the library downtown shelving books and doing odd jobs, but he was always back in time to open the shelter, and Susan had given him permission to be in the building during daytime hours.

Susan helped Charlie set out leftovers for breakfast and for those who'd be packing lunches tomorrow. Fortunately, they were under capacity this week, with eleven men and a family of five. Two of the guys who worked the night shift hadn't checked in yet, and the rest of the men were either in bed already or in the dayroom watching TV.

Charlie took the dishrag from her and finished wiping off the serving bar. "I've got everything under control here. You go home."

"I will in a few minutes. But I think I'll go catch up on some paperwork first." She could probably trust Charlie to keep things under control until the night shift showed up, but sure as she did that, something would go wrong. She unplugged the coffeemaker and checked the stove one more time, making sure everything was off. The fire—a year and a half ago now—had made everyone extra cautious.

She settled in at her desk, but a minute later Charlie wheeled into the office holding up a bottle of red liquid—cheap wine, by the looks of the label.

"What on earth . . . ?"

Charlie wore a triumphant smirk. "Found this behind the refrigerator."

"You're kidding?"

"Well, it sure ain't mine." He looked offended.

"I know that. But you're sure it's not just—"

Before she could finish her sentence, Charlie had the lid off the bottle. He waved it under her nose.

"Whew . . . Okay, okay . . . It's the real deal." Great. Now she had to deal with it. This was the part of the job she hated.

"You know whose it is, of course."

She eyed him. "I have my suspicions."

He harrumphed. "You'd almost think that jerk wanted to get caught."

"Charlie—"

"Sorry." He waved a hand. "I'm just sayin'."

"I'll handle it." She took in a deep breath and blew it out.

Thankfully, Charlie wheeled out of the office and headed for the dayroom—no doubt to a spot where he could still listen in on the altercation that was sure to ensue.

She slid her chair back and went to find Earl Eland. If he failed the Breathalyzer test, it was three strikes. She couldn't afford to look the other way, but if Charlie hadn't been watching to see how she handled this, she would have quietly discarded the bottle and pretended she never saw it.

She didn't think Earl would give her any trouble if she asked him to leave—especially if he was drunk. But on the off chance he refused, she did not want to have to call the police. The *Courier* would love nothing more than a juicy story about trouble at the shelter.

Earl was in the dayroom with the other residents, glued to a sitcom.

Being careful not to make eye contact with Charlie, Susan cleared her throat. "Earl? Could you come here for a minute?"

He pointed at himself and gave her a questioning look, as if he hadn't understood her.

She nodded and motioned for him to follow her. He eased out of the shabby recliner and shuffled to the office.

She closed the door and looked him in the eye. He didn't look drunk, but, then, she wasn't sure she'd ever seen him completely sober. She walked around her desk, picked up the wine bottle, and held it up.

His face gave away nothing.

She unlocked a desk drawer and retrieved a Breathalyzer kit. "I'm sorry, Earl, but I need to have you take this."

He looked away. "Rather not."

"Earl, you're putting me in a tough spot here. You know the rules."

"I know . . . I know."

"Is this yours?"

He looked directly into her eyes. "I can truthfully tell you that it's not." His impish half grin gave him away.

She almost laughed. He was probably telling the truth—because he'd stolen the bottle. Or "borrowed" it from one of the lowlifes he hung out with. She replaced the Breathalyzer kit in the desk, closed the drawer, and locked it. She'd probably be sorry, but if he failed that test, she'd be forced to kick him out. She simply didn't have it in her tonight to deal with the fallout.

"Okay, Earl, here's the deal." She looked at him hard, hating how often this job made her sound condescending and snobbish. "I'm going to trust that you're technically telling me the truth. This bottle is going into a random Dumpster in an unidentified town on an undisclosed date"—that earned her another grin—"and you are going to recognize that you've been given a chance you probably didn't deserve, and you're going to appreciate it and not blow it because, unlike God, I do not have an unlimited amount of grace to offer. Is that understood?"

"Understood." He grinned big enough to reveal the gaps where important teeth were missing.

"And I'll be mentioning this incident to your social worker and you'll have to work something out with her. Okay?"

He nodded, looking only slightly penitent. "I think I'm gonna hit the hay, if that's okay with you, Blondie."

"I think that's a very good idea." *Before I punch your lights out.* She'd let him get away with calling her "Blondie" before, so she couldn't very well say anything about it now. Though it hadn't sounded so disrespectful before.

Earl reached for the door just as the night-shift volunteers came through.

Susan glanced at her watch. "You guys are early."

"And you're still here," Garrett Edmonds said. "When do you ever sleep?"

"The early shift didn't show."

"Susan! You should have called," Bryn said. "We would have come earlier."

"I know, but that's not what you signed up for."

Garrett and his wife, Bryn, were newlyweds who often volunteered for the overnight shift. Bryn had served many hours of community service for claiming responsibility for the fire that killed David, along with Bryn's first husband, Adam, and three others, including Garrett's first wife, who had also been a firefighter. It had been a careless accident—Bryn had left a candle burning in the upstairs office.

But Susan had never blamed Bryn. That act of negligence had changed so many lives, but it could have happened to anyone. If anything, Susan blamed herself for not having had stricter rules in place.

"Well, we're here now." Bryn put her purse in a drawer of the file cabinet and shrugged out of her jacket. "So would you please go home and get some sleep?"

Susan gave her a grateful smile.

"Everything calm here tonight?" Garrett asked.

"Mostly." She told them about Charlie finding the bottle of wine, and about Earl's transparent denial. "I haven't searched the rest of the place, but I'm guessing that was the extent of his stash. The bottle is over there. You guys can take it home if you trust it."

Garrett hooked a thumb toward Bryn, laughing. "I don't trust her with it."

"Garrett!" Bryn feigned a glare. "That's how rumors get started!"

"Just kiddin', babe." He winked, then turned to Susan, serious again. "I'll dispose of it if you want me to."

"I'd appreciate it. And I do think I'll go home now, if you guys don't mind."

"Go!" Bryn shooed her out. "I'll do a quick walk-through. And you"—she poked a finger at her husband—"get some sleep. He's on Saturday school duty tomorrow," she explained.

Susan made a face. "Too bad. Well, I just put fresh sheets on the sofa bed, so you're set. Sweet dreams."

Garrett shot her a boyish grin. "I bet I can get her to let me stay up another hour," he said in a stage whisper.

Bryn pointed at the sofa like a drill sergeant.

"I'm going, I'm going . . ."

"I'm going, too," Susan said, reaching for her jacket and purse.

Seeing the young couple together touched her deeply—such obvious love between them, and, oh, the depth of forgiveness they'd had to find . . .

It had caused quite a stir in the community when Bryn and Garrett ended up getting married. But, like Susan, most of the town sympathized deeply with Bryn. Which one of them hadn't walked off and left a candle burning at least once? But Bryn bore deep scars from the tragic consequences of her carelessness. To think that she bore the responsibility for the death of her own husband—and of Garrett's wife . . . Susan shuddered.

Yet seeing the easy, affectionate way Bryn and Garrett had with each other made Susan ache for David in a way she hadn't dared to in a long time. She pushed the thought from her mind and pulled the lanyard heavy with keys from around her neck and handed it to Bryn, wishing she could hand off the weight of her worries so easily.

She'd become a thorn

in his side . . .

3

Saturday, May 16

*P*eter Brennan slammed the hood of the truck and resisted the urge to swear. It was the second time this month the station's brush truck had blown a head gasket. At least that was what it looked like to him. But for all he knew about mechanical stuff, it could be the transmission.

Why did this stuff always have to happen on his Saturday off? Guess the fish in Ferris Park pond would have to wait. Weren't weekends off supposed to be one of the perks of age and seniority? Okay, so he wasn't that old, but he was, after all, the head honcho. That ought to be worth something.

He kicked at the oil stain on the floor of the bay and slipped a Tootsie Pop out of the breast pocket of his uniform. He peeled off the red-and-white wrapper and wadded it into a tight ball. His looking under the hood of a vehicle was about as helpful as his looking into an empty oven to see what was for dinner. Neither was likely to produce any results.

Never mind that they were paying him to be the county's fire chief, not chief mechanic and bottle washer.

The custom-built Ford F-350 brush truck was almost twenty years old, but the county's budget wouldn't let the fire station replace it anytime soon. Pete ran a hand over the dented side panel. This old jalopy was almost as much a hero as any of his men, but it was time to put the thing into retirement. He'd driven it out to a pasture fire ten miles west of town last night, and, thankfully, it had waited until the return trip to break down again. God forbid the day it stalled out at the scene of a fire. The brush truck was still their first responder, and in these wooded hills it was often the only pumper they could get on site without playing lumberjack first.

He clenched the white lollipop stick between his teeth. Shoot, with the money they were putting into replacing head gaskets, they almost could have bought that new BrushFighter he had his eye on. The next rookie he trained had better be a crack mechanic. He sighed. Wishful thinking. He was lucky to have the small crew he had. And lucky his men were willing to pull double shifts and double duty while they were so shorthanded.

His cell phone rang, and he wiped the grease off his hands before unclipping it from his belt. He shifted the Tootsie Pop to one side of his mouth and talked around it. "Chief Brennan."

"Hey, Pete. It's Susan Marlowe. I hope I'm not catching you at a bad time."

He sighed. There wasn't a good time for Dave Marlowe's wife—widow. She'd become a thorn in his side, and not just because she reminded him of the Grove Street fire—a tragedy that weighed heavy on his shoulders. Recently she seemed determined to push her homeless shelter off on a community that was increasingly antagonistic toward it.

He'd made the mistake of loaning Susan his firefighters as volunteers when she was getting the shelter back up and running after fire had gutted the original. Scenes from that night still haunted him. The building—an old hospital—had gone up in nothing flat, and a quarter of his firemen with it.

Admittedly, Susan was doing a good job running the shelter. He had to admire how doggedly she'd worked to get the place functioning again in the empty office park across the street from the burn site. But a series of arson fires at the shelter last year had soured people on the idea of having a shelter open here. Him included. He just hadn't been brave enough to say so to her face. But maybe it was time. "What can I do for you, Susan?"

"I know you're as shorthanded as we are, but the new smoke detectors are in and I was hoping you could send somebody to check them out. Byron Fleming and some of the guys from his church put them in. It's not that I don't trust them, but I'd feel better if somebody official looked at them."

Great. He couldn't very well refuse that request. "Sure. I'll get somebody over there later this week. Do we need to call first?"

"Not if you come after five. There's always someone here. Or I can meet you down here anytime. Just let me know."

"Will do." He tried not to sound too friendly, but that was hard to do with Susan, who—in spite of her misguided judgment where the homeless shelter was concerned—was one of the nicest people he knew. And it didn't hurt that she was as pretty as a summer day.

He hung up the phone, gave up on the brush truck, and headed for the parking lot. He'd call a real mechanic tomorrow. He'd worked double shifts twice this week, so he wasn't going to feel a lick of guilt about going home a little early. They could always call him back if they had to go on a run.

But when he drove by the homeless shelter a few minutes later, he found himself pulling in. May as well check this off his to-do list.

S usan unlocked the door and greeted the men who were loitering in the courtyard, waiting for the shelter to open. "Hey, Bobby, Earl. How's it going?"

Earl Eland gave her a knowing smirk, and she promised herself that if he had so much as a hint of liquor on his breath, she would give him the boot.

It was ten 'til five and balmy outside, so she left the men waiting outside and locked the door behind her. Sometimes, especially if it was cold, she let them in early, but she wasn't in the mood tonight.

First Presbyterian was on the list to provide dinner, but the pastor's wife had called earlier to say there'd been a misunderstanding about the schedule, so they were having pizza delivered. The woman apologized all over herself, but Susan assured her the residents would actually be thrilled with pizza for dinner.

She went back to check the fridge. There was a fruit salad left over from last night's supper that she could add to the Bailey kids' plates. With a glass of milk it could pass for a nutritious meal.

Someone pounded on the front door and she ran back to answer. Either Charlie had lost his keys or the pizza was early. The shelter clients knew better than to ask to be let in early.

She unlocked the door, making a mental note to move *install peephole* to the top of the priority list of shelter needs. She opened the door to a bluster of wind and Pete Brennan, still in uniform. Two Tootsie Pop suckers peeked out of his shirt pocket.

"Pete. Hey, come on in. That was fast."

He shrugged. "Figured I'd better get to it while I was thinking about it. Is this a good time?"

"Absolutely. Do you need me to show you where all the smoke detectors are?"

"No, I can find them. Unless they're behind locked doors." He started through the dayroom, craning his neck. "These ceilings are higher than I remember. I've got a stepladder out in the truck . . . Let me—"

"Oh, we've got one you can use." Susan fingered the keys on the lanyard around her neck. "Let me unlock the kitchen and storage rooms for you, too."

"Just how many hours a week do you put in?"

"Here?"

He gave her a look. "You work somewhere else?"

"No. Sorry. Dumb question. I put in twenty hours . . . a good twenty hours." It was closer to thirty. Forty some weeks, but she wasn't about to tell him that.

"And you don't take a salary?"

"Not yet."

He shook his head. "Crazy lady."

Ignoring him, she went for a ladder. She returned to find him teetering on a dining chair, reaching for a smoke alarm.

"Here"—she plopped the four-foot ladder beside him and locked it open—"before you break your neck."

He grinned down at her and stepped over onto the very top of the ladder, an even more precarious position than the chair.

She rolled her eyes but watched him, holding her breath as if doing so could keep him upright.

The fluorescent lights overhead played up glints of silver at Pete's temples that she'd never noticed before. Not that it made him any less attractive. The opposite, in fact. But she was pretty sure he was a couple of years younger than she was, and she couldn't help but wonder if he'd been gray before the Grove Street fire. The tragedy had aged them all.

He inspected and tested the alarm, then jumped down, grabbed the ladder, and moved to the next one.

It was all she could do not to follow him from room to room making sure he didn't fall. But it was past time to unlock the doors, and the pizza would be here any minute.

She was checking people in and opening lockers when Pete reappeared, looking uneasy.

"Everything okay?"

He nodded, but not convincingly. Looking pointedly at two residents who stood nearby, he motioned toward her office. "When you have a minute, I need to talk to you."

She finished quickly, and when the clients had started on their nightly chores, she motioned Pete into the office. "Is there a problem?"

He glanced over her shoulder through the window that looked out over the central hallway. "Um . . . you might want to check the laundry room. Looks like somebody's thinking about opening a bar in there." He chuckled. "Unless that's *your* stash."

"What?" She gave a little growl. *Earl!* "I am going to kill somebody."

He held his hands up. "Hey, don't shoot the messenger."

She ignored his attempt at levity. "Charlie found a bottle of wine behind the refrigerator last night. I think I know who put it there."

"So, what's the protocol on something like this?"

"This is the third"—she shook her head—"at *least* the third time he's either come in drunk or snuck alcohol in. I never should have let him get away with it the first time. I've got to ask him to leave."

"And how's that going to go over?"

"Probably not very well . . . Especially since I can't really prove it's his. But he practically admitted it last night."

"You're not going to try to kick some guy out by yourself, I hope."

"Well, I'm not going to call the police to do it. I have enough trouble without getting them involved." She wondered if Pete was aware of all the flack the shelter was getting from the community. He'd have to live in a cave not to.

"Susan—" He looked frustrated. "That's just flat foolish. You don't know how this guy will react."

"Well, what would you suggest? I don't have a lot of other options."

He stared at her, closemouthed, but she could almost see him biting his tongue. Finally he said, "What exactly do you plan to do if he tries to fight you?"

She narrowed her eyes and curbed a smile. "I think I could take him."

He threw back his head and laughed. But just as quickly he turned serious again. "Let me at least come with you when you confront him."

She opened her mouth to protest, but just then Charlie rolled by the open door, his lap piled high with pizza boxes.

Pete turned to follow her gaze. He took in a deep whiff. "Man, does that ever smell good."

"Stay and have some."

"Oh, no. I couldn't—"

"Seriously . . . Please join us. This is compliments of the Presbyterians, and they had enough for a full house delivered, but we're way under capacity. It'll just go to waste." That wasn't exactly true—the men would polish off any leftovers before they went to bed—but suddenly she really wanted him to stay. And not just because she needed moral support to kick Earl out.

Pete shrugged. "Well, if you're sure. Pretty hard to resist Mac's Pizza, and it sure beats the PB and J I was going to have at home."

"Consider it a tip for checking out our smoke alarms."

"I'll consider it a tip for being your bodyguard when you kick the bartender out."

She nodded, resigned. "Okay. But let's let the poor guy have one last meal before we throw him out on the mean streets."

She turned and headed for the dining room, but she heard him sigh behind her.

"I don't know, Susan . . . You really are way too nice, you know that? You'll never survive in this business if you don't get just a little mean."

Now it was her turn to bite her tongue. What she really wanted to say was, "And just what do you think I've been doing these last three years at this 'business,' if not surviving, Chief Brennan?"

. . . firehouse rumors
were often true.

4

$\mathcal{E}$arl, I have to ask you to leave."

"Why?"

"You know why. We don't tolerate alcohol consumption here." Susan glanced at her watch. "I'll give you a few minutes to gather up your things."

Pete was surprised how casual yet confident she sounded. He'd positioned himself at a table in the TV room adjacent to Susan's office and sat there trying to look unobtrusive while every nerve stood on end. If Earl Eland so much as twitched an eyelid the wrong way . . .

Susan glanced his way as she followed that little weasel out of the office. Pete smiled to himself. She was right—she probably could take the guy. But Pete didn't trust him. And the more he observed, the more nervous he felt about Susan working alone here every night. He wouldn't have allowed it if she were his wife. But then, she wasn't. And, yes, there were usually volunteers from the churches on site with her, but from what he could see, none of them had the training necessary to handle the kind of emergency that might arise in a building full of homeless addicts and losers.

He checked his thoughts, wanting to be fair. But so far he'd seen nothing to change his mind about the shelter being a bad idea. A town the size of Hanover Falls had no business hosting these people. Worse, they probably wouldn't be in the Falls at all if the shelter didn't provide them a place to loiter. If not for this refuge, they'd move on to Poplar Bluff or Springfield where there were already established shelters. David Marlowe had never said much to him about Susan's passion for the homeless other than to call the shelter her "little project" in a tone that said he wasn't exactly a fan either.

It wasn't fair to judge the guy, but for a while there'd been rumors floating around that Dave had an "extracurricular" woman. Unfortunately, firehouse rumors were often true. And if so, Dave Marlowe may have had ulterior motives for belittling anything Susan was passionate about. But Pete had never appreciated the gossip that went around a small town. He'd always liked Dave and had chosen to give him the benefit of the doubt.

Watching Susan now, Pete shook his head. How a guy could cheat on someone like Susan, he didn't know. They always said the wife was the last to know. For her sake, he hoped she'd never heard the rumors— true or not.

Earl fidgeted while he waited for Susan to unlock his locker. She handed him a raggedy backpack, then put some loose items in a plastic grocery sack. "I'm sorry, Earl," she said, handing him the bags.

He kicked the locker. "Yeah. You're sorry all right."

He said it with a smirk that gave Pete the creeps.

Susan set her jaw and headed for the door, keys in hand. But before she'd gone three steps, Earl spewed a string of curses, then hauled off and put a fist through the drywall.

Pete shot out of his chair and crossed the hall in three paces. He grabbed the man by the collar, wishing it was the scruff of his neck, and lifted him an inch off the ground before slamming him into the lockers.

"Pete!" Susan's voice climbed an octave. "Stop it!"

Earl's feet bicycled comically in midair. "Put me down or I'll call the police!"

It was all Pete could do not to plant the man's face in the hole he'd just punched in the wall. Pete's firefighters had put up most of that drywall. He'd have made the little runt patch it while he watched if he hadn't wanted the guy out of here so bad.

Still gripping him by his filthy collar, Pete escorted Eland to the door and shoved him through it. But the scrappy man turned on him, hissing like a mangy cat and clawing at Pete's face.

Pete grabbed Eland's arm and shoved him against the wall. "You want a fight? I'll give you a fight." Adrenaline pumped through his veins. *Lord, don't let me hurt the guy.*

"Pete! Let him go!" Susan gripped his arm from behind. "Let him go right now!"

He dropped Eland, and the man grabbed his gear and scrambled for the door. Good riddance.

"Pete!"

He turned, expecting to see gratitude on Susan's face.

Instead, she glared at him. "What in the world were you thinking?"

He blinked, then exhaled and glared back. "You're welcome. I told you he was trouble! Now what would you have done if I hadn't been here?"

Wide-eyed, she answered through gritted teeth. "I would have asked him to patch the wall, and when he was finished, I would have asked him to leave."

"You actually think he was going to stick around and repair a wall because you asked him to?" He shook his head. "You're out of your mind."

"And you're not? You could have killed him!"

"Believe me, he was in no danger."

"You didn't have to be so rough with him. He was just trying to save face in front of the guys." She motioned over her shoulder to the little gallery of onlookers gathered in the doorway to the dining room. "You just made it worse!"

Pete rubbed his neck, suddenly aware of muscles he hadn't stretched in a while. "Excuse me for stepping in." He started for the door.

"Wait, Pete." She put a hand gently on his forearm. "I'm sorry . . . I know you were just trying to help."

"Yeah, well, I won't make that mistake again." He pulled his arm away. "I came here trying to keep an open mind, but all this has done is make me realize why so many people are against this place."

"That's not fair." Her eyes held a desperate gleam. "You're right. I shouldn't have tried to handle that on my own. I should have expected trouble and—"

"You got that right."

The gleam in her eyes turned icy. "He wouldn't have been so defensive if you hadn't been lying in wait for him."

"Lying in—" He rolled his eyes. Was she serious? "I wasn't even in the room!" He pointed back to the TV room. "And you're lucky I *was* lying in wait." He'd had all the abuse he was going to take. Tucking his chin to his chest, he headed for the parking lot.

He slammed the door of his pickup and gunned the engine. Why did he bother getting involved?

His life was starting to seem like a long list of failures. He tried to push the thought away, but it was hard to ignore the evidence against him.

He turned out of the parking lot, strangely gratified at the dust his tires kicked up behind him.

Even before the Grove Street fire, the pattern had begun. A five-year battle with infertility had finally taken his marriage hostage. He'd been separated from Lana for over five years before she'd asked for a divorce. He didn't fight it. He'd given up on reconciliation long ago—it was hard to reconcile with someone you never saw. The divorce had become final a week before the fire, and she'd remarried that Christmas. *Merry Christmas, Pete.*

His grief and sense of failure had gotten lost in the chaos surrounding the fire and its aftermath. Then one night last winter he'd come home and opened the *Courier* over a frozen dinner, only to be hit with the birth announcement: Lana and her husband were the proud parents of twin daughters.

He set his jaw and pushed the memories away. If he let himself feel anything, he'd regret it later.

He punched the accelerator and headed for home.

*Why did she
expect these people
to be trustworthy?*

5

Saturday, May 23

Susan bid the night-shift volunteers good-bye and made her way across the dark parking lot. The air smelled like fresh-mown grass, and though the thermometer had hit eighty today, the night air was chilly. She shivered in her short sleeves and rubbed a thumb over the teeth of her car key.

When she'd first started the shelter, the walk to the car had been the most frightening thing about every shift. Strange since she lived a mile outside of town on a deserted dirt road. She'd gotten over her fears long ago, but tonight it seemed like a scary place again. Earl Eland was probably miles from Hanover Falls by now—if he wasn't sitting downtown in jail. She made a mental note to contact his social worker tomorrow and let her know what had happened. She was not looking forward to that conversation.

Something skittered around the corner of the building and she jumped. But it was just the night breeze tumbling a fast-food wrapper across the parking lot.

Pete Brennan had insisted she was foolish to be here alone. "Crazy" was his precise word. And the confrontation with Earl last week had ensured she'd never convince Pete otherwise.

If she was honest, the incident had rattled her a little. Why did she expect these people to be trustworthy? Sure, a few of them were. But most of them had need of the shelter precisely because they had issues—addictions, anger issues, mental illness—that rendered them unable to handle ordinary life. And unworthy of trust.

She unlocked her car, checking the backseat as soon as the light clicked on. She peered over her shoulder before climbing in and quickly locked the car doors again.

She felt bad about what had happened with Pete. It'd been eating at her all week. He'd only done what any decent man would do—what David would have done had he been sitting in that TV room when Earl threw his fit. And if she was honest with herself, she had to admit she liked the way it had made her feel to have a man worry over her, want to protect her. Sure, Pete had overreacted—big-time—but his intentions were good. He didn't know Earl like she did, so why wouldn't he think the man might be dangerous?

She owed Pete an apology. She'd tried to offer one the night she threw Earl Eland out—or rather, the night Pete threw him out. But it hadn't gone well. She'd been too proud and too afraid that he'd see anything she said as conceding that the shelter had no value.

Pulling out of the gravel lot, she glanced at the clock on the dashboard. It wasn't yet ten. She'd drive by the station and see if Pete was still there. Doubtful—it was a holiday weekend. But the longer she waited, the easier it would be to blow off an apology she knew she needed to make.

Parking her car behind the fire station a few minutes later brought a swell of memories crashing back. When David was with the Clemens

County crew, she'd often brought sandwiches or cookies to the guys. Since that awful night of the fire, she'd avoided driving by the station whenever possible. The last time she'd used this back door was the day she'd come to pick up David's personal things. Pete had spared her the difficult task of cleaning out David's locker and had her husband's belongings waiting in a small cardboard box. There was nothing of real value there, but Susan had taken the box home and put it on the floor in his closet where it sat to this day.

Eighteen months. Almost nineteen now, and most of David's clothes still hung in that closet untouched. She'd tried to get Davy and Danny to help her go through their father's things the first time they came home from college after David's death. "Some of Dad's shirts are like new. He'd like it if you took what you want and got some good out of them," she'd said.

They'd halfheartedly pawed through the closet, and Danny had taken a couple of polos. Davy had gone through the motions, tried on a couple of jackets, but had taken nothing—and gotten out of there as fast as he could.

The one time she'd opened the door to finally clean out David's closet, the scent of him had overwhelmed her. Shoe leather, his musky aftershave. And maybe it was her imagination, but she smelled the smoke from a hundred fires that had clung to his hair and his clothes, even when he'd done most of his laundry at the station.

She'd closed the door and mentally marked the task off her list. If she ever moved or if the boys ever changed their minds—then she'd deal with it. As it was, she didn't need the storage space and she didn't have the time or energy to handle the emotional chaos the job was bound to provoke.

She walked toward the back door that led to the Station 2 break room, wishing she'd thought to stop and pick up a treat for the guys. They'd always appreciated her homemade cookies and muffins, and David usually came home with requests for her recipes.

Feeling suddenly nervous, she had to force herself to open the door.

Familiar noises and the pungent smell of smoke hit her the moment she stepped inside, and for an instant she was transported back in time. David had carried that distinctive odor in his hair and in the cab of his pickup when he'd brought his bunker gear home with him whenever he filled in for Station 1, or if he came straight home after a middle-of-the-night fire. She'd forgotten what a different world she'd lived in when David was alive, and for the first time in a long time, the ache of missing him returned, as sharp and fresh as it had been in those first weeks.

She didn't recognize the fireman standing at the utility sink washing turnout gear. Two others sat at the table playing cards, but before she could ask for Pete, Lucas Vermontez appeared from around the corner.

He stopped short. "Susan! What brings you here?" His million-watt smile warmed her instantly.

"Hey, Luc."

"Don't you know it's Memorial Day weekend? Shouldn't you be at the lake or off on vacation somewhere?"

"I could ask you the same question. But, hey, you're looking good!" It was true. Lucas still walked with a slight limp after being severely injured in the fire that had killed David. But the average person would barely notice. She'd heard he was back working with the station to train accelerant detection dogs.

A gangly chocolate Labrador trotted out from behind Lucas, and Susan knelt to pet him. She missed having a pet in the house. Danny had taken the family dog with him when he moved to his apartment in Indiana.

"What's his name?" she asked, scratching the affectionate pup's ears.

"Smoke."

"Perfect. I love it," she said, smiling up at him. "So is this one yours or the station's?"

"Don't tell Jenna, but technically he's mine."

Susan laughed. She remembered that Luc's girlfriend was not a fan of dogs.

"I'm using him to train the guys in working with a detection dog, but I'm hoping to take him through Tulsa's training program. The one Sparky graduated from."

"What do you hear about ol' Sparky?" The black Labrador had belonged to Charlie—before the fire. Susan had allowed a few of the residents at the old shelter to keep a pet as long as they could afford to have it neutered, properly registered, and its shots kept up-to-date. Owning an animal seemed to foster a sense of responsibility—and a dog might be the only loyal companion some of the shelter's clients ever had. Still, it presented its share of problems and she'd yet to reinstate that pet policy in the new shelter. She had enough trouble with the *humans* at the shelter.

"There's a fire inspector in Springfield who's working with Sparky. Sounds like it's going pretty well."

"I'll tell Charlie," she said. "He'll be glad to hear it."

"So, what can I do for you?"

"Is Pete—Chief Brennan—around?"

"I think he's out in the bay. Hang on and I'll get him."

"Oh, no . . . don't bother him. I thought I might catch him on break and—"

"Believe me, he won't mind being bothered," said one of the rookies Susan hadn't met.

Lucas gave her his trademark grin. "That's for sure. He's playing mechanic tonight."

"Only time I've ever heard the chief swear." The rookie laughed and hit a remote that opened a small garage door to the bay. He hollered Pete's name, and a few seconds later Pete strode through the opening, wiping his hands on his uniform pants.

"Hey, Susan." He flashed her a grin, then—as if he'd just remembered their last encounter—his smile faded. "What's up?"

She glanced from Lucas to the rookie, then back at Pete. "Would you have a minute to talk?"

The guys took the hint and disappeared into the fitness room. "I don't think anybody's in the kitchen," Pete said. "I need to wash up anyway."

She followed him past the laundry area, where a row of turnout gear hung drying, and into the sparely furnished kitchen.

Pete pushed up his sleeves and turned the water on with his elbow. While he scrubbed, she looked around the room, remembering the times she'd brought supper or dessert for David and the crew.

The guys were like one big family, and those nights she'd spent here had felt like family reunions with some of her favorite people.

After the shelter fire, they'd had trouble filling the positions left by the fallen firefighters. Hanover Falls was a small town and the pay wasn't anything to write home about. She didn't know half the guys here now. And the ones she did know were different men since the tragedy. They all bore the scars of what had happened to their station, their city. Lucas had lost his father in the fire. And their fallen comrades were as close as brothers—even to those who'd come on the Clemens County crew afterward.

Pete dried his hands and motioned for her to take a seat at the long table. He pulled out a chair and straddled it backward. "What can I do for you?"

Feeling awkward and suddenly remembering why she'd come, she sat down across from him and breathed a quick prayer. "I just wanted to say that I'm sorry for the other night. I . . . I know you did what any man would have done, and it wasn't fair for me to jump all over you like I did."

He gave a single nod. "I appreciate that."

She couldn't tell if he was being smug or gracious but decided to pretend it was the latter. "I know you don't think a whole lot of the shelter, Pete—that's getting to be a bigger bandwagon all the time—but I just want you to know that the entire time the shelter's been open, I've never felt threatened or in danger or—"

"There's always a first time, Susan."

"May I finish?" The emotions from the other night roared back.

He held up a hand and gave the floor back to her. "Sorry."

"If there's ever anything I can't handle, I have people I can call. We're two minutes from the police station. Sure, I'd love to have a bouncer at the door every night when we open, but we both know that's not possible. And it's getting less possible all the time."

He frowned. "What do you mean by that?"

"I don't know who or what is fueling it, but this city turned sour on the shelter after the fire, and it seems to be getting worse by the—"

"It's not just the fire, Susan. You surely know how Dave felt about the shelter from day one."

So David had talked to Pete about his reservations. "I think I put my husband's fears to rest. And they were just that—a husband's fears for his wife's safety. Not always completely reasonable or justified."

Pete shrugged as if he didn't agree but didn't care to argue the point.

"David supported what I was doing, Pete." Her voice broke and she swallowed hard. *Oh, Lord, don't let me start crying.* But she hadn't counted on having to defend her husband—her marriage! "Maybe he wasn't crazy about it at first, but he came around. For Pete's sake, he had the—"

Pete's chuckle made her realize she'd invoked his name—well, the name he shared with *Saint* Peter. But she wasn't going to let him humor his way out of this discussion. "Well, it's true, Pete. David had the rookies giving every free hour to help fix up the old hospital!"

Pete softened and nodded. "I know Dave helped out. And, hey, don't forget I loaned you some of the guys to drywall and paint the new shelter, too."

In the heat of defense, she had forgotten. "Of course you did," she said, backpedaling. "And I appreciate it."

"But that doesn't mean I'm buying what you said about never having any problems. What does your board think?"

She looked away. "I don't exactly have a board," she admitted. Since the fire, no one wanted to attach their name to the shelter. "But I have advisors I trust. It's not like we're running a for-profit business, Pete." She wouldn't tell him that her "advisory board" consisted of Charlie and Bryn and Garrett Edmonds.

"I seem to recall Dave talking about Charlie and some other guy getting into it because their dogs couldn't get along."

"Yes . . . Zeke. He didn't get along with anybody." Zeke had only been at the shelter two weeks at the time of the shelter fire, but he'd been the prime suspect in the tragedy in the beginning. Susan hadn't thought about the man for months, but Pete's comment made her remember clearly.

She sighed. "I admitted him against my better judgment. He didn't want to show any ID, or have his photo taken. I should have known something wasn't on the up-and-up."

"That's not my point, Susan. If two guys get into it at the shelter, there's not one thing you could do to stop it. Shoot, if two *gals* get into it, you'd still be pretty powerless to do anything about it."

She ignored that last comment. "The only reason Zeke and Charlie didn't get along was because their dogs were always fighting."

"Maybe it worked the other way around," Pete said.

She shrugged. After Bryn had turned herself in for accidentally starting the fire, Zeke Downing was no longer a suspect, despite his criminal record. "What's your point anyway, Pete?"

He raised an eyebrow. "I'm just helping you remember that you *have* had trouble at the shelter before. And what about the whole thing with James Friar and that girl? You don't call that trouble?"

Why was he dragging out this ancient history? "That had nothing to do with the shelter."

"But it happened at the shelter, right?"

"Friar had a history with that girl long before he assaulted her."

"But it happened at the shelter." It wasn't a question this time.

She was starting to suspect Pete was fighting for the sake of fighting. "If you're trying to make a point about the shelter attracting riffraff, you can just save your breath, because Friar and that girl were both born and raised right here in the Falls. They didn't migrate to town because of the shelter. That seems to be what the anti-shelter faction is arguing. Yes, Springfield sends us a few clients when they're full, but *most* of our residents are from here or towns within a twenty-mile radius—"

"I think you're being mighty generous to call them *clients*—or *residents*. *Inmates* is more like it, and—"

"Pete—"

He waved a hand at her. "I don't care if they're from Timbuktu. That has nothing to do with anything. My point is, it's not safe for you to be there by yourself."

"You know what?" She stood. "My safety isn't your problem, Chief Brennan. Unless it involves a fire. But I appreciate your concern. I really do." She retrieved her keys from her coat pocket and took a step toward the door. "And, again, I'm sorry for the way I behaved the other night. You overreacted, of course, but there was no excuse for me jumping all over you the way I—"

"You want to go get something to eat?"

She stopped. "*Excuse* me?"

"I haven't had supper yet. It's a simple question, Susan. I'm hungry. And I'm wondering if you want to go get something. With me. Together. The two of us." He wore a grin that completely disarmed her.

Eyeing him, she drew back a step as if a little distance might make his intentions clearer.

He pushed up his sleeve and checked his watch. "I think Java Joint is still open."

"Java Joint?" she repeated, trying to figure out what he was up to.

He leaned forward. "Yeah. Java Joint. It's a cute little place down-town that—"

"I *know* what the Java Joint is, Pete."

His smile turned mischievous. "Well, then I guess I'll just have to assume you're still weighing the offer."

Weighing it, she was. And the most surprising thing . . . She wanted to go. With him. She wasn't even that hungry, but it didn't matter.

Somewhere along the way she apparently nodded in the affirmative, because five minutes later she was sitting in the darkened cab of Pete Brennan's pickup, heading downtown.

*She hadn't been on a date
in twenty-five years . . .*

6

*P*ete carried their trays to a table in the corner of the almost-empty coffee shop. Susan followed, still not sure how she'd gotten herself into such an awkward situation.

In the opposite corner, a high school couple made goo-goo eyes at each other and Susan tried valiantly not to make comparisons. She was not on a date. This was simply an impromptu dinner between two long-time friends. Never mind that Pete had paid for her meal.

She hadn't been on a date in twenty-five years—unless she counted the rare occasions during their marriage when she and David had gone the dinner-and-a-movie route. Ordinarily, when they weren't at one of the boys' ball games or music events, they were fixing up the house or working on the yard.

Of course, with David's crazy schedule at the station, even those times had been few and far between.

"Do you want a straw?" From among the ever-present bouquet of Tootsie Pops in his breast pocket, Pete pulled out a straw that he'd grabbed at the counter.

"Thanks." She accepted it and took her time peeling the paper off, waiting for him to settle into the chair across from her.

They'd ordered sandwiches and chips, and even though she'd eaten with the residents at the shelter at six, she was suddenly famished. She said a quick blessing under her breath and ate with gusto.

A minute later, she realized Pete hadn't taken one bite but was watching her eat, barely managing to curb a smile.

Feeling self-conscious, she wiped at her face. "Do I have mustard on my nose or something?"

"No. You're good."

"Then . . . what?"

He smiled. He had a nice smile. White, even teeth and a dimple that gave him a boyish quality.

"I like a woman who knows how to eat," he said.

His comment did nothing to allay the feeling that this whole thing was far too close to a date. She managed a laugh. "Well, glad I could entertain you."

He picked up his own sandwich and bit off a hunk. "You go ahead," he said over a mouthful. "I'll let you eat in peace."

They ate in silence for a few minutes, and she found herself simply enjoying his company and happy to leave the conflict from earlier behind.

When he'd finished his sandwich, he said, "Will your boys be home for the summer?"

"I doubt Davy will. He quit school to take a full-time job. And probably not Danny either. I look for him to stay up there and take some summer classes so he can graduate at Christmas."

"I'm sorry . . . remind me where 'up there' is."

"Oh . . . I wouldn't expect you to remember. Danny's at Bethel College in Indiana."

"That'll be nice to have him finished with school. I hear college costs as much as a small home these days."

"More like a *large* home. The boys both got the fallen firefighter scholarship last year. That helped . . . made losing their dad a little easier, I guess." She regretted the words as soon as they were out. How could anything have made that time easier?

But Pete's smile warmed her. "Almost like their dad is still providing for them, huh?"

"Yes. Yes, it is." She could have kissed him. And she should have known Pete would understand how much it meant to her for her sons to get the NFFF money. "I hadn't really thought about it like that. Maybe I can use that for leverage to get Davy to go back to school. I just hate that he dropped out."

"Well, college isn't for everyone."

"No, but . . . Davy needs some direction. He's been . . . shall we say, 'a challenge' . . . since he was big enough to ride a bike." She laughed, but it wasn't funny. They'd gone through one rough patch after another with that kid. He'd run away from home twice the summer he was eight. He was missing all night the second time, and they'd finally sent search parties looking for him at four that morning. She'd been so furious, she was afraid of what she'd do when they found him. But when he moseyed up from the meadow at sunrise as if nothing had happened, she'd hugged him tight and cried like a baby.

They enjoyed a few years of calm after that, but when Davy was eleven, he'd started setting fires. Nothing that did any serious property damage, but it soon became obvious there was more to it than just a boy's curiosity with matches. They'd finally taken him to a counselor who determined that setting fires was Davy's way of getting his father's attention. David did work long hours, and shifts at the station meant he was often gone overnight. The counselor's explanation made sense to Susan, but David had been furious at the implication he was to blame. The whole thing had seemed catastrophic at the time. Strange, because now Susan could barely remember how it had all shaken out. Davy's pyromania had been replaced by binge drinking and the rare vandalism incident in high school, but by the time they sent him off to college, he seemed ready to take on the world. Until David died.

"I think I'm too easy on him sometimes," she told Pete. "I suppose I'm afraid I'll set him off."

He nodded, but she got the impression he didn't want to tackle that topic.

The young lovebirds in the corner left their booth, and as they went out the door, a woman slipped in. Pete watched her, momentarily distracted. It reminded Susan of the way David had looked at other women. Maybe all men did. But David had been an admitted flirt . . . always noticing a pretty woman. This one definitely would have caught his eye. She looked familiar. Or maybe she just looked like some actress who'd been in the news recently.

Susan took a sip of her soda. The straw made a gurgling, empty sound. She held up her cup. "I'll be right back. Do you need a refill?"

"Here, let me . . . I could use some more coffee, too." He took her cup from her. "Diet Coke, right?"

She nodded, impressed he remembered. "Thanks."

Pete slid from his chair and went to refill their drinks.

Susan busied herself gathering up their empty sandwich wrappings but looked up when she heard someone say Pete's name. It was the attractive woman who'd just come in.

Pete looked surprised to see her, even though Susan was quite sure he'd noticed her when she first came in.

"You're out past curfew, aren't you?" he said.

"Look who's talking!" The woman flashed him a bright smile. "You're out pretty late yourself."

Susan watched as he refilled her Coke, wondering if he'd introduce her to Pretty Woman.

He held up his own coffee cup in his left hand. "Gotta get fueled, you know. Are you working?"

"On my way home. We did a fire in Columbia this week."

"Really? I didn't know you ever worked that far out."

"Hey, I'm not proud. I'll work for anybody who'll pay me." She laughed.

She had a pretty, musical laugh, and Susan felt a strange niggling of jealousy. It didn't help that despite the plain khaki uniform and messy ponytail, the woman was gorgeous.

They continued to chat while Pete filled his coffee cup, and Susan gathered, from their conversation, that the woman was in the firefighting business—maybe a firefighter. Her athletic build lent credence to that guess.

A teenage boy behind the counter called out an order number, and the woman turned. "That's me. Are you eating here? Save me a place."

Pete had his back to Susan, and she strained to hear how he'd reply.

"Oh . . . I'm, uh . . . with someone." Pete held up his coffee cup and her Coke as if to prove it.

The woman looked over his shoulder, obviously panning the café to see who had accompanied Pete. Susan looked away, but not quickly enough.

Pretty Woman gave her a knowing glance and flashed a smile, then turned her attention back to Pete. "Ah, I see . . . Well, another time, then."

Susan didn't think it was her imagination that the woman spoke loudly enough for Susan to hear.

"Yeah, sure thing." Pete gave a little wave.

The woman's gaze trailed him—a little too appreciatively—as he walked back to the table. Following his path, she caught Susan's eye again briefly and tossed her a look that, if they'd all still been in high school, Susan would have interpreted as a challenge. Again, she had the feeling she should know the woman.

Pete seemed unaware of their brief exchange, and when he sat down, he offered no explanation. But the leisurely mood had evaporated and he seemed antsy.

After a few awkward moments, he drained his coffee cup and crushed it in his fist. "Well . . . I guess I'd better get you back to your car so you can go home."

"Okay." She pushed her chair back and gathered her purse and jacket. "Thanks for dinner."

"No problem." He carried his squashed cup to the trash can near the exit.

She followed him, but before he opened the door, he glanced out the window and scanned the parking lot. She got the distinct impression he was checking to see if Pretty Woman was still here.

She could take a hint. *Cut it out, stupid. This wasn't a date anyway, remember?*

As they drove back to the station where her car was parked, Pete seemed to be deep in thought. She searched her brain for a conversation topic but came up blank. It felt like back in high school when Samuel Clegg had asked her to prom, then started dating Julie Svensen before prom night rolled around. He'd honored his invitation, but it was clear the entire night that Sam wished he was anywhere but out with Susan Rickman.

"See you around." She waved as she climbed out of the pickup.

"Yeah . . . See you, Susan. Thanks for keeping me company."

"Sure." *Anytime, chump. I've got nothing better to do.*

How sad that it was true.

On her way back through town, Susan decided to drop by the shelter. The two volunteers for tonight were new—a couple of men from the Presbyterian church. Not that she didn't trust them—they'd been through the training like all the volunteers—but she'd sleep better if she saw for herself that things were going okay. And it didn't hurt for the volunteers to know that the director often dropped by unexpectedly.

There were still a couple of men awake in front of the TV and she found the guys in the office playing cards.

"Back so soon?" asked the man who'd introduced himself as Jerry Simmons earlier this evening. She remembered him from the volunteer-training sessions she'd led a couple of weeks ago.

She unlocked her desk drawer as if she had a purpose besides checking up on them and was careful not to lie. "I was out and about anyway. Just thought I'd make sure you guys were getting along okay."

"Everything's going fine," the younger man said. He laid down an ace, then turned to Jerry. "Where'd you put that note?"

"Oh, yeah . . ." Jerry went to the bulletin board and untacked a slip of paper. "Some guy stopped by looking for you. Said you'd know who he was. I sure hope you can read it because we couldn't make heads or tails of it."

He handed her the note. It was scribbled in pencil and Susan saw what Jerry meant. It was nearly illegible. She could make out the phrase, *I'm back in town*, and what looked like *talk to you* but what else it said was anybody's guess. Except for the signature, which was printed very clearly: *Herb Downing*.

Downing? Could that be *Zeke* Downing? The shelter resident who'd disappeared after the fire? She didn't remember him going by any name other than Zeke. That seemed like a nickname, but even the news accounts from police reports had referred to the original suspect in the fatal fire as Zeke. Strange that Pete had just brought Downing's name up earlier.

She turned the note over, hoping for a better clue. "Did the guy say what he wanted? Was he trying to check in to the shelter?"

"That's what we thought at first," Jerry said. "He . . . well, he kind of looked like—" His Adam's apple bobbed in his throat and Susan knew he was searching for a polite way to say it.

"Like someone in need of a homeless shelter?"

"Exactly." Jerry looked relieved. "But he didn't ask about staying. Just said to give you the note."

She fingered the paper, straining to read the scribbling. "I have no idea what this is supposed to mean."

Both men shrugged.

"So he must have knocked on the door?"

"Actually, he showed up while we were locking up. Not long after you pulled out. I didn't see which way he came from, but he left on foot . . . headed toward downtown."

"That's odd. Can you describe him?"

The younger man thought for a minute, then looked to Jerry as if he might have an answer.

Jerry shrugged, looking sheepish. "It was dark out . . . The guy never came inside. He was—probably about my height. White guy . . . maybe fifty-five or sixty. He was wearing a cap."

"I guess it's a good thing this isn't a criminal investigation," the other volunteer said. "I couldn't tell you anything more than what Jerry's already said."

She looked at the note again. "Did he sound like he was—in his right mind? This note looks like it might have been written under the influence of . . . *something*."

"I didn't think he seemed out of it, did you?" He looked to Jerry, who agreed.

"Oh!" She held up a hand. "Hang on." She went to the file cabinet in the corner where they kept archived files. She thumbed through till she came to a folder that held clippings about the Grove Street fire. She slipped an article from beneath a paper clip and handed it to Jerry. "Is this the guy?"

The two men bent over the fuzzy newspaper photo. "I wouldn't want to swear under oath or anything," Jerry said, "but it sure could be him."

The other volunteer nodded.

Downing had been wanted for questioning by the police immediately after the fire. But they wouldn't have any reason to talk to him now. The case was long solved.

"Well, okay . . ." She replaced the clipping and filed the folder away again. "I'll see what I can figure out. Right now, I think I'll head home if you guys have everything under control."

She rummaged in her purse for her keys and held them at the ready before letting herself out. She was thankful she'd parked next to the building. But as she walked to her car, a shiver went through her. She wasn't given to premonitions, but she had the oddest feeling someone was watching her.

She cast about cautiously, making sure the parking lot was empty. Then she let her imagination invent a protector and pretended she was being walked to her car, muscular arm firmly around her shoulders. But the instant she was behind the wheel with the doors locked, she discarded the foolish fantasy.

She couldn't so easily shed the question it begged. If she were merely fantasizing, why had it been Pete Brennan's strong arms she imagined around her, instead of David's?

Except there were things her sister didn't know.

7

Friday, May 29

*H*ey, Andi, there's a fire chief from Illinois on Line 2. They're wanting to talk to you about the K-9 program. You want to take it?"

Andi glanced at the clock above the door to her office, then to her secretary. "Can you get a number and tell them I'll call back Monday morning?" She lowered her voice to a whisper. "I'd love to get out of here by five."

"No problem. I'll get the number."

"Thanks, Shelly."

Andi sorted through the last pile of forms on her now-tidy desk and filed everything away in appropriate file folders in the bottom drawer. The canted sunlight revealed a fine layer of dust coating her desktop and she went to find a bottle of Windex and a roll of paper towels.

She carefully dusted three photos that had a place of honor on one corner of her desk: Andrea L. Morley receiving a citation from the state fire marshal, Andi and Rebecca on the Plaza in Kansas City, and a photo of the Springfield Chamber of Commerce ribbon-cutting ceremony for her office.

Her business was thriving. She'd built a name for herself since the Grove Street fire. She'd gotten a lot of face time on the networks—national as well as local—after the fire. Even now, more than eighteen months later, she still got called to make a statement whenever some anniversary of the fire rolled around.

Over a year and a half now, and the networks were still milking that fire for stories. She didn't need the reminders. She accepted the interviews even though it bothered her, brought on nightmares. But like Rebecca said, she'd be foolish to turn down the free advertising. Except there were things her sister didn't know.

She picked up the nameplate from her desk and dusted the flimsy metal. *Andrea Morley, Fire Inspector.* Once upon a time that title had been a source of deep pride. Not that it wasn't still. It was just too bad her father hadn't lived long enough to see her prove him wrong about what she would become. Then it would have meant something. Maybe then it would have justified everything else that happened.

She gave her nameplate one last swipe and replaced it on her desk. The triumph of her position—first female fire inspector in the tricounty area—had long since paled.

Now what enticed her most was the idea of settling down with a man she loved and having three or four cute little kids call her "Mommy." She yearned for that life. To put everything else behind her and start over. But how could she do that? She'd paid a high price to get where she was. Higher than anyone knew. And she had to live with that knowledge every day of her life.

She was thirty-seven and the life she'd only dared to dream about before Dave Marlowe came into it was quickly slipping from her grasp. It still amazed her that despite how she'd grown up, she'd somehow attained the world's definition of success. Yet all she wanted now was what any girl in Shannon County could have started in the backseat of a car on a Friday night.

She couldn't let herself think too long about the choices she'd made recently. She would have gone crazy after the fire if she hadn't filled her hours with work.

She waited for her computer to complete a backup, then shut it down. Getting involved in the K-9 program had been extremely gratifying, but it could be a 24-7 job added to her full-time work as a fire inspector. It looked like she'd be able to place Sparky, the dog who'd started it all, with a fire station in Langhorne County, and she was talking with Lucas Vermontez about training another dog, a pup named Gulliver.

She'd been disappointed to learn that Lucas was practically engaged. His girlfriend was one lucky woman. But after running into Peter Brennan in Hanover Falls the other night, she'd seen the fire chief with new eyes. He was cute. Not as old as she'd first thought, despite a few strands of gray at his temples. And he'd been as friendly as ever.

A red flag went up, remembering who he'd been with that night. But surely he wouldn't have flirted in front of Susan Marlowe that way if she was a girlfriend. Besides, she happened to know Pete was single. Divorced.

A sigh escaped before she could contain it. Another dream she'd given up on—finding a never-married man. Any man her age who'd never been married was highly suspect. And what did that say about *her*? Another sigh.

"You okay in there?" Shelly called from the reception desk.

"I'm fine. Just ready for it to be the weekend."

Shelly appeared in the doorway again. "News flash. It *is* the weekend. Why don't you get out of here?"

Andi laughed. "Okay. I think I will. You, too. It'll all be here bright and early Monday morning."

"Yes, ma'am." Shelly gave a comical salute.

Andi gathered her briefcase and jacket and headed for the door. She hated that she'd become so desperate. Not so many years ago she'd had her choice of dates on any given Friday night. But even as a teenager, she'd been strangely drawn to the ones she couldn't have. The ones who already had girlfriends or who were headed to college or the army or the mission field. Why had she always been drawn to the ones who couldn't offer her what she really wanted?

She shook off thoughts that threatened to take her to a dark place. It was Friday and she had tonight and two more spring days stretching out before her. Maybe she'd call her sister and see if she wanted to go out for drinks, or maybe catch a movie. Being with Rebecca was always good for a laugh.

*P*ete lifted the lid off the massive pot on the back of the stove and breathed in the mouthwatering aroma. It wafted through the fire station's large kitchen. Homemade spaghetti sauce, a gift from Vermontez's mom. Emily was another Grove Street fire widow. She'd remarried several months ago and moved to Springfield, but lucky for the weekend crew, she'd sent a pot of her specialty sauce home with Lucas for the guys of Station 2.

Pete stirred the savory sauce and meatballs with a wooden spoon while he waited for the linguine to cook. He might be the fire chief, but he was also the self-appointed fire *chef* any time he was on duty. He didn't mind—enjoyed it, actually—and in three years nobody had challenged him for the job. There were some crackerjack cooks on his team, too. Only six of them manned the station tonight, along with three probies, which meant they would eat hearty.

He replaced the lid on the pot and checked the noodles again, fishing one out of the steaming water with a pasta scoop. Almost done. "Vermontez! Ring the dinner bell!"

He heard laughter and hollering in the next room and chuckled, picturing exactly what was going on. The probies were racing—doing air-pack times. To pass the test, they had forty-five seconds to go from pants and boots to full gear, no skin showing, and breathing from an air pack. It was a challenging exercise, yet Pete had confidence every one of them would pass that test.

But there also wasn't a one of them who would risk his share of a spaghetti dinner for a win. The dinner bell sounded and shouts rang through the station, out to the bays and back. Within three minutes eight hungry men lined up in the station's utilitarian kitchen, man-sized plates in hand. Pete portioned out noodles while Vermontez ladled generous servings of sauce over each plate.

They ate fast, history having taught them that every meal was subject to interruption. Some of them straddled high stools at the bar, others leaned against the counter and stove, holding their plates under their chins, sopping up every last drop of Emily's sauce with slices of white sandwich bread straight from the bag.

"Good stuff, Vermontez." Randy Elsinger, the newest rookie at the station, spoke over a mouthful. "You grew up on this stuff, huh?"

Lucas put down his fork long enough to flex a bicep. "Where do you think I got these guns?" he said.

"*Vermontez* don't sound Italian to me."

"It's not Italian," Pete challenged. "It's Cuban."

"It's *American*," Lucas said. "You think nobody but Italians know how to make spaghetti? Don't tell my Cuban grandmother."

Elsinger grinned. "I don't care if it's Chinese, as long as it gets me guns like Vermontez has."

"Ha, he's got nothin' on me." Jake Young rolled up his sleeve and flexed, and a rowdy competition for the biggest "guns" ensued.

Pete watched them horse around, a warm spot growing in his chest. It startled him to realize that he was playing high school football when some of these young bucks were born. But this was what he liked about his job. The feeling of *family*. Yeah, the job had its downsides. Working on weekends being one. Risking his life being another.

Sometimes—like tonight—he felt more like a father to these guys. Since the fire, the men they'd hired on were babies . . . some of them not yet twenty-five. Barely shaving. But the camaraderie he had with his men went way beyond being colleagues. They were brothers. And he knew every man in this room would die for him if asked.

A heaviness crept over him. He wished it were as easy as being "asked." He would have died for his crew that November night when five of them had lost their lives. Sometimes it still didn't seem real. But then the memory of the charred bodies lined up in that parking lot would come, and the responsibility hung heavy on his shoulders.

He'd gone over the events of that night a hundred times, in a hundred different ways, and finally convinced himself that there wasn't a thing he could have done that would have altered the outcome. But that didn't change the fact that he felt responsible for his men—and for Molly, his lone female firefighter—who'd died in the blaze that night.

He pushed his chair back and carried his plate to the counter.

"Hey, chief, you're not having seconds?"

"Not tonight." He rubbed his full belly. "Gotta watch my youthful figure."

Their laughter floated behind him.

Chief. He held the title of fire chief. The lives of his firefighters were in his hands. Losing even one man was a heavy burden to bear. Not once had anyone intimated that he was at fault, but sometimes when he walked around town, he felt the stares and imagined the whispers. *That's Pete Brennan. He's the chief who lost all those men in the homeless-shelter fire.*

He dumped his plate in the sink and ran the water good and hot. It didn't do any good to let the thoughts fester. He watched the orange grease swirl down the drain and forced his mind back to the present.

She regretted her
comment . . . the minute the
words left her mouth.

8

Monday, June 1

"Susan, somebody's asking for you out there." Charlie Branson hooked a thumb over his shoulder, indicating the hallway.

"Do you know who it is?" Tonight's volunteers had already checked in and were in the dining room helping clean up after supper. She wasn't expecting anyone.

"Says she's from the *Courier*."

"Great." She huffed under her breath.

"You want me to tell her you're not here?"

"No. It's okay. I may as well talk to her before she hounds me to death." She'd refused to talk to the reporter who'd called last week wanting a response to two letters to the editor that had appeared in last week's paper.

She pushed away from her desk, smoothed her polo shirt over her hips, and tucked her hair behind her ears, hoping she didn't look too unprofessional. She wasn't running a charm school after all.

The young woman waiting in the hallway jumped up when she saw Susan.

"Hi. I'm Bee Quinton." She extended a hand.

Susan shook it. She recognized the name—and its unusual spelling—from bylines in the *Courier*. Susan guessed her to be in her mid-twenties, fresh out of college, stars in her eyes.

"I'd like to ask you a few questions about your shelter."

"Why don't we talk in the office?"

The woman's eyes darted from the hallway to the dayroom entrance where Charlie pretended to be dusting. She looked the way Pete had the other night—distinctly out of her comfort zone.

But Susan tried to give her grace, remembering how she'd felt the first time she volunteered at a shelter, when she and David lived in Springfield before the boys were born. It was that early experience that planted a seed that had sprung to life once the boys were gone from home. Feeling adrift and depressed after Danny left for college, she'd found purpose again in getting the shelter open here in the Falls. Perhaps that was the story she should focus on when she spoke with this young woman.

But five minutes into the interview, it became clear that this reporter had an agenda, and it wasn't a warm, fuzzy story she'd come for.

With pen poised, she was suddenly all confidence. "How do you respond to those people—who seem to be a majority—who would like to see the shelter shut down?"

"What makes you assume it's a majority? Have you taken a poll?"

The reporter didn't miss a beat. "I imagine it's distressing to think that this thing you've fought so hard for is coming under such fire from the community. It probably feels like people don't understand your passion for this project. I would imagine your board of directors must be concerned."

Susan feigned a smile. "I have an idea, Ms. Quinton. How about if you ask the questions and *I'll* answer them?"

She regretted her comment—and her snarky tone—the minute the words left her mouth. She was giving Miss Busy Bee exactly what she wanted.

But Bee Quinton appeared unfazed. "So what are your plans for the shelter? Are you at all swayed by popular opinion? By the flood of letters calling for the shelter to be shut down?"

Susan swallowed hard and shot up a prayer that her words could be full of grace and "seasoned with salt," as the daily devotional she'd been reading just this morning had put it. "Frankly, I haven't seen a flood of letters, Ms. Quinton. I know there are some who don't think Hanover Falls needs a shelter. I wish those people would come visit some evening. In fact, I invite them to come. We could use the extra help. And as for popular opinion, you may want to talk to the one hundred and fifty-five volunteers who keep the shelter running smoothly each month by giving their time, making meals for the clients, providing upkeep and repairs on the building. I don't think those people would waste their time if they felt the shelter should be shut down. The churches of the community have been wonderful to provide the manpower—"

"And how do you respond to those who believe that the shelter brings an undesirable"—she groped for a word—"*element* into the city?"

Susan looked around, praying Charlie or the other residents hadn't heard the insensitive comment. "First of all, Ms. Quinton, shutting down the shelter is not going to *eliminate* any persons from this town. If the shelter shuts down, the men, women, and children who stay with us while they try to get back on their feet will go back to living in their cars and under the overpasses and on the streets of Hanover Falls."

That seemed to shut the reporter up momentarily and Susan took advantage of her silence. "If there are those who see the shelter's residents as 'undesirables,' I'd ask them to come and volunteer at the shelter for one day. Not only would it put their fears to rest, but I think they would see that the people the shelter serves are not all that different from them. In truth, there but for the grace of God go any of us." A mixture of passion and anger boiled inside her and she worked to modulate her voice. "In this present economy, none of us know whether we, or a loved one, might need the services of a place like the Grove Street shelter *tomorrow*. And I, for one, am glad there's a place like this to help."

Bee chewed the end of her pen. "It's interesting you can say all that in light of the sexual assault that occurred at the shelter shortly after it opened in the first location, in spite of the tragic fire that killed your husband and four other firefighters, in spite of the arson fires that have plagued the shelter since it reopened, in spite of—"

"None of those things have anything at all to do with the shelter itself. Would you close down a hospital simply because an assault happened there? Or because a fatal fire destroyed the building?"

"Yes, but the rape that occurred here involved two residents—"

"To set the record straight, it was not a rape. I don't mean to make light of the situation. It was a serious assault, but it—"

"Yes, that's exactly the point. People are concerned that the shelter brings that kind of people into our town—"

"The facts are that both of the parties involved in that incident were longtime residents of Hanover Falls. They were both raised right here in the Falls." Her voice refused to cooperate. She felt like she was fending off Pete's verbal blows from the other night all over again.

"And the arson fires? How do you reassure residents that they're safe from such attacks themselves?"

"I think you are distorting the facts, Ms. Quinton." *Breathe, Susan. Don't lose your cool . . .*

"Detractors would say that you're the one distorting facts, Ms. Marlowe. How do you answer that?"

Susan shot out of her chair and turned her back on the reporter. "This interview . . . this *interrogation* is over!" She strode toward the door and held it open, counting to ten lest she say something she'd regret even more.

Charlie wheeled through the doorway and parked his chair between her and Bee Quinton. "Is everything okay, Susan?"

She forced herself to calm down and measured her words. "Everything is fine, Charlie. Ms. Quinton was just leaving."

The reporter scribbled on her notepad for a few seconds, then slipped it into her bag and, without a word, marched down the hall.

Wednesday, June 3

Y ou're not gonna like today's *Courier*." Charlie tossed the weekly paper on Susan's desk.

She gave him a questioning look, but he only shook his head and pointed her back to the newspaper. She scanned the headlines, then unfolded the paper. Her heart sank when she came to the bold words sprawled across the entire page just below the fold: SHELTER DIRECTOR CLAIMS "INTERROGATION," DECLINES FURTHER COMMENT.

"This is ridiculous. I talked to her for ten minutes. What did she want from me?"

"Well, you did call it an interrogation."

She glared at him. "Whose side are you on anyway?"

"Don't worry. I know where my bread is buttered. I'm just sayin'."

She sank into her chair and read the first paragraph of the article, struggling to be objective. It definitely took a certain slant, siding with the faction in the community that was against the shelter. But everything Bee had written was true, and Susan was quoted accurately.

"I come off like an arrogant jerk."

"Well, you're not that," Charlie said.

"But maybe I shouldn't have talked to her when I was angry."

"Well, I didn't want to say anything . . ."

He knew her too well. She forced a smile and returned to reading:

> Referring to the fatal fire eighteen months ago, Peter Brennan, Clemens County fire district chief of operations, said, "For obvious reasons, the shelter is a difficult topic for the fire department. Anytime you have an institution run almost completely by volunteers, there's a risk that things will slip through the cracks. But the department has been actively involved in the renovation . . . and making sure the shelter's fire alarm system is up to code."

She could have hugged Pete. He'd stood up for her. Even gone out on a limb, revealing that the fire department had offered manpower and safety checks.

She would thank him. Right now, in fact. "Thanks, Charlie."

"Yeah, yeah, I can take a hint." He maneuvered his chair through the tight space between her desk and the row of mismatched file cabinets.

She felt bad for dismissing him. Seemed she did that far too often lately. But right now it seemed more important to talk to Pete.

He'd never noticed
what a startling blue
her eyes were.

9

$\mathcal{P}$ete crossed the parking lot, keys in hand. For once he was getting out of here at a decent hour. Not that he had anywhere important to go. He clicked the remote to unlock the doors and jumped in the pickup.

With the weather warming up, he'd been grilling steaks and burgers the evenings he was home. His doctor wouldn't be crazy about the amount of red meat in his diet lately, but he more than made up for it in the weight room each morning. Had to do what he could to keep up with the young guns on his crew.

His fishing gear was in the back of the truck. Maybe he'd drive through for tacos tonight instead and go straight to his fishing hole.

He started out of the parking lot, unwrapping a chocolate Tootsie Pop while he waited for a car to pass. But when it slowed and started to turn in, he recognized the vehicle. Susan Marlowe.

He cringed. He felt for the woman. The *Courier* had not been kind to her. He felt a little guilty because he'd seen it coming when the reporter talked to him.

He'd done what damage control he could with Bee Quinton and was actually pretty pleased with the way he'd been quoted. In fact, Quinton had left out the few things he'd had second thoughts about after the reporter left. He wondered why the paper had such an interest in this story. Maybe it was a legitimate curiosity in what was causing the most buzz in the community right now, but he'd gotten the impression that Quinton had an agenda.

He eased the truck forward and rolled the window down. "You again?" He was trying for humor, but she didn't smile. "Everything okay?"

She slid her sunglasses on top of her head. He'd never noticed what a startling blue her eyes were. The color of a peacock's feather. And striking with her pale blond hair.

"I wanted to talk to you about something, but . . . I can come back tomorrow if you have someplace to go."

"Actually, I was just going to get something to eat." He saw his dream of a quiet evening at the river evaporate. But then, Susan Marlowe wasn't a bad alternative. "Want to join me? Just drive-through, but . . ." He shrugged.

"That could get to be a bad habit."

He wasn't sure how to take that. "A bad habit, huh?"

"Not . . . you. The drive-through." She patted her flat belly.

"Or I could throw a couple of chicken breasts on the grill and make both our doctors happy. I'm a pretty good cook."

She hesitated, looking conflicted about that invitation.

He was starting to feel a little conflicted himself. This was the second time he'd practically asked the woman on a date. But he laughed and motioned toward the fire station. "Or we could just go inside and talk. But I warn you, my stomach will be growling."

"I could help you cook."

"It's a deal." He put the truck in gear. "Do you know where I live?"

"If you haven't moved in the last couple of years, I do. On Mill Road, right? But I forget which apartment."

"Two-ten. You can just follow me." He crunched the hard candy and hit chewy chocolate.

She nodded, looking as if she still wasn't sure she wanted to accept his invitation. But without another word, she rolled her window up, slid her sunglasses back on her nose, and circled the drive.

Watching her car in his rearview mirror as she followed him back to his apartment, it struck him that he may have just invited a woman to dinner who planned to eat his lunch.

*P*ete's apartment was about what Susan expected, only maybe a little neater—which wasn't saying a lot.

"Excuse the mess." He scraped newspapers and a collection of wadded-up Tootsie Pop wrappers off the sofa and kicked two pairs of shoes underneath a bench. "I worked this weekend . . . didn't get a chance to clean."

Susan followed him into the kitchen, which was surprisingly tidy, though when she opened the refrigerator she realized why. Apparently the man rarely ate at home. She found the chicken in the freezer and thawed it in the microwave while Pete got the grill going out on the tiny deck off of the living room.

Once the chicken was grilling, he popped the tops on two cold cans of soda and offered her one. "Maybe I should have stopped off at the grocery store on the way home." He rifled through bare cupboards. "Not sure what I have to go with this. Potato chips? That's a vegetable, right?"

She laughed. "Sounds good to me."

"Come talk to me while I watch the grill."

She grabbed her soda and followed him out to the deck. He flipped the chicken with tongs, closed the lid on the grill, and leaned back against the railing. "So what did you want to talk to me about?"

A gust of wind blew between the apartment buildings and she shivered and rubbed her arms.

"You cold? Hang on, I'll get you a jacket." Without waiting for an answer, he went back in the house and returned holding out a heavy flannel shirt. "It's clean."

"Thanks." She slipped into it, pushed the sleeves up on her wrists and tugged the collar around her neck. The fabric smelled like Pete—evergreen and woodsmoke, and a hint of raspberry Tootsie Pop. Or maybe that was just her imagination. The warmth felt good on her shoulders.

"I wanted to thank you for what you said to that reporter. I know you kind of went out on a limb for me—"

He shrugged. "I just told her the truth."

"Yes, but I still appreciate you . . . practically defending me."

He turned away and opened the cover on the grill. The scent of roasting chicken made her mouth water.

Pete closed the grill again and turned to study her. "Listen, I wasn't defending you. I don't think you need defending. And besides, the paper didn't necessarily print everything I said." He muttered something she couldn't understand.

"What are you saying, exactly?"

"I'm not saying anything." A slow grin bloomed on his face. "I'm smarter than that."

She tilted her head. "Did you say something against me?"

"Not you."

"The shelter, then?"

"I don't think it really matters. All you need to know is that the paper didn't misquote me."

She eyed him with suspicion. "This is interesting. Given the way they edited my statements, you've got me wondering."

"Well, wonder to your heart's content. That's all I'm saying. Chicken's just about ready."

Now he had her curious. Oh, what she would give to have heard the entire conversation between Pete and Bee Quinton.

They took their plates inside and ate at the kitchen bar. The combination of grilled chicken and potato chips was surprisingly delicious. She'd have to walk an extra mile tonight, but maybe it'd be nice enough she could walk at Ferris Park and then she wouldn't mind so much.

They ate in companionable silence for a few minutes before he turned to her with a glint in his eye. "So you gave the queen bee a run for her money?"

"I'll tell if you'll tell."

"Playing hardball, huh?"

"No. But I'm sure not dishing if you're not."

"I'll just say that I didn't like the direction the lady's questions were taking. I may or may not have given her a piece of my mind."

She laughed. "Good thing she didn't try to talk to us at the same time."

He looked up from his plate. "You get enough to eat? I think I've got some ice cream in the freezer."

"Oh, goodness. More than enough." She pushed her plate away, strangely satisfied by the interesting menu.

"Told you I was a good cook."

She laughed. "I wouldn't quit your day job."

"Hey!" But his smile said he was enjoying their time together as much as she was.

⁓

*I*t was after ten when Susan got home. She loved her house, but living a mile out in the country, she still dreaded coming home alone to an empty house.

After doing her check-the-closets-for-boogeymen walk-through, she went to the kitchen, took a cup of yogurt from the refrigerator, grabbed a spoon, and took the snack to the great room. Thinking about her impromptu dinner with Pete tonight warmed her. She wasn't quite sure what to do with the feeling. Maybe it was just that being with him reminded her of what it had felt like to be loved and cherished. To feel like a woman. To make someone laugh and know that you'd brightened his day.

Sure, she felt that way at the shelter sometimes, interacting with the residents, but except for Charlie, none of her relationships were long-term—and certainly not romantic—not that what she and Pete had shared was romantic.

Yet. She felt herself blush and laughed out loud at the craziness of it. Why had she even let her thoughts follow such a crazy trail?

She flipped on the TV. The ten o'clock news was on and she caught the tail end of a teaser for an interview that would air later tonight—about the Grove Street fire.

For the first year after the tragedy, they'd done a little story the first of every month. She hadn't been able to watch them. But with the mystery of what had caused the fire solved, and more than a year and a half gone by since the fire, the stories had stopped.

A year and a half. It shocked her a little. Eighteen months since she'd become the widow of David Marlowe. *Thanks a lot for the reminder, KSPR.* She'd be glad when the media got tired of rehashing the story once and for all.

The phone rang and she turned off the TV, grateful for the distraction. "Hey, Mom."

"Davy! What's up?"

"Nothing much. Just hadn't talked to you for a while. I didn't wake you up, did I?"

"No . . . I just got home."

"Man, your boss must be a slave driver." It was good to hear the teasing in his voice.

"Ha ha, very funny. No, I had dinner with . . . a friend," she said finally.

"What, you can't remember who you had dinner with?"

She feigned a laugh. "Sorry . . . brain freeze for a minute there." No use opening that can of worms, especially when she didn't know herself whether her time with Pete was a date or just food with a friend. "Speaking of work, how're things with *your* boss?"

He grunted.

"That bad?"

"Bad enough that I applied for another job."

Oh, boy. Here we go again. "Doing what?" Her oldest son had dropped out of college after his dad died, and he'd floundered between four or five part-time, minimum-wage jobs ever since.

"It's web design. Sort of. It's only part-time, but this guy has more work than he can handle and he wants me to—"

"Davy, why don't you go back to school? If this is part-time, you can still work, too."

"Mom—don't start."

"It just makes sense. There's scholarship money and I'm just afraid the longer you wait—"

"I know, I know. The longer I wait the less likely I'll finish. That's what Dan said, too."

"Well, your brother's right."

"I'll think about it."

His tone said, *End of discussion.* He'd struggled desperately after losing his dad, but she thought he was doing better lately. She didn't want to push it.

She forced small talk for a few minutes, before Davy made an excuse to hang up. She'd ruined it with her lecture. Again.

She searched for the remote and found it underneath a sofa cushion. The news was still on, and she started to click to another channel, but the story about the Grove Street fire was playing and she couldn't make herself click away. They were interviewing one of the fire inspectors who'd worked the tragic fire. It was a woman—Andrea Morley, the caption on the television screen said.

Something about the woman seemed familiar, but Susan didn't remember her from the Clemens County crew David had worked with. Of course, fire stations from several counties in southern Missouri had been called in that night. And Clemens County didn't have inspectors on staff.

The woman answered a question Susan didn't hear and hung her head, obviously emotional. When she looked up at the camera again it was as though she was looking directly at Susan.

And then Susan realized why she looked so familiar. It was the woman Pete had been talking to at Java Joint the other night. But she felt like she knew her from somewhere else. Probably from seeing her photograph in the newspaper.

If she was a fire inspector, she'd probably known David, too. Something niggled at her, and she had that same uncomfortable feeling as when she'd seen the woman before.

The woman on the TV got a pensive expression on her face, and in that instant Susan realized where else she knew her from: it was the woman from the cemetery. In Springfield. David's graveside service.

She would have thought nothing of it if she'd seen the woman at the service in the Falls. Half of Clemens County had been there. But why would a fire inspector have come to Springfield to attend what was essentially a private family service?

A weight moved into the pit of her stomach and rested there. There was something about this woman, about the reason she would have been at David's graveside. Something that struck terror in Susan.

Why? David had never given any indication that anything was wrong. Or had he? After the boys left home and she started the shelter, their lives had grown in different directions. She'd written it off to adjusting to the empty nest, maybe a touch of midlife crisis for both of them. David had done some silly, out-of-character things—like going bungee jumping and posing for the annual fireman's calendar. The calendar was a fundraiser and never exactly in bad taste, but still, it was beefcake . . . They'd had a big fight when she found out about it, but ultimately she conceded that if it was the worst thing he ever did during his midlife crisis, she was pretty fortunate.

But she and David had become more distant than she wanted to admit those last two years of his life. She couldn't pretend otherwise.

She clicked off the TV.

She was being ridiculous. And even if her worst fears were true, what could she do about it now? David was gone. It was foolish to go looking for trouble. She had plenty of that as it was.

*What in the world had
she gotten herself into?*

10

Saturday, June 6

Susan stood in front of her closet drawing a complete blank. Everything she pulled off the rack was inappropriate for one reason or another. What she usually wore to the shelter was too casual, what she wore to church was too dressy, and everything else was either out of style or made her look like president of the PTA.

Unless you counted her accidental trip to Java Joint with Pete two weeks ago, she hadn't been on a date since she and David did dinner and a movie the weekend of the last anniversary they'd celebrated.

She pushed the thoughts away. Now wasn't the time. She had a date and she wanted to enjoy it. She smiled thinking about Pete's phone call the other night. He'd sounded as surprised as she was that he was asking her out.

"We're probably too old to be going out on dates," he'd joked, "but . . . you wanna go out? On a date?" He'd been as jittery as any teenager asking a girl out for the first time. She liked that Peter Brennan—*Chief* Brennan—wasn't above being nervous with a woman.

But they were only going to dinner in Springfield, not to the Ritz. She finally settled on khakis, a crisp white shirt, and a new fitted jacket she'd picked up at a consignment shop a couple months ago but never had a chance to wear. The evenings were still cool enough that layers were a good choice. With the wardrobe dilemma solved, she headed for the shower.

She'd told Pete she'd meet him at his house, since she needed to stop by the shelter first and make sure dinner had arrived and that the volunteers had things under control before she left town. She was learning to trust Charlie to handle just about anything that came up, but it made a good excuse not to have Pete drive out to her place to pick her up—and a better excuse not to have him bring her home after their date. A chill went down her back. What in the world had she gotten herself into?

Pete was sitting in his pickup in front of his apartment when she pulled in. He backed out and motioned for her to take his parking space. She locked her car, grabbed her purse, and checked her reflection in his passenger window before she climbed in. She hadn't worn makeup in forever, but she kind of liked what it did for her forty-something complexion. Maybe she'd get back in the habit.

"You clean up nice," he said, grinning like a little boy, but giving her a quick, very guylike once-over.

"You, too." She looked away, feeling uncomfortable yet flattered at the same time. "I hope you're as hungry as I am."

He chuckled and hit the accelerator. "I'll drive fast."

Two hours later they'd finished dinner and were contemplating dessert at T.G.I. Friday's when Pete looked up from his menu, his gaze going over her head. Recognition lit his face.

"Well, hey, Pete. What are you doing in the big city?"

Susan turned to look behind her. The woman from Java Joint, the fire inspector from the TV interview, stood there beaming at Pete.

"How's it going, Andi?" Pete seemed awfully happy to see her.

She was beginning to think these run-ins weren't accidental.

But this time Pete slid from the booth and stood. "Andrea, this is Susan Marlowe."

Andrea had positioned herself behind Susan's chair, making it almost impossible for her to make eye contact without craning her neck. She stood and offered her hand.

Andrea took it, an unreadable expression shadowing her face. At first Susan wondered if this woman and Pete had a past together. But then Andrea's expression changed to something all too familiar, and Susan realized she was making the connection: Susan was one of the Grove Street widows.

Pete must have recognized the look, too. "You knew Dave Marlowe, Susan's husband. Andi's a fire inspector the county's worked with. Maybe you've met . . ."

"I don't think so. Nice to meet you." Susan made an effort to be friendly, but she was half-afraid Pete was going to invite the woman to share their table.

Unsmiling, Andrea ignored her and turned back to Pete. "Well, I won't keep you from your evening, but I saw you and just wanted to come over and say hi."

Pete gave a lame wave. "Yeah . . . good to see you."

Susan watched as Andrea slipped into a booth across from another woman who looked enough like Andrea to be her twin.

"That's gotta be her sister," she told Pete. "Andrea was the one you were talking to at the coffee shop the other night, right?"

He nodded and winked. "You think she's stalking me?"

"Ha! You wish," she teased.

He waved her off and the simple action filled her with inexplicable relief. Maybe because it seemed to deny he had any interest in Andrea. It was obvious the reverse wasn't true.

"Andi was the lead inspector on the Grove Street fire. The shelter fire. I thought you probably knew her."

"I recognize her from the news."

"Yeah. She made quite a name for herself when all that was going on. National TV and all that." He looked at the menu. "Have you decided on dessert?"

"Do you want to split something?"

"Oh, no, you don't. Don't pull that kind of bait and switch on me."

"What do you mean?"

"I told you one of the things I liked about you was that you know how to eat. Don't make me share the best part."

She laughed, remembering their supper together at Java Joint.

"Tell you what," he said. "I'll eat half of whatever dessert you order, but I'm getting my own, too."

"Deal. I'll have the Brownie Obsession."

"Good choice."

They ordered coffee, and while Pete demolished his cheesecake and most of her gooey chocolate concoction, Susan stole glances at the sisters. When the two of them got up to leave, they turned heads all over the restaurant. Susan got the distinct impression the sisters were accustomed to doing so. And they enjoyed it.

But when Andrea slipped on her jacket and lifted her hair into a ponytail to free it from her collar, Susan took in a sharp breath. Something about the woman's innocent actions, about the pensive expression on her face, brought back the memory of her brief encounter with Andrea Morley at David's graveside—the heavy grief Andrea had worn on her face that day.

Her skin prickled, and she felt light-headed.

She couldn't shake the feeling that there'd been . . . *something* between David and that woman.

"Are you okay?" Pete repeated himself twice before she realized what he was saying.

"I'm fine." She pushed her cup and saucer away. "I—I just ate too much."

He laughed. "If you ate too much, then what in the world did *I* just do?"

The sisters had apparently left the restaurant, but she couldn't get Andrea Morley out of her mind. She was sure David had never mentioned Andrea—or Andi, as Pete called her—and that fact alone seemed to give credence to her suspicions.

Susan remembered the expression Andrea wore that day at the cemetery. There'd been something more on her face than the sadness one felt at a colleague's death, or even over the community's tragedy of the fatal fire, as horrific as that had been.

It had been something *personal*.

"Are you sick?" Pete was eyeing her as if he feared she would lose her supper right there at the table.

"I—don't feel very well. I'm sorry. Could we just go home?"

"Okay . . . sure." He motioned for their server.

She waited by the door while he paid the bill. Later, in the car, she felt his eyes on her.

"You're not going to hurl, are you?"

She turned to look at him and had to laugh at the comical expression on his handsome face. "I'm not that kind of sick."

"Oh? Then what kind of sick are you?"

She hesitated. She doubted Pete would really want to hear what she was thinking. But right now, she desperately needed someone to bounce things off of.

"I think . . ." Inhaling deeply, she tested the waters. "There was something about . . . that woman." She gestured in the general direction of the restaurant.

"That woman?" He reached up and adjusted the rearview mirror. "Andi?"

Was she imagining things, or did Pete hesitate a split second too long?

But he looked her in the eye. "I'm not sure what you mean." His comment seemed perfectly guileless.

She never should have started down this path. Pete and Andrea worked together, seemed to be friends. She didn't even know the woman. She had no real foundation for her fears. "I'm sorry. It just . . . it brought back a lot of memories." Which was true.

He reached over and touched her hand lightly. "Of course. Of course it did. I'm sorry. I should have realized." He was suddenly intent on the road.

Susan wished there was something she could say to get back to where they'd started the evening, laughing and joking.

They rode for ten minutes in silence before Pete reached over and put a hand on her arm. "Are you going to be okay?"

She nodded. "I'm fine."

It was a lie, but how could she even begin to tell him the awful thoughts that had taken her mind captive?

*He didn't want
the evening to end
on a sour note.*

11

Pete nudged the cruise control up a notch. He was so out of practice at this talking-to-women thing. And frankly, Susan wasn't making it any easier.

No sooner was the thought out than she adjusted her seat belt and turned toward him in the seat, looking sheepish. "I didn't mean to put a damper on the evening."

"Well, hey, the evening's not over yet." He grinned, trying not to give away his thoughts. He didn't want the evening to end on a sour note. "How are you feeling?"

"A little better. Thanks."

"Do you want to get a cup of coffee before I take you home?"

She looked pleased but slid the sleeve of her jacket back and checked her watch. "I need to stop by the shelter and make sure the overnight shift showed up. It's a new couple and I never did get hold of them to confirm."

"You want me to swing by there first?"

"Would you mind? It'll just take a few minutes for me to talk to the volunteers and do a quick walk-through. I'd love a cup of coffee, though. My treat this time."

"You've got yourself a deal."

The rest of the drive back to the Falls, they talked about the station and her sons, and a movie they'd both seen recently. By the time they pulled into the shelter parking lot, Susan seemed in much better spirits and Pete was feeling like maybe he still had the knack after all.

*S*usan could tell the minute she unlocked the door to the shelter that something wasn't right. Two women volunteers she'd met a few times before stood at the desk, cell phones in hand. Their anxious frowns eased as she walked through the door, but they pounced on her, both speaking at once.

"The overnight volunteers showed up but the husband got into an argument with Benny—"

"—because the guy didn't think he was doing his chores right."

"Well, he wasn't, after all."

"Still, he shouldn't have—"

"Okay, okay." Susan held up a hand. "One at a time, please."

Charlie wheeled in from the dayroom and took up the story, filling in the details. "Benny spit a few choice words at the volunteer, and he and his wife stormed out of here."

The younger woman actually wrung her hands. "I'm so sorry, but I have to work at six in the morning. I just can't stay all night."

The other volunteer shrugged and reached for her purse on the desk. "I'm really not comfortable staying by myself."

Susan sighed. "I understand. You two go on home. I can stay. Did everything else go okay? Are Josh and Tony back from work?"

"Everyone on the list is accounted for," the older woman said.

"I'll give Susan the full report," Charlie assured them in his take-charge tone.

"I need to go let my ride know I'm staying," Susan told Charlie.

"You don't need to stay." Charlie hoisted himself up in his wheelchair, the muscles in his arms flexed. "I can handle it."

"I appreciate that, Charlie, but I'm really not comfortable having just one person in the office."

But he waved her away, dismissing her with a shake of his head. He'd been after her for months to let him take charge of the overnight shifts, but every time she considered it, visions of the fire stopped her. That night it had taken three of them to get all the residents out. And like that night, they had children staying in the shelter this week—a single mom and her two preschool sons. She dared not leave Charlie in charge by himself.

She was surprised at how much she did not want to go out and tell Pete to head on home. She'd enjoyed their time together immensely and had to admit she felt "all fluttery," as Danny would have said, about going out for coffee with Pete. She was flattered that he wanted to keep their evening going. At least the night had ended on a good note. She still needed to work out in her own mind what the whole Andrea Morley thing meant, but at least she hadn't let it ruin her evening with Pete.

"I'll be right back," she hollered after Charlie. "Don't set the security alarm yet."

"I won't."

She followed the volunteers to the parking lot. Pete's truck was still running and he rolled his window down when she came around to talk to him. She explained what had happened. "I'm sorry, but I need to stay."

"You got a coffee pot in there?"

She nodded, her hopes rising. "Might be some leftover cake, too."

He turned off the engine and unlatched his seat belt.

"You don't have to stay, Pete."

He grinned. "You don't offer a man cake and then try to back out of the deal."

She laughed and crossed the parking lot beside him, feeling more lighthearted than she had in a long time.

The entryway carried the faint scent of cigarette smoke. Pete couldn't shake the on-edge feeling he got every time he walked into the shelter. He only knew that a five-alarm fire would have been preferable. Even tonight, when all the clients were apparently in bed for the night, the place put him way outside his comfort zone.

He didn't know how Susan did it day after day. Especially when, on a moment's notice, she had to change plans and drop everything to fill in for volunteers who either didn't show up or didn't keep their commitment.

Susan headed for the coffeemaker on a small table in the volunteers' lounge connected to her office. "Do you want decaf tonight?"

"Whatever you're having is fine."

Susan's assistant manager rolled into the lounge in his wheelchair, looking at him with open curiosity.

"Pete, you remember Charlie?"

"Sure." He went over to the man's chair and shook his hand. "Pete Brennan. How're you doing?"

"Doin' okay," Charlie said. He looked pointedly at Susan. "She doesn't have to stay, you know. I could handle it."

Pete cleared his throat and opened his mouth—to say what, he didn't have a clue.

Susan saved him the trouble. "I appreciate it, Charlie, but I don't mind. And Pete's going to stay. We were just going for coffee, so we'll have it here instead."

"Suit yourself. I can take a hint."

Pete didn't think he was imagining the pink blush that crept up Susan's throat. But she didn't argue with Charlie, and he spun his chair in a circle and wheeled out of the room.

Pete went over to the coffee table. "What can I do?"

"Just have a seat. I'll go see if I can rustle up that cake."

She was back a few minutes later with two wilted-looking slices of bakery cake on paper plates. He took them from her and placed them on the center cushion of the old sofa, taking a seat at one end.

She poured coffee into Styrofoam cups and joined him on the opposite end of the gaudy floral sofa that divided the room.

"Thanks for staying." She lifted her cup in an awkward toast. "I really appreciate that."

"I don't mind," he said over a bite of cake. The stuff wasn't half bad.

"You don't have to stay all night. I'm here by myself—well, with Charlie—all the time. But I'm glad to have you keep me company for a while," she added quickly.

"You really don't mind, do you?"

Her brow lifted in a question.

"Being here. Spending so many hours."

"I don't. It sort of feels like home. Especially now that . . ." She didn't finish.

He knew she meant now that Dave was gone. "I can imagine. I don't like going home to an empty house either, and I've been doing that for a lot of years now."

"How long ago was your divorce?"

He looked toward the ceiling, doing a quick calculation. "Been divorced almost two years, but we were separated five years before that."

"Wow. I didn't realize it had been that long."

"Yeah, well, wouldn't expect you to."

"You never had kids, though."

He looked at her and knew she wasn't just baiting him. "That was the problem."

Susan cocked her head, a question in her eyes.

"We couldn't have kids. Not my fault, the doctors said, but kind of funny that she had kids right away after she got married again."

"Ouch."

"Yeah, it stung a little." He found it easy to admit that to Susan. "Lana married money. I'm guessing they did that . . . procedure . . ." He grappled for the word.

"In vitro?"

"That's it. We—*I* couldn't afford it. Didn't really want to do it even if we'd had the money. Not that I didn't want kids—" He stopped, surprised that it could still choke him up.

"I'm sorry," she said simply.

"Don't be. Water under the bridge. And I didn't mean to hijack the conversation. I don't even remember what we were talking about." But before the words were out, he remembered. They'd been talking about going home to an empty house.

He had a feeling Susan remembered, too, but she changed the subject. "How about another piece of cake?"

He groaned and patted his belly. "Better not. Gotta keep the six-pack from becoming a keg, you know."

She laughed and pointed across the hall. "Somebody donated an old treadmill. You can go a few rounds on that before you leave."

"I think I'll just pass on the cake."

She jumped up and took his plate and wadded napkin to the trash. "Do you want to play cards or something?"

"Cards?" He rubbed his hands together. "Are we playing for money?"

Susan feigned a gasp. "Don't you dare start that rumor, buster. I can see the headline in the *Courier* now: 'Gambling Ring Busted at Local Homeless Shelter.'"

Pete laughed. "Sorry. Didn't mean to give you a heart attack." He settled deeper into the sofa. "Okay, an innocent round or two of gin rummy . . . or is the gin a problem, too?" He winked.

"I think we can probably get away with that kind of gin." She shuffled and dealt a ratty deck of cards.

They played and talked for the next two hours. Around midnight Pete turned over yet another winning card. "Gin!"

He scooped up the cards and stacked them again. "One more hand? Maybe your luck will change." He twirled an imaginary mustache.

She shot him a look that said, "I doubt it, bub," but he could tell she wasn't bothered in the least by being the loser of the night.

She pushed back her chair and stretched. "I'd probably better do a quick walk-through. It'll only take a few minutes, but if you want to go home, feel free. It's getting late."

He checked his watch. "If I go, how are you going to get to your car?"

"Oh . . ." She looked befuddled. "I hadn't thought about that. But don't worry, I can work it out. If it's as nice as it was today, I'll just walk."

"In those shoes?" He eyed her sandals.

She shrugged.

"I can stay. If I can catch a few winks on the sofa I'll be fine. I don't have to work till three tomorrow."

She seemed to consider his offer. "We've got a couple of empty beds in the men's wing. That would be more comfortable than this lumpy sofa."

"I doubt that," he mumbled. He didn't realize he'd said it aloud until the words were out. No way was he going to share a dorm with a bunch of homeless men. "I'll be fine on the sofa."

She shot him a wry smile. "Then where will I sleep?"

"Oh." He frowned. "I guess that won't work."

"Pete, go home. Sleep in your own bed. Seriously. I'll be fine. Charlie's here. Besides, I stay here by myself all the time."

He knew it was true, but he felt like a jerk abandoning her. "At least let me stay till you do the walk-through. I'll tuck you in."

She laughed, but the look in her eyes said she would hold him to that.

She came back a few minutes later. "Everybody's out cold. You go. I'll be fine."

"Tell you what," he said. "I'll come and pick you up in the morning. We'll go for breakfast and then I can take you back to your car."

She looked pleased. "Perfect. We don't lock up 'til eight in the morning, so you can even sleep in a little."

"What time does your church start?"

"Not 'til eleven. Yours?"

He'd walked right into that one. "I'm not sure. It's . . . been a while since I've gone."

"Do you want to go with me?"

"We'll see. Maybe." He felt bad about leading her on since he had no intention of going to church—with or without her. He didn't have anything against God, but he wasn't crazy about some of His children. Not to mention, Sunday was his only morning to sleep in.

Looking for an excuse to change the subject, he went to empty their cups in the tiny kitchen, hoping he wouldn't run into any of the residents. But true to Susan's report, all was quiet in the shelter. When he came back, Susan was already curled up on the sofa with a fuzzy blanket and a book.

"Night-night." He grinned at her and playfully tucked the blanket around her shoulders, patting her head as if she were a small child. "Okay, I'm outta here."

"I'll walk you out." She started to throw off the blanket.

But he gently pushed her back down and tucked the blanket around her again. "I didn't tuck you in for nothing. I can let myself out."

She smiled sleepily. "You're sweet." Beneath the blanket she jingled the keys on the lanyard around her neck. "The door should lock behind you, but double-check it, would you?"

"Sure. Okay . . . Well, I guess I'll go. Call me if you need anything."

"Don't worry about me. I'll be fine." She covered a yawn.

"You do look pretty comfy there."

"I am." She smiled up at him, looking vulnerable and very pretty in the golden glow of the lamp on the side table. He wanted to kiss her. It would have been the most natural thing in the world.

He leaned over the back of the sofa and everything in him said, *Kiss her, you fool*. But something stopped him. Instead, he brushed a kiss in her hair.

She stilled and a little sigh escaped her—one of contentment, if he remembered anything about what it was like to have a woman in his life.

"Sleep tight," he said.

He grabbed his jacket off the back of the door. Then he hightailed it out of there before he gave in to the temptation to kiss her the way he'd been wanting to all night.

Five minutes later,
still no Pete.

12

Sunday, June 7

Susan closed the checkbook, turned off the calculator, and blew out a breath. She wasn't even halfway through the pile of bills on her desk, and there was only thirty-two dollars left in the shelter's account. Donations were way down, but she didn't have time or energy to do a fundraiser. She glanced at the clock above her desk. Ten after eight. Breakfast was over, the clients had left, and Pete would be here any minute.

She locked her desk and went to the door. "Charlie?" she hollered down the hall. "You going to church this morning?"

He stuck his head out of his room. "And Sunday school, too."

"Do you want a ride?"

"Too early . . . but thanks."

"I'd offer to come back by and pick you up, but I'm going to breakfast with a friend."

"It's a nice morning. The exercise will do me good." He cleared his throat. "This wouldn't be the friend who was here last night, would it?"

She felt herself flush and turned away, tempted to deny it. But Charlie would have picked up on that in a heartbeat. And made something out of it, too. "Yes. Pete's picking me up in a little bit." She started for the office, calling over her shoulder, "You have a good day now. I probably won't come in until tomorrow evening, but all the volunteer slots are covered through next week."

"Don't you worry. I've got everything under control."

In the mirror of the small restroom off her office, she checked her makeup and hair. She'd gotten ready in the semidark of her office early this morning. Not exactly conducive to getting beautiful. She desperately needed a haircut and highlights but kept forgetting to call for an appointment. She gave her hair one last fluff. It would have to do. She locked the office and went outside to wait for Pete.

It was a beautiful morning and she stood in the parking lot enjoying the crickets' song, the coos of a pair of mourning doves, and the raucous honks of a skein of geese winging their way toward Ferris Park. How long since she'd taken time to enjoy the symphony of spring?

But twenty minutes later she was still waiting. Should she call Pete? She had his number on her cell phone, but if he'd just overslept, she didn't want to be the one to wake him. It was sweet of him to stay with her last night.

Five minutes later, still no Pete. She didn't think he'd gotten called out on a run. She usually heard the sirens from the shelter.

She waited a few more minutes, then started walking in the direction of his apartment where her car was parked. He had her number, so if he took a different route, he'd surely give her a call. For his sake, she hoped he was still sleeping. But she knew he'd feel bad when he woke up and realized he'd forgotten to pick her up.

And she was disappointed about missing breakfast with him. She'd been looking forward to it. She wasn't sure what to feel about that kiss—if you could call it that. She'd liked it. No doubt about that. But she wasn't sure it meant the same thing to Pete that it had to her.

His friendship had been a pleasant surprise in the midst of a tough time, and she hoped it continued. But hadn't she and her friends always said you could never "just" be friends with a guy? Still, maybe that wasn't such a bad thing.

The sun beat down on her and she shed her hoodie and tied it around her waist. Maybe she'd skip church this morning. If anyone missed her—which she doubted—they'd just think she was tied up at the shelter. She'd used her work there as an excuse more than once.

She thought about Pete not knowing what time his church started and his admission that it had been a while since he'd attended. A firefighter's schedule didn't make it easy to be involved in church, but David had managed to be there whenever he could. She'd always appreciated that. Although the doubts that had crept in recently made her wonder if she'd ever known her husband as well as she thought she had.

She slowed her pace, enjoying the lush canopy of oak and maple leaves that arched over the street. She didn't want to think about David, about her suspicions. Today, for the first time in many months, she felt truly hopeful. About life, about love. And she wasn't so naive as to deny that Peter Brennan played a big role in that.

She looked up the street wondering if she'd missed him, tempted to call him, even if it did wake him up. She didn't dare think too hard about what might be blooming between her and Pete.

She didn't want to jinx it.

The sun was warm on his face and blinded him when he opened his eyes. He rolled over and threw off the covers. What time was it anyway?

When he looked at the clock, his heart lurched. He was supposed to pick up Susan forty-five minutes ago!

He jumped into last night's jeans and pulled on a rumpled T-shirt. He gargled with mouthwash and grabbed the phone on his way out the door, combing his fingers through messy hair with his free hand. He scrolled through his contacts, searching for her number. But before it came up, his phone started ringing. He answered without looking at the screen. "I am *so* sorry.—I'm on my way."

Dead silence for a few seconds, then, "Boy, that was quick. Do you know where you're on your way *to*?"

Not Susan's voice. He held out the phone and looked at the name on the ID screen. Andrea Morley. "Sorry, Andi. I thought it was someone else. What can I do for you?" He unlocked his pickup and climbed in.

"Sorry to bother you on a Sunday. I figured I'd get the answering machine. But as long as I have you on the line . . . I've got an invitation here to a career day—a community education thing for teenagers. I was wondering if you and some of the guys at the station might be willing to come for a couple of hours. Wear your uniforms, show 'em how cool it is to be a fire chief, you know?"

He ignored her teasing tone. "When is it?"

"Two weeks. The twentieth. It's a Saturday."

He looked at his watch as he backed out of the drive. He wouldn't blame Susan if she was furious with him about now. "Can I get back to you on that?"

"Sure." She sounded deflated. "I need to let them know early next week, but just give me a call. We'd have room for three or four people in the booth. You wouldn't have to prepare anything . . . just man the booth and answer questions. Recruit some future firefighters."

"I'll talk to the guys and call you later this week."

"Thanks, Pete. And listen, I have some information about the event. I'm headed for the Falls and I could drop it off at the station if you're going to be there."

"What time?"

"I'm about twenty minutes from Station Two."

"Sure. Go ahead and drop it off. If my office is locked, just leave it at the reception desk."

"You won't be there? I was hoping maybe—"

"I don't mean to be rude, Andi, but I really need to run."

"Oh. Sure. Well, thanks again."

He flipped back to Susan's number, making a mental note to remember to follow up on Andi's call. He wasn't crazy about doing these events, but he'd done them often enough that at least they didn't make him nervous anymore. And Andi had promised he didn't have to give a speech or anything.

"Hello?" Susan answered with a lilt—and what he hoped was a smile—in her voice.

"I bet you're wanting to throttle me right about now."

Her laughter was a relief. "If you forgot me and went to breakfast without me, I'm ticked. If you were sleeping like a baby, then that makes me happy. You were very sweet to stay with me last night."

Her reaction left him reeling, and he realized why. He'd been expecting a Lana reaction to his tardiness. If he'd pulled a stunt like this with Lana, he would have paid for weeks to come.

Susan was no Lana, and he felt the anxiety drain away at the mere sound of her voice.

"I'm heading home to get ready for church. Probably no time for breakfast now, but would you be up for lunch?"

"Sure. Do you want to just come by the station around noon?"

"Wait . . . Aren't you coming to church with me? You've still got time . . . It doesn't start for another hour and a half."

"Um . . . Sorry. Something's come up and I need to run by the station. I'm good for lunch, but I'm going to have to take a rain check on church."

"I'll hold you to it."

He hung up, smiling. She'd do it, too. And maybe that was okay.

She felt like crawling in a hole and just staying there.

13

They had a guest speaker at church, and the service got out a little earlier than usual, but Susan went ahead and drove out to Station 2. There were only four cars in the parking lot. *Must be operating with a skeleton crew this weekend.* Hopefully it would be accident—and fire—free.

She let herself in the front door and followed the sound of voices back to Pete's office. She approached slowly, prepared to sidestep the doorway if she saw he was in a meeting. Feminine laughter, mingled with Pete's, floated from the office.

The door was partially open and she could see Pete with his feet propped up on his desk, hands behind his head. If it was a meeting, it was an informal one.

She lifted a hand to knock on the doorjamb but stopped short when she realized it was Andrea Morley in the chair across from Pete. Even in profile, it was apparent how animated he was, how enthralled he was with the conversation. *With the woman.*

Exactly the way he'd looked at *her* last night. At least the way she imagined he had.

She wanted to turn and walk away. Just leave, before they realized she was here. But if she did that, she'd spend the rest of the day obsessing—about her suspicions about David. About Andrea and Pete.

And about *her* and Pete . . . what they'd shared last night. If she'd only imagined the affection growing between them—or if he was just toying with her—it wouldn't hurt any less to find that out now.

She swallowed and sucked in a shallow breath, then tapped on the door before she could change her mind.

Pete looked up. "Susan. Hey . . ." His expression changed, almost imperceptibly, and he quickly put his feet on the floor and motioned her in.

She stepped inside, feeling like a third wheel. An *older* third wheel. "I didn't mean to interrupt. I can wait in the car." She gave Andrea a little wave. "Hi."

Andrea waved back, not smiling, not speaking. In fact, she seemed a little perturbed at the interruption.

"Um . . ." Susan cleared her throat, barely able to make her voice obey. "Are we . . . still on for lunch?"

Pete and Andrea exchanged a look.

"I think I'd better take a rain check," Pete said.

"Lunch and church, too, huh?" She couldn't resist.

Pete smiled and Andrea looked confused, but he didn't bother to explain. And Susan wasn't about to.

"I'll call you," Pete said. He started to get up.

She waved him off. "I can show myself out . . . Have a good weekend."

She backed out of the room, then turned and hurried down the hall. At the front doors, she fumbled in her purse for her keys and dropped them on the tile floor. Her face on fire, she stooped to retrieve the keys, hoping no one had heard the clatter.

She felt like crawling in a hole and just staying there. But why? She had no reason to feel embarrassed. Pete had agreed to lunch with her, after all. Her imagination had been working overtime lately, but she wasn't imagining that Pete's meeting with Andrea *could* have been business.

Yeah, go ahead and tell yourself that, Marlowe. You know better. Or at least you should. Who scheduled a business meeting on a Sunday? And Andrea had been beyond cool toward her. The woman had been rude. But then, Pete hadn't exactly been warm and fuzzy either. Fine. She could take a hint.

Her heart literally felt heavy in her chest as she crossed the parking lot to her car.

But if there was something going on between those two, why had Pete acted the way he had with *her* last night? His actions had not been those of a man who was already involved with someone else. And if they were, she was finished.

Or maybe you're just blowing everything out of proportion like you always do. She didn't own Pete, and their plans to have lunch today hadn't actually been a date. Pete's job—even more than David's had been—was on call, high stress, and high priority. Even if she'd misunderstood the whole thing with him and Andrea, she still had to realize that Pete wouldn't always be able to drop everything to spend time with her.

By the time she turned onto the dirt lane that led to home, she'd gotten her head on straight and decided to turn her disappointment into opportunity. No obligations for the rest of the day. She could crawl into a hot bath, finish that novel she'd started weeks ago, putter in the kitchen. The day was hers. She didn't get many of those.

She cranked the wheel, turned into her driveway, and drove up to the old farmhouse nestled in the woods. The flowerpots hanging from the eaves of the wide wraparound porch begged for attention. They hadn't been watered in almost three days and the drooping blooms showed it. She made a note to water them while her bath was running. She couldn't afford to replace the flowers, and they were a luxury she didn't want to live without.

She stopped in front of the garage, put the car in Park, and got out to open the garage door. She made a mental note to call about getting an automatic opener installed before next winter. David had always thought that was an unnecessary luxury, but if there was anything good about being alone, it was that she didn't need anyone's permission to make a decision like that.

Let Pete and Andrea Morley have their little tête-à-tête. What did she care?

She hefted the heavy door up and got back in the car. But instead of putting the car in gear, she rested her forehead on the steering wheel. Who was she kidding? She cared plenty.

She'd let Pete get to her last night. It had felt nice to be starting— she thought—a new friendship. But she'd hoped it was more than that. And she'd let herself dare to think that she was starting a new romance. Something she'd given up on the day David died.

No. Before that.

She lifted her head and stared into the empty garage. She and David had made love twice a week, almost without fail. But she'd begun to feel as if her husband wasn't really present with her in those moments. He'd quit telling her that he loved her unless she forced it. Things had changed between them.

The truth was, she'd lost David long before the fire took him from her.

Feeling bone weary, she pulled the car into the garage and went in to change into shorts and a T-shirt. She grabbed the watering can and filled it from the spigot behind the house. She watered the plants on the back deck, then filled the can again and carried it to the front porch.

She started to water the geraniums in the hanging baskets but stopped short when she noticed a slip of paper sticking out from beneath the welcome mat. It looked like the delivery-attempt notice UPS used, but she wasn't expecting a package.

She picked up the dust-coated paper. She rarely entered the house through the front door. How long had the note been out here? She perused handwriting that was familiar and very difficult to decipher.

Need to talk. Try to reach at G.S.S.

Susan read the cryptic note again and turned the paper over. It was blank on the sticky side, and the logo at the top was nondescript with no indication of where the note had come from. She couldn't even think what G.S.S. stood for, but after a minute she guessed it might refer to Grove Street Shelter, though no one had ever used those initials for the shelter. Its official name was Grove Street Homeless Shelter, but even those initials—GSHS—were rarely used in reference to it.

But connecting the note to the shelter, Susan couldn't help but remember the note from "Herb Downing" that the volunteers had handed her. This handwriting was too similar to be a coincidence. If it was Zeke, did the note refer to when he'd tried in the past to reach her at the shelter, or was he instructing her to try to reach *him*? It wasn't clear. And there was no indication of when he intended to connect with her.

She put the note in her pocket and finished watering the plants. She puttered in the yard until it grew too warm, then tried to read for a while. But her mind kept returning to the note. When the clock flipped to four-fifty, she went in to call the shelter, hoping Charlie would pick up.

A female volunteer whose voice she didn't recognize answered the phone.

"This is Susan Marlowe . . . Is Charlie there?"

"Oh, hi, Susan. He was outside just a minute ago when I came in. I can get him for you . . ."

"No, that's not necessary. I just wondered if a man had come by there . . . looking for me?"

"Not that I'm aware of, but let me ask the others."

After a brief, muffled conversation, the woman was back on the line. "No one here is aware of anyone asking for you. Do you want us to give them your number if they come by later?"

"No," she said too quickly. "Don't give out my number, but if someone does come by, could you ask him to wait, and then call me right away? I'll come in to meet with him."

"Sure. We'll be glad to do that," the volunteer said. "I assume we call this number on the bulletin board?" She read off the number.

"Yes. That's my cell phone. But don't give anyone that number, okay?"

"Oh, no. Of course not."

"If he does show up looking for me, just call me. Or dial the number for him if he prefers to speak to me on the phone."

"Will do."

"And would you make a note for the overnight crew?"

"Of course."

Susan thanked her and slid her phone shut. She sighed and sank onto a stool at the kitchen counter. So much for the notion of a quiet day at home.

Susan seemed to think
she had some claim on Pete.

14

$\mathcal{A}$ndi clicked her tongue and lobbed the soggy tennis ball into the pond. "Go get it, boy!"

She laughed as the yellow dog bounded into the water after the ball. Gulliver still had a little too much puppy in him to keep his nose to the job, but she thought he'd come around. Especially if she could get Lucas Vermontez to help her train him.

She shook her head. No. She was as bad as Pete Brennan, keeping two women on a string. She knew Lucas liked her, but maybe not in the way she'd hoped, since she'd heard he was practically engaged. So he was off limits. She'd learned her lesson.

But Pete was fair game. Though he'd never done a thing to give the impression he and Susan Marlowe were together, Susan seemed to think she had some claim on Pete. Well, Susan had another "think" coming. That woman had already kept her from the only man she'd ever loved. She'd better keep her paws off Pete Brennan.

Andi brushed grass from the knees of her jeans and retrieved the tennis ball again. She could tell Pete liked her. He always teased her and made it a point to talk to her whenever they ran into each other.

He'd turned a little cool after Susan Marlowe had stopped by the station this afternoon, but she warmed him up, and they ended up having a great time together at lunch.

He hadn't asked her out again, though, in spite of her broad hints. Pete might take some coaxing. But then, she'd never been one to back away from a challenge.

She threw the tennis ball again and Gulliver leapt into the air. The Humane Society volunteer had told her Gulliver was a Labrador mix. He had enough Lab in him to give him a good sniffer, but judging by the size of his feet, Andi was starting to think he had some mastiff in him, too—or Saint Bernard? Something huge.

Sparky, the first dog Lucas had trained, had an uncanny knack for sniffing out accelerants. She'd already gotten a call from the Langhorne County fire department praising Sparky's performance and thanking her for talking them into starting up a K-9 division at their station. Sparky had spoiled her for any other dog, though Gulliver was winning her heart.

She'd only had Sparky for a few weeks when she turned him over to the Langhorne County station. She still borrowed him anytime she needed a dog with a good nose, but, even so, she'd shed a few tears driving away without him. It was going to kill her to let Gulliver go. Especially after she worked with him for another six or eight months.

She'd have to talk to Lucas about fixing her up with another pup after Gulliver was trained. But eventually she'd have to let that one go, too. *Getting them trained. Letting them go.* The story of her life. With men and now with dogs.

She had a sudden image of Dave, that thousand-watt smile lighting his face. She pushed the image away, feeling sad that she'd never been able to mourn him the way she needed to. But—like too many things in her past—she was starting to admit that what she'd had with Dave was wrong. Even though ultimately nothing had happened between them—not really—they'd both gotten high on the promise of what could be. But she never should have let it go on for so long.

Seeing Susan again today made her remember that day in the cemetery at Dave's graveside service. Seeing the mantel of grief Susan Marlowe had worn—and Dave's sons—she'd put herself in Susan's shoes for the first time that day. And she'd hated the way it had made her feel. As though she'd done something wrong. Maybe she had. Rebecca seemed to think so. But her sister didn't understand.

She and Dave started out as friends. Dave was a good listener and easy to talk to. And, yes, he was cute. And he made her feel like she was the most beautiful woman in the world. What woman wouldn't have been attracted? What she and David had together had come slowly and naturally, taking them both by surprise.

It had all seemed very innocent. She knew better now. And in the moments when she was being honest with herself, guilt dogged her like a hungry wolf.

She threw the ball harder than she intended. Gulliver raced to the water and paddled in after it. Andi chased after him, not wanting him to swim too far out. Making her voice stern, she called him back. But he kept swimming, heading for the other side of the pond.

The sun was sinking fast, reflecting vibrant orange on the glassy water. Andi sprinted around the perimeter of the pond, trying to beat Gulliver to the other shore. But no matter how fast she ran, she couldn't escape thoughts of Susan Marlowe.

David's wife—*widow*—didn't know about her and Dave. They'd always been careful. But if she ever found out . . .

The thought twisted her stomach in a knot. If Susan ever found out the truth—the whole truth—she would have every right to hate her.

She exhaled, staring out across the park but not really seeing. Sometimes—if she thought about things too hard—she came close to hating herself enough for the both of them.

*P*ete slammed the hood of the truck and gathered the empty motor oil containers, tossing them into the trash on his way to the utility sink.

He'd been mad as a grizzly all day. And no one to blame but his own stupid self. He'd acted like a jerk toward Susan, and there was no true reason he could give her that wouldn't cause her to hate his guts.

He rehearsed a litany of lies, but he refused to complicate an already complicated relationship with deceit. The sad truth was, he'd let Andi Morley get to him. The woman had a way of making a man feel very— well, manly.

In his defense, it wasn't every day he had two women flirting with him. Shoot, it wasn't every *year* he had two women flirting with him. He didn't know many guys who wouldn't want to keep their options open. But he could hardly give Susan that version of his story.

He wasn't so sure Andi wasn't just playing him. And for such a professional, accomplished woman, she could be pretty needy. But he'd fallen for her flattery hook, line, and sinker.

Even the look of disappointment on Susan's face when he'd asked for a rain check on lunch hadn't been enough to make him reject Andi's invitation. Not that he owed Susan anything. He was a free man, and he'd be a fool not to explore all his options.

But Susan hadn't deserved the brush-off he gave her. Especially after the time they'd shared together last night. He'd probably led her on as bad as Andi had led him on.

He scrubbed with the bar of harsh soap, then yanked the paper toweling so hard the whole roll came loose from the dispenser. This dating stuff was not for the faint of heart.

But he couldn't exactly call Susan and say he was sorry. That would be a lie. He *did* feel bad for acting so cool toward her, and he was sorry if she'd felt hurt or embarrassed, but how could he explain that without risking that he'd embarrass her further?

The sad truth was, he *wasn't* sorry he'd spent the afternoon with Andi. She was an amazing woman. Needy or not. She was accomplished and self-confident, and stunningly beautiful when she wasn't covered in soot. Attractive even when she was, actually. She'd never paid that much attention to him before. And he'd never figured he stood a chance with her.

Not that Susan wasn't amazing, too. He liked her a lot. She had a strength—and a vulnerability—that was oddly alluring. But Susan was steady, no-nonsense. And she wasn't the type to take a relationship lightly. If they started something—and maybe they already had—Susan would expect it to be serious.

And lasting. He wasn't sure he was ready for that either. Ever.

Andrea, on the other hand, gave the impression she was on to greener pastures if he didn't pay attention now.

He blew out a breath and headed through the break room. *Andi.* Why did he find her so attractive? Why did he even entertain the idea of being with her? Especially when he thought about the hurt look on Susan's face when he'd cancelled their lunch plans.

Wrong, Brennan. He swiped at a smudge on the stainless-steel counter with a wad of paper towels. He hadn't *asked* Susan for a rain check. He'd flippantly told her he'd have to take one. Why did being a first-class jerk come so easy for him sometimes? He was a nice guy. Deep down.

He was. The Pete Brennan who offered to stay with Susan at the shelter, who'd stepped in when that drunk put a fist through the wall, *was* a good guy. He was pretty sure he'd done those things out of the goodness of his heart, and not for selfish motives.

So then why did he turn around less than twenty-four hours later and act like such a swine?

The TV droned from the break room where Lucas Vermontez and a couple of rookies were watching old reruns. They only got two channels out here, but he refused to pay for cable when they were on such a drum-tight budget.

Pete stuck his head through the doorway. "I'm heading out, guys. I might leave town, but I'll have my cell if anything comes up."

"See you Tuesday, Pete." Lucas waved from the primo spot on the dingy sofa. Beside him, Smoke, the dog he was training, perked his ears and barked.

The rookies echoed Lucas's good-byes, and Pete headed for the parking lot, confident the station was in good hands. He'd assembled a fine team over the past year and a half since the fire. Clemens County Fire District would never recover from the tragedy that had taken five of his best people, but it was a point of pride for Pete that they'd been back up and running almost immediately in the wake of the devastating loss. They still could use a couple of full-time firemen and depended on volunteers to pick up the slack, but that had been true even before the fire.

The sky was darkening as he pulled out of the parking lot. And, like always since the Grove Street fire, he muttered a prayer as he left the station. "God, keep the guys safe tonight. Keep the Falls safe." Lately he felt a little silly talking to a God he wasn't sure even listened to the likes of him. But he figured it couldn't hurt.

He wasn't sure why he'd told the guys he might leave town, other than he didn't want to sit at home all night and feel sorry for himself. And he had the whole day off tomorrow. He'd probably go fishing. Too bad Andi worked on Mondays. It was tempting to call her. But he wasn't going to be the pursuer. If she was really interested in him, let her prove it.

Oh, call her, said the imaginary devil sitting on his left shoulder.

Susan is the one you really ought to be calling, said the angel sitting on his right.

He laughed at the crazy places his imagination took him sometimes. For all he knew, he'd only imagined the hurt expression on Susan's face this morning. *Don't kid yourself, Brennan. She was hurt, and you know it.*

So what was he going to do about it?

She studied his face,
trying to think why his
voice sounded familiar.

15

Wednesday, June 10

It was eleven thirty when Susan pulled into her driveway, mentally running a hot bath in the whirlpool tub. It had been a crazy night at the shelter and she was exhausted. The only good thing about it was that she hadn't had time to stew over the fact that Pete Brennan had never called her.

She stopped the car and got out to open the garage door. Rolling the heavy door up, her breath caught. Davy's car was parked on the other side of the garage. What was he doing home? It was a nine-hour drive from Indiana.

His car hadn't been here when she'd run home for a few minutes after supper at the shelter. He must have driven all night. But when she'd talked to him last week, he hadn't said a thing about coming home. Her imagination immediately gave her half a dozen scenarios to worry about.

She ran back to her car and drove it into the garage, not taking time to pull the garage door down behind her.

She let herself in the door between the garage and kitchen. "Davy? Is that you? Where are you, bud?"

"In here, Mom. Where've you been?"

She stopped in her tracks. He was slumped on the sofa in front of the TV in the great room. "What on earth are you doing home? Is everything okay?"

He frowned. "Long story."

She gave him a quick hug, then shrugged out of her jacket and perched on the arm of the sofa beside him. "Well, I've got all day."

She flipped on a lamp on the side table, illuminating her son's face. His hair flirted with his collar and his cheeks sported several days' growth of whiskers. He was too thin.

"What's going on?" She slipped the remote from his hand and turned off the TV.

He didn't protest. "I quit my job."

Biting her tongue, she framed a response. "Okay . . . So now what?"

"I don't know. I just . . . need to sort some things out."

Help me handle this right, Lord. She moved a throw pillow aside and slid down beside him on the sofa. "So talk to me."

He shrugged. "I don't know what you want me to say."

"Why would you put it like that? I want the truth, of course."

"I don't even know if I know the truth, Mom."

"What happened? Did you get fired?"

"No. I told you I quit."

"What about that part-time job you told me about?"

He shrugged again. "It didn't work out."

"Don't you think . . ." She might bite a hole through her tongue, but she was going to hold her temper. "It might have been wise to have another job lined up before you quit that one."

"I'm sorry, Mom, I just couldn't stand it for one more day. It was sucking the life out of me."

She refrained from suggesting that he wouldn't know the meaning of having the life sucked out of him till he'd lived here for a few days.

"What's so funny?"

She wiped the smirk off her face. "I didn't realize I was smiling. I just think—well . . . how pleasant do you think it's going to be living with your mommy at the ripe old age of twenty-one?"

He grimaced, which made her laugh genuinely.

"I'm only twenty, Mom."

"Nice try." She patted his arm. "Not for long. Davy, I understand if you need to hang out here for a few days to get your head together—I could actually use your help around here and maybe at the shelter. But don't get too comfy because this is short-term. Very short-term."

"But—"

"Like weeks, not months." How could two brothers be so different? Where Danny almost couldn't move out fast enough, they'd had to practically boot Davy out of the nest. And she knew that if she made it too easy, he'd still be living here when he was forty.

His eyes narrowed. "I don't see how I'm going to get this sorted out in *weeks*."

"Listen, son, it's not that I don't enjoy having you around, but it would not be a good thing for either one of us to have you get too comfortable here." A lump came to her throat. "I'm just doing what I know your dad would have done under the same circum—"

Davy shot off the couch and glared at her. "Don't! Do *not* throw that in my face!"

His reaction set off alarms in her head. And brought back memories of the years they'd struggled during his adolescence. Where on earth was this anger coming from now? She eased off the sofa and went to him, but he turned his back on her and headed downstairs to his room.

She started to go after him but thought better of it. Her shoulders slumped. They were both too tired tonight. She'd try to talk to him in the morning.

Right now, that hot bath seemed vital.

Sunday, June 14

Susan hurried toward the side entrance to the church, struggling to navigate the gravel parking lot in her heels. She hated coming in late, but something told her she needed to be here this morning. Maybe she could sneak in without being noticed.

She was probably foolish for even hoping, but in the back of her mind, she still had visions of Pete showing up at church. She hadn't talked to him since a week ago when she'd gone to the station to find him there with Andrea Morley. He'd given her no reason—that day or before—to think he had any intention of going to church with her. Still, something within her couldn't put aside that inkling of hope. He owed her an apology, and wouldn't that be a great way to show her how sorry—

"Susan Marlowe?"

She whirled around to see who'd called her name. A man of about sixty stood in the shade of a tree at the edge of the parking lot. He doffed his cap and held it in his hands. "It is Susan, isn't it?"

"Yes. I'm Susan Marlowe." Something about the way he stood—as if he was on edge—made her cautious. "May I help you?"

The man looked at the ground, kicked at a rock with the scuffed toe of his boot. "You don't remember me, do you?"

She studied his face, trying to think why his voice sounded familiar. "I'm sorry . . . should I—" Suddenly the memory jogged. "Zeke?"

He looked hesitant, then nodded.

She let out a breath. "Oh, my goodness. You . . . you left me a note . . ."

"So you *did* get it? That was three weeks ago."

She nodded. "You left one at the shelter, too, right?"

He nodded again.

"I wasn't sure what it meant. And I—I didn't know how to reach you."

"I figured."

"How are you?"

"I'm okay, I guess."

He looked good. Jerry and the other volunteer had said he looked "in need of a shelter," but now he was clean-shaven, with his hair neatly trimmed, his clothes clean and pressed.

Zeke looked around the parking lot. "I need to talk to you."

"Okay . . ."

"But not here." His eyes darted from one end of the parking lot to the other as if he was looking for someone.

She scrambled to think how to handle this. "We could go inside. There are empty Sunday school classrooms—"

"No!" He looked pointedly toward where her car was parked about twenty feet behind her. He must have been watching her. Or following her? How else would he have known to find her here? She felt her guard rise another notch. Clean, pressed clothes or not, she wasn't about to get in a car with this man. "How about the shelter? We could talk there . . ."

"They rebuilt it," he said. It wasn't a question.

"We could go there and talk."

"Is anybody—" Zeke stopped midsentence and looked past her.

She turned to follow his gaze and saw a car pulling into the church parking lot. Another latecomer, no doubt. But Zeke bolted, all but running, and looking over his shoulder as if he were being pursued.

"Zeke? Wait!"

But if he heard her, it made no difference. He fled down an alley and disappeared.

Shaken, Susan hurried back to her car and checked to make sure she'd locked it. She started back toward the front doors of the church.

As she reached for the handle the elderly couple serving as greeters opened the door. "Good morning!"

She hesitated for a moment, wondering if she should report her encounter with Zeke. But what was there to report, really? And the sanctuary the church offered felt safer than going out and getting in her car, certainly safer than going home.

Davy. He'd promised to be in church this morning, but he'd still been in bed when she left and she didn't remember seeing his car in the parking lot.

Because of the note on her porch, she was pretty sure Zeke Downing knew where she lived. He could have gotten her address from any Hanover Falls phone book. But for him to know where she went to church, to seek her out here . . . She shivered. It was almost as if he was following her.

She took a deep breath. She didn't believe there was any real reason to be afraid of Zeke Downing. But she'd feel better when Davy got here.

She entered the sanctuary and took a seat at the back where she could watch for Davy. She scanned the pews, desperately hoping he was already there. But within a few minutes she knew he wasn't. It didn't surprise her that he'd overslept. But he'd promised. Attending church was one of the conditions she'd set for him living at home.

She participated in the worship time half-heartedly, one eye on the door. She was not in the mood for another knock-down-drag-out with her son. Maybe she was being too strict. He was an adult, after all. But if that was so, then he ought to start acting like one.

Twenty minutes later, when the pastor dismissed the children for children's church, she slipped out of the sanctuary.

One of the ushers caught her before she could escape. "Everything okay?"

"Everything's fine, Frank," she assured him. "I just need to leave a little early. If my oldest son—you remember Davy?—happens to show up, would you ask him to give me a call?"

"Sure will," Frank said. "But you're missing a good sermon . . . I heard it in the first service."

"Maybe I'll get the CD," she said, feeling strangely as if she'd been caught in a lie.

In the parking lot she checked the backseat and under the car before she climbed in, and—feeling a little foolish—locked herself in after she shut the door. She rummaged in her purse for her phone and dialed Davy's cell phone.

It rang five times before his voice mail picked up. "This is Davy. You know what to do."

She gave a low growl and clicked End. If she left a message now, she might say something she'd regret later.

She started the car, but a moment later her phone rang.

"Yeah, Mom? What's up?" Davy sounded groggy.

"Where are you? Is everything okay?"

"Sorry . . . I overslept."

"Yeah, I noticed. But that's not why I called." She told him briefly about the encounter with Zeke Downing. "He's on foot, so I honestly don't think he'll try to come out there, but I'd feel better if you'd lock the house. And don't answer the door if he does show up there. I don't think he's dangerous or anything"—she prayed that was true—"but you don't need to talk to the guy."

"You sure you're okay, Mom? You sound a little shook-up."

"Oh, I'm fine." She tried to sound perky. "But I do think I'll go talk to Pete about it. I don't have a clue what this guy wants, but this isn't the first time he's tried to contact me."

"Well, don't do anything stupid."

"Now you sound like Pete."

He gave a short laugh. "Oh, and sorry about church. I'll be there next week."

"You could go tonight, you know. Evening service starts at six."

"Oh, yeah . . . I didn't think about that."

She hung up and blew out a breath of frustration. She knew Davy had no intention of even trying to make that evening service. It had been a lot easier parenting grown sons when they lived five hundred miles away.

She didn't know what was going on with Davy, but something was eating at him. He'd been home for four days, and he'd barely spoken a dozen words to her. He slept 'til noon and got up sullen and lethargic.

And she had no idea what to do about it. At times like this, she always convinced herself that David *would* have known what to do, what to say to Davy. In spite of his long hours and crazy shifts, David had always been a good dad, always tried to make enough time for the boys. She desperately missed his matter-of-fact way of handling crises.

Now she tried to imagine how he would have handled this one, what he would have said about Davy quitting his job and moving back home. About him not keeping his agreement to go to church.

And she came up empty. Completely empty.

She liked this turn of events.
The whole day suddenly
seemed brighter.

16

"*H*ey, Susan. How's it going? You looking for Pete?"

Lucas Vermontez sat on his haunches in the break room, roughhousing with a gangly yellow puppy.

"Hey! Who's this?"

"This is Gulliver, one of the fire inspector's newest protégés. She brought him by for a visit. But"—Lucas nodded toward the garage bays—"turns out this guy and Smoke aren't too fond of each other, so Andi took Smoke back to kennel him."

"Andrea Morley . . . She's here?" The implication threatened to capture Susan's breath.

"Oh, you know her?"

"Yes, we've met." She wanted to turn around and leave—and never come back.

Too late. Just then Andrea sashayed in from the back.

Pete was nowhere in sight.

Andrea stopped short when she saw Susan. "Oh, hi." She turned away and patted Gulliver's hindquarters, talking nonsense to the dog.

Susan was surprised to recognize insecurity in the gesture. The woman had seemed anything but insecure when they'd met before. Susan forced a calm she didn't feel into her voice. "Hello, Andrea."

Thankfully, Lucas interceded. "Pete should be back in a few minutes. He ran to grab some pizza. I'm sure there'll be plenty if you want to stay."

"Oh, no. I can't stay," Susan said.

The fact that Lucas didn't include Andrea in his invitation told Susan that Andrea must have already been here when they'd decided to order pizza. Susan had no desire to be caught in a situation like last time. "I'll catch Pete later," she told him. "Thanks."

She gave a brief nod in Andrea's direction and turned to leave.

Just then the front door opened and the savory aroma of fresh pizza preceded Pete into the station. As if the scent had emitted a three-alarm warning, firefighters appeared from all directions. Susan stood at the edge of the room and watched as they crowded around the pass-through. In less than two minutes all that remained on the counter were four soggy takeout boxes.

Pete seemed to notice her for the first time and came over with a paper plate loaded with pizza. He held it out between her and Andi. "I can share."

They both declined. Andrea laughed and gave Lucas a playful punch—much the way Susan had seen her flirt with Pete. "What was that about 'I'm sure there'll be plenty'?" she teased.

Lucas shrugged and gave a sheepish grin. "Oh! I'm sorry," he mumbled over a mouthful of pepperoni. He held out his plate. "Here. I can share, too. I thought . . . you said you didn't want any." He studied Susan with a teasing spark in his eyes. "Both of you said that, as I recall."

"I wasn't about to risk my life getting in the path of hungry firefighters," Susan joked, determined not to let Andrea Morley cow her.

"How are you?" Pete asked, turning slightly away from Andrea and giving Susan a quick wink.

She wondered if he'd singled out Andrea with the same winsome wink. No doubt.

She reminded herself that she'd prayed all the way here that she could be wary and not read anything into Pete's actions that wasn't there. She'd thought that still being just a little irked at him would work in her favor, but she was learning that it wasn't easy to stay mad at this man for long.

"Everything okay?" He tore off a man-sized bite of pizza.

She bit her lip, not wanting to mention what had happened with Zeke in front of the others. Pete motioned for her to follow him into the kitchen.

Andrea seemed not to notice, since she was busy flirting with Lucas, a fact that offered Susan a little comfort since she knew Lucas and Jenna were in a serious relationship. Maybe that was just the woman's way of relating to men. But if Susan's suspicions were true, Lucas being "spoken for" meant nothing to Andrea Morley.

Fuming at the thought, Susan trailed Pete into the kitchen. Without preamble she said, "I had an interesting experience at church this morning. I thought you should know about it."

He looked at her as if he was afraid she was going to nag him about his church attendance.

She grinned. "Don't worry, I'm not going to preach at you." She told him about her encounter with Zeke in the parking lot.

He frowned. "That's strange. Do you think he'll show up at the shelter tonight?"

"I kind of doubt it, though I wouldn't be surprised to find another note from him waiting there." She refrained from mentioning the note she'd found on her front porch.

"Did you tell him to write legibly next time?"

She knew he was being facetious, but she answered seriously. "I'm not sure he knows how, Pete."

"Well, I don't like it. Any of it. If the man has something to say to you, why doesn't he say it and quit stalking you?"

"I really don't think he's dangerous, and besides—"

Pete started to interrupt, but she held up a hand, cutting him off. "I know, I know . . . I'll be careful. Don't worry."

"You're not staying there alone tonight, are you?"

"At the shelter? Not for long. Bryn and Garrett are coming in around ten or eleven."

"Susan." His tone held warning.

"I'll be fine."

"Well, just in case, I'm coming, too."

She looked at him askance. She hadn't expected that. "Pete . . . you don't need to . . ." But she let her words trail off. She honestly hadn't expected him to offer, hadn't even considered that he might. But she liked this turn of events. The whole day suddenly seemed brighter.

When she left the station a few minutes later, she didn't even mind so much that she'd left Andrea flirting with Pete.

*P*ete cinched the garbage bag, shouted a good night to the skeleton crew at the station, and jogged out to the Dumpster with the trash. He tossed the bag in and slammed the unwieldy lid shut. It was almost dark, but the night air was still warm and moist. It made Pete remember how much he dreaded Missouri's humid summers.

He hoped they'd turned on the air-conditioning at the homeless shelter. He still wasn't sure how he felt about promising Susan that he'd work a shift at the shelter with her tonight. Frankly, he wasn't sure how he felt about anything lately. He'd always thought he was a man who knew what he wanted, what he believed, what he stood for. Lately he didn't know squat.

And it was the women in his life who were causing all the trouble. Although, maybe the fact that he was going home to shower and spruce up before he saw Susan tonight told him more than he'd have liked.

He buckled his seat belt and turned the key in the ignition. He couldn't deny that he was flattered by Susan Marlowe's attention. And that he found her extremely appealing. But then there was—

A knock on his side window startled him out of his reverie. Andrea Morley jumped up on the running board and smiled through his window. *Speak of the devil.*

The yellow dog she'd gotten from Vermontez stood at attention on the ground below her.

He rolled the window down, forcing his eyes away from the revealing neckline of her shirt. "Hey, what's up?"

She reached down to ruffle the dog's fur, keeping her eyes on Pete. "You headed home?"

He nodded.

Andi had spent most of the afternoon working with Vermontez and the two mutts. But even though she'd flirted with Lucas, Pete got the distinct impression that she was doing it in an attempt to make him jealous. It might have worked if he hadn't caught her—more than once—watching to see if he noticed.

She tilted her head. "I wondered if you wanted to go get a cup of coffee."

"Sorry, it's a little late. I have—" He looked pointedly at his watch. "I've got something going on tonight."

"Hot date, huh?" Her grin seemed innocent enough, but she was fishing.

"Depends on what you call hot."

She flipped her curly ponytail off one shoulder. "Going to a fire or something?"

"Ha! Good one." He wasn't about to tell her where he was headed. "I hope not."

She leaned her forearms on the doorframe of his truck, her perfume wafting under his nose. "Well, maybe next time."

"Yeah. You planning to be back in the Falls next week?"

"I don't know. Depends. Maybe."

She was onto him and beating him at his own game.

He revved the engine just enough to make her straighten and back away from the car.

Her eyes narrowed, but she said nothing.

He gave a little wave and threw the truck in reverse, regretting that he hadn't somehow worked it out to get a rain check on that cup of coffee with her. "See you around."

He had a feeling Andi was a woman who liked a man who played hard to get. And he'd be lying if he said he wasn't tempted to play a round or two of that game.

*It felt funny ordering
him around.*

17

"Sorry to bother you . . . Looks like you were in the middle of something," Pete stood at the front door of the shelter, looking far more vulnerable than he'd looked at the fire station this morning.

Susan laughed and opened the door wider. "You are *not* bothering me! Come on in." She finished drying her hands off and locked the door behind him. Supper was over, and she'd been cleaning out the small refrigerator in the dining room when he called to say he was in the parking lot. To be honest, she'd half expected him to bail at the last minute. But she was glad he was here.

"Things have been pretty quiet tonight," she told him, leading the way to her office. "I sent the evening shift volunteers home right after supper. Our numbers are way down tonight."

"That's good, right?"

"I guess so. I don't have even a dozen beds spoken for tonight. But this happens every summer. Once the weather gets nice, people are more mobile, and a lot of our regulars start sleeping outside. In the parks and . . . wherever."

"Oh. So it doesn't necessarily mean the homeless population is decreasing?"

"No, but in the last couple of weeks we've helped two of the guys—and that sweet family with the twins, remember?—find housing and get back to work, so in this case I'd say low numbers are a good sign."

"That's good." He hung his jacket on a hook beside Susan's and rolled up his shirtsleeves. "So what can I do?"

Just stand there and look gorgeous, she thought. But she said, "The food will be here in a few minutes. If you want to help me put the dining chairs down and wash tables off, that'd be great." It felt funny ordering him around. He was there on her account, not as a typical volunteer.

"You got it."

He followed her to the dining room, and they worked in amiable silence together. Later, with the dining room cleaned up, she showed Pete back to the volunteers' lounge in her office. He shuffled a deck of cards while Susan rummaged in a drawer for the scorepad they'd used for their gin rummy marathon last time Pete was at the shelter.

"I bet you wouldn't have been so quick to save that scorecard if I'd been ahead," he teased.

"Just shut up and deal," she deadpanned.

He rolled his eyes but did as she ordered.

The familiar sounds of the shelter provided background music—the hum of the washer and dryer, clients fighting over the shower, and the evening news blaring on the TV in the dayroom.

Susan had to halt their card game several times to dispense clients' medications, hunt down laundry soap and shampoo, and remind a couple of the guys about their assigned chores. Pete jokingly accused her of conveniently being interrupted just when he was about to win.

Later, after most of the residents had drifted to bed, she and Pete watched some legal thriller on TV while they worked on a jigsaw puzzle that last night's volunteers had started.

A commercial came on and Pete plunked one of the last few pieces of the puzzle in place. "You don't think they'll be mad if we finish their puzzle, do you?"

"They'll never know." She winked at him and tore out a handful of pieces from the section of the puzzle they'd spent the last hour working so hard on.

"Hey!" The shocked look on Pete's face cracked Susan up.

She laughed harder when he mimicked her and ripped out another hunk of the puzzle.

She threw her arms and torso over the puzzle, protecting it. "They might be mad if they come in and there's *negative* progress."

He chuckled, and they worked together to fit a few puzzle pieces back in for good measure.

The movie got boring and Pete—who had commandeered the remote—turned the volume down. They talked for a while before Susan realized what time it was.

"Let me do a quick walk-through . . . make sure everybody's accounted for."

When she came back, Pete was snoozing with his head back on the sofa. When she closed the door, he started awake.

"Sorry," he said, jolting upright. "Just resting my eyes."

She laughed. "You always snore when you rest your eyes?"

He gave her a guilty grin. "Everybody down for the night?"

She nodded. "Even Charlie. And he's usually up 'til after midnight. Go on home, if you like. Bryn and Garrett will be here soon."

He looked at his watch. "Not for another hour. Don't they come on at ten?"

"Around then." She didn't dare tell him that she'd told the couple they didn't need to come until eleven. She knew they'd come early like always. "I'll be fine. Charlie's here."

"I thought you said he was asleep."

"He is, but I can wake him up if I need him."

He looked skeptical. "What's Charlie going to do—run the intruder over with his wheelchair?"

"I'm really not expecting Zeke to show up, Pete. Go home. Seriously. You've done enough."

"No. I'll stay." He unfolded himself from the sofa and stretched, then took a seat at the table where the puzzle was.

"I think Zeke would have shown up by now if he was going to. But suit yourself. And . . . thanks, Pete."

"No problem. I don't like that this guy has been harassing you."

"I wouldn't call it harassment."

He shrugged. "Still, if the man has something to tell you, why doesn't he just come out with it? Why would he write a cryptic note and track you down at church, then run off before he actually tells you anything?" He idly picked up a puzzle piece and tapped it on the table. "You really don't have any idea what he wants to talk about?"

She shook her head. "I couldn't even make a wild guess."

The entry door in the hallway opened and they both jumped at the sound, staring at each other with wide eyes.

Then Susan heard voices in the hallway. "It's Bryn and Garrett," she said, laughing.

Pete looked relieved, and Susan rose and went to greet them. "You guys are way early."

"We were on our way back from seeing Bryn's dad," Garrett said, shedding his jacket. "Figured we may as well come on by. Maybe you can get home at a decent hour for a change."

"Well, it's been a super quiet night," she told them. "Pete—Chief Brennan—is here but I'll send him home now that you guys are here."

Pete appeared in the doorway of her office. He lifted a hand in greeting. "Hey . . . How are you?"

"Good," Garrett said. "I didn't know you were working here, Pete."

"Whenever she can talk me into it." Pete shot Susan a teasing look that she chose to ignore.

Bryn touched her husband's arm. "I'll be right back. I'm going to go get that stuff out of the car."

"You'll do no such thing," Garrett said, looking at her pointedly. "That stuff is heavy."

Bryn giggled and smiled up at her husband. "You may as well make our announcement. You know you're dying to."

Garrett broke into an ear-to-ear grin. "We're having a baby."

"Oh! That's wonderful!" Susan gathered Bryn into a hug. She'd begun to suspect as much the last few times she'd seen Bryn. Her face had a certain glow, and her clothes fit her differently. Susan was thrilled for them and overcome with joy for this couple who'd had too many trials thrown at them so early in life.

Pete shook Garrett's hand. "Congratulations, man. That's great news."

In spite of Pete's smile, Susan didn't miss the shadow that crossed his features. There must still be a tender place inside him because he'd never had children of his own.

"When are you due?" she asked Bryn.

"Christmas Day," Bryn said, beaming.

"Not the best timing." Garrett patted Bryn's tummy. "This poor kid will have to compete with the holidays."

Pete laughed. "Yeah, tough to share a birthday with Baby Jesus. But, hey, think of the tax deduction."

They laughed together, and Susan and Pete offered further congratulations. Garrett went out to get some groceries for the shelter from his car, and Pete slipped around the corner into Susan's office. He returned with his jacket over one shoulder.

"I'm going to head out if that's okay," he told Susan.

"I'll walk you out."

He didn't argue like she was afraid he would.

Garrett was coming in the door as they went out. "Back in a minute," Susan told him.

"No problem. Take your time."

When the door closed behind them, Pete turned to Susan and touched her arm. "Just be careful, would you? And you might want to warn Bryn and Garrett not to open the door to Downing if he shows up."

"They won't. Our policy is to not admit anyone after ten p.m. unless the police bring them here. I doubt Downing is going to ask for a police escort."

That seemed to satisfy Pete. She thanked him again for coming.

"Let me know if I'm in trouble for messing up that puzzle, would you?" He winked. "I'll make restitution."

"You mean you'll come in and fix it? I'd like that," she said.

He only gave her a cocky salute in reply, then turned and headed for his pickup.

She watched him walk to his truck, wishing she didn't like the man more every minute she spent with him.

Monday, June 15

*H*ey, Pete, I won't keep you . . ." Susan's sigh came across the line. "I just wanted to let you know I talked to Bryn and Garrett Edmonds, and they said Zeke Downing never did show up at the shelter last night. I'm sorry."

"Hey, it's a *good* thing he didn't show, right?" Pete leaned back in his chair and put his feet up on his desk. "Nothing to be sorry about."

"I just meant I'm sorry you wasted a whole night waiting for something that never happened."

"I didn't feel like the night was wasted. I beat your socks off at gin rummy, didn't I?"

"I told you I won't go so easy on you next time."

Her laughter made him smile into the phone. "Yeah, well, we'll see." He was glad they'd managed to find this easy way with each other again.

"Seriously, though, thanks, Pete. I appreciated you being there. Again. You know, if you keep this up, I'll have to add your name to the permanent list of volunteers."

"Yeah, uh . . . I don't think so." He was dead serious about that, but he didn't feel like opening that can of worms right now.

He found that the more time he spent at the shelter, the less intimidated he felt by the residents. He wouldn't say he relished interacting with them, but last night he hadn't felt nearly as nervous about walking through the front doors. He was even able to greet a few of the residents by name and joke with one of the little boys staying there. It killed him to see families with children at the shelter. Better there than on the street, of course, but how that must hurt to not be able to provide even the basics of food and shelter for your family. He couldn't imagine . . .

He'd enjoyed his time with Susan more than he wanted to admit. After she walked him out, he'd driven around the block and come back to park on the street across from the parking lot. He'd waited for Susan to finish updating Garrett and Bryn Edmonds, then watched her walk to her car, thinking how easily he could have been that Zeke character, lying in wait for her.

He hadn't driven off until she was locked in her car and on the road in front of him. When he got home, he called the sheriff's office and asked them to keep an eye on Susan's place. He felt better knowing her son was at the house, but with that loony all but stalking her, he didn't like that she lived out in the country.

"So, are you working tonight?" Susan's voice in his ear pulled him back.

"Uh-huh. Pulling a double shift so Vermontez can take his woman shopping for an engagement ring. Apparently Jenna has a birthday coming up."

"Aww, that's sweet."

"Yeah, that's me . . . sweet, as they come."

She laughed. "I was talking about Lucas, but you're sweet, too. You really are."

She sounded so sincere that he would have blushed if they'd been face-to-face. Yet he was glad they weren't face-to-face. Because he was pretty sure Susan wouldn't think him quite so sweet if she knew he had sort of a date with Andrea Morley next weekend.

He still wasn't quite sure how that had happened. And, technically, it wasn't a date. Andi had said so herself. But he knew it was every bit as much a date as his volunteer stint with Susan had turned out to be. In other words, there would be food, there would be fun, and there would be a whole lot of flirting going on.

He had to make up his mind which one of these women he was really interested in before he ticked them both off and ended up with neither.

"Well, I'll let you go," Susan was saying.

He jerked his attention back to the phone.

"But I just wanted to let you know," she said, "that the bogeyman never showed up."

"That's good. We'll just hope he stays away for good."

He didn't tell her that he'd been researching back issues of the *Hanover Falls Courier* and the *Springfield News-Leader* for stories about the fire. And he did not tell her what the sheriff's office—with a quick search of the criminal records database—had learned about the recent activities of one Zeke Downing.

"There's something
you're not telling me."

18

*S*usan got out of the car and went around to close the garage door. She had to yank with all her might to get it to budge. The stupid thing had been sticking, and she'd asked Davy at least twice to take a look at it. But as far as she knew he had yet to even glance at the thing.

Davy's car was parked outside the garage, because he'd unloaded box after box of his belongings into the second bay and was apparently too lazy to stack them at one end of the garage.

She gathered two bags of groceries from the backseat and bumped the car door shut with one hip.

It was officially the first day of summer, and it felt like it. Her shirt was damp from the exertion. Inside, she deposited her things on the kitchen counter, put away a few groceries, and went to start a load of laundry. "Davy? Have you eaten?"

No answer, but back in the kitchen she pulled some hamburger patties from the freezer and put them under the broiler. A full five minutes later, Davy appeared at the top of the stairs, uncombed, looking like he'd just crawled out of bed.

"Are you hungry? I've got some burgers on."

"Not hungry."

"What did you have for supper?"

He grunted an unintelligible answer and turned away, heading for the stairs again.

"Davy, wait."

He turned back, looking sullen and impatient.

She pulled the broiler pan from the oven and tried to make her voice bright. "What did you do all day?"

"What does it matter?"

"All right! That is enough!" She slammed the pan down hard, and grease splattered. Almost immediately a small colony of blisters raised on her wrist.

She ran to the sink and ran cold water over her arm. She felt Davy staring at her. Wrapping the dish towel around her wrist, she turned to face him.

"You okay?" His demeanor had softened considerably.

"I'm fine." She started cleaning up the mess, and he went through the motions of helping her.

When they'd wiped up the grease spots on the counter and floor, she flipped the burgers and put them back under the broiler. But she'd lost her appetite.

"So . . . Let's try this again. What did you do all day?"

"Mom . . . You don't want to hear it."

"Try me."

He shrugged. "Slept mostly. I—I don't feel so good."

"Are you sick?" He didn't look sick.

Another shrug.

She pulled out a stool at the bar and perched there. "Davy, what is going on? There's something *you're* not telling *me*."

"No." The harshness was back in his voice. "There's something *you're* not telling *me*."

"What are you talking about? What do you think I'm not telling you?"

"Maybe there's something you just won't let yourself see."

He hopped up on the counter and sat there, swinging his legs, kicking at the bottom cupboards with his heels, daring her to make him stop.

Her anger flared, but she decided this wasn't a hill to die on. Not now. "What are you talking about, Davy?" What had she done to make her son so angry?

"I'm talking about Dad." He shook his head and huffed. "God . . ." He spoke the word like a curse.

Had this anger she saw in him been simmering for the last year and a half? And she'd been too caught up in her own grief to see? Not certain she was on the right track, she chose her words carefully. "Davy . . . you're not still blaming God for what happened to Dad, are you?"

He gave her a look she remembered from his high school years. One that said she must be the stupidest woman on earth. "How can you act like nothing happened, Mom? Like everything's just fine?"

"Honey . . . What happened was very hard. But we have to go on. We don't really have much choice but to go on without Dad."

He shook his head and rolled his eyes. "That's not even what I'm talking about."

"Davy. Slow down. I'm trying to understand, honey, but—" *Stay calm. Stay calm . . .* "You're not talking . . . about Dad? About his death?"

"Not his death. His stupid life."

"What? You—you're going to have to explain what you're talking about. I'm sorry, but I'm in the dark here."

With a sigh, and without explanation, Davy turned on his heel and went downstairs. She heard him rummaging around in his bedroom.

She stared at the spot where he'd been standing. Had he just walked out on her without explanation?

She jumped up, ready to storm down after him, but he came back up before she reached the stairwell. He held out a small white card. He wouldn't meet her eyes.

She took it from him, straining to read the tiny print. *Morley Fire Inspection Services.* Andrea Morley's business card." She looked up. "I don't see what—"

"On the back," he said, sounding like the words were strangling him.

She turned the card over. Scribbled in a feminine hand was a simple note: *July has always been my favorite month.* Beneath that was the name *Andi*, with the *i* dotted with a jaunty little heart, like one a lovesick teenage girl might draw.

She was suddenly light-headed. Feeling off-balance, she reached for the counter behind her. She studied Davy, trying not to let him see her turmoil. "I don't understand. Where did you get this?" *Please, God. Let there be another explanation.*

"In his jacket. Last time I was home before . . ."

At Christmas. "Dad's jacket?"

He nodded.

She turned the card over, read it again. "And you think . . . ?" She couldn't finish the sentence. "What does that even mean . . . July?"

He gave her that look again. "Think about it, Mom."

She feigned a pitiable laugh and backed into the corner where two counters met, propping her elbows on either side for support. "What are you getting at?"

"July?" There was disgust in his voice. "It's that stupid calendar Dad was in. *He* was July."

"Oh, Davy. I don't think . . ." But was it true? She and David had gotten into a huge fight after she'd found out he posed for the firemen's fundraiser calendar.

In his photo David had been shirtless, wearing his turnout pants low-slung with suspenders, and flexing an admittedly impressive bicep that bore his Maltese fireman's cross tattoo.

She'd tried to laugh it off in public, but she'd been embarrassed for her husband. He was an elder in their church, for crying out loud. "You're not a twentysomething bachelor anymore, David," she'd reminded him.

"That's right, I'm fortysomething," he'd said, giving her a perfunctory peck on the forehead and flashing the smile that captured her heart when he *was* twentysomething. "And very happily married with two sons, just like the bio on the calendar says, thank you very much."

And she'd let that be the end of it. Until now.

She looked down at the business card and read the message again. If someone had given her a card like that, she would have torn it up and tossed it in the trash. Why had David kept it? She felt sick to her stomach.

Davy was glaring at her, as if *she* was the object of his disgust. "You have a better explanation?"

"She's a fire inspector, Davy," she said. As if that could explain it all away.

"Yeah, a *woman*."

"She and Dad . . . probably worked together all the time."

He rolled his eyes. "You got the together-all-the-time part right."

"David Michael, what is wrong with you?"

"Do I have to spell it out for you, Mom?" His eyes brimmed with unshed tears.

Andrea and Pete's cool dismissal of her was all too fresh. She couldn't make herself meet her son's gaze. "You think your dad was having an *affair*?" Her voice rose an octave on the word, and she hated herself for even speaking it out loud.

"I know he was." It came out in a monotone, leaden and dead.

The way she felt. "How . . . how do you know, Davy?"

He hung his head. "I should have told you. I should have said something and then maybe we could have stopped him."

"Davy, stop. Let's sort this out. Tell me what you know."

"I saw them. Dad"—he flicked the card like he was shaking out a lit match—"and this woman."

She took a step back and eased onto the sofa. "How do you know it was her? Where did you see them?"

"In Springfield. At that coffee shop out by the campus. I don't think it's open anymore. I was with Brandi. I thought I saw Dad's car in the parking lot. I figured you guys were on a date or something." He let out a humorless laugh. "I was going to go in . . . say hi. But when we drove around to park, I could see them through the window. I should have told you. Right then. Now—" His voice broke. "Now it's too late." His shoulders heaved with silent sobs.

The knot in her stomach tightened like a vice. "Davy, they were probably . . . just having a meeting. A business lunch." A tiny spark of hope flared inside her. Maybe there was a perfectly logical explanation.

But Davy narrowed his eyes. "Yeah. Business. I'm sure that's why they were hanging all over each other." He spit the words at her, as if it were her fault.

But her son wasn't making this up. The pain in his eyes proved that. And it hurt more than she thought possible.

Shame and humiliation flooded her. *David.* She hated him right now. Hated his guts. How could he have done this to her? To his sons?

She tried to come up with something plausible to defend him. But how could she? With everything Davy knew, if she tried to convince him that his father was innocent, she'd only be trying to convince herself.

And she was already convinced otherwise.

It stung to be treated like the enemy. Especially when she felt more like the victim.

19

Tuesday, June 23

$\mathcal{D}$avy had left the house unlocked and a blast of hot air hit Susan's face the minute she opened the door. Why hadn't he turned down the thermostat? It was like an oven in here.

"Davy?"

No answer.

"Davy, I'm home." She went down the hall and set the temperature at seventy-two. The electric bill might be as much as the mortgage, but she wasn't going to be miserable in the few precious hours she got to spend at home.

She started a load of laundry and went downstairs. "Davy?" She knocked on the door of his room. It was ajar, and she pushed it open against an avalanche of dirty laundry. Giving a little growl, she stooped to gather an armload of limp socks and underwear.

Davy's car was on the drive, right where it had been when she'd left this morning. He must be outside. Maybe he was finally doing some of the chores she'd nagged him about. She carried his dirty clothes up to the laundry room and added them to the load she'd started earlier.

Since Sunday, when Davy had told her about seeing his dad with Andrea Morley, her firstborn had all but shut himself off from her. Oh, he answered her questions about how his day was or what he wanted for dinner, but his demeanor made it clear he didn't wish to engage. At least not with her.

It stung to be treated like the enemy. Especially when she felt more like the victim. Davy had been almost despondent since revealing that he'd known about his dad's affair.

She'd been too wrapped up in her own grief and anger to know what to say to Davy, how to comfort him. Now she needed to give him time to start grieving his father all over again and to deal with the disillusionment he must be feeling. Heaven knew she had to do the same.

But she worried about her son. Worried he might be depressed. Worried he'd do something stupid. What David had always referred to as "a permanent solution to a temporary problem." Susan probably worried about that more than most parents, since David had answered too many suicide calls over his years at the station. And it was the young men who usually succeeded at their attempts.

She shuddered and fished her cell phone out of her purse. She punched Davy's number.

No answer. Not even his voice mail. It just kept ringing. He'd been helping out at the church, doing odd jobs for a little extra cash, but he hadn't said anything about working today.

If it had been Danny, she wouldn't have given it a second thought. She would have known he was out with friends, being the life of the party. So much like his dad.

But Davy was more of a loner. He'd had a few dates in high school, and he'd always had one or two guys he hung out with, but it worried her that he hadn't reconnected with anyone since he'd come back to the Falls. Most of his friends had left town for college, and the few that hadn't had jobs and new friends.

She went out through the garage and looked in his car, trying not to entertain the images her mother's mind wanted to conjure. The tension went out of her when she saw the car was unlocked and empty.

An acrid whiff met her nostrils and she looked around for its source. Smoke. Cigarette smoke. The boys had done their share of partying when they were in high school, but smoking had never been part of it. They'd both hated it when David occasionally lit up a celebratory cigar when one of the guys at the station welcomed a new baby.

She sniffed the air again. She wasn't imagining it. There was the smell of woodsmoke—a bit unusual in itself in this warmer weather—but mixed in with the smell of wood burning was the distinctive scent of a lit cigarette.

She traipsed through too-tall grass around the side of the house to the backyard. So much for thinking Davy might have mowed the lawn. She didn't want to get into it with him, but this was ridiculous. He'd reverted to acting like an irresponsible teenager. And she'd let him.

She sighed again. The mowing wouldn't get done tonight. It would be dark in an hour. She started to turn back toward the house, but something caught her eye. She squinted and shaded her eyes against the setting sun. In the woods to the west, she thought she saw a flash of light.

There it was again. She looked higher in the sky and saw a thin spiral of smoke rising above the trees, white against the purplish evening sky. It was too dry for a bonfire . . . Probably just someone burning trash, though she couldn't remember seeing smoke in that spot before. Bill Harker, who owned the adjacent acreage sometimes burned off his meadow, but not in June. And not as dry as it had been this year.

Her imagination had conjured too many fires since the shelter burned, but a fire could be disastrous for these woods she loved. She couldn't take a chance this one wasn't real. She ran to the kitchen for the binoculars, but when she came back, she couldn't see anything where she'd seen the smoke before. She still smelled cigarette smoke, but maybe her imagination was working overtime.

Distracted and trying to think what to do, she went inside and pulled a package of meat out to thaw. At least she could offer to grill when Davy got home. Maybe he'd take her heart-to-heart talk better over a burger and baked beans.

She washed and sliced fruit for a salad and wrapped some potatoes in foil.

With her hands full, she maneuvered through the back door to start the grill. The sky was gray now, with only a haze of light on the horizon. Putting the potatoes and grill utensils down on the table, she attempted to start the igniter. The stupid thing hadn't been working right, and half the time she ended up having to light it by hand. But it caught on the second try, and she put the potatoes on the top rack to start cooking.

But when she lifted her head, she gasped. Past the meadow near the tree line, a ball of fire burned and, even as she watched, smoke rose higher into the night sky. Bill Harker wouldn't be so foolish to burn tonight, and after dusk. Something was wrong.

Davy! Surely he hadn't—The images that gripped her were a kaleidoscope of those from when Davy was a troubled boy, those from the Grove Street fire, and others from her imagination, too horrific to give voice to, even in her thoughts. Where *was* her son?

She felt paralyzed, torn between running down to the meadow and going back inside to call the fire department.

She did have the presence of mind to turn off the grill. It wouldn't do to save the woods and burn down the house. She hurried inside and grabbed her cell phone, dialing 911 as she ran toward the woods.

Please, God . . . Please don't let it be Davy.

For once, he hoped she was working at the shelter tonight.

20

$\mathcal{P}$ete couldn't remember Susan's exact address, but he knew the location and directions the dispatcher was reading off were close to her property. For once, he hoped she was working at the shelter tonight.

He punched the accelerator on the pickup and focused his eyes on the night road. Smoke rose against the charcoal sky and he saw it before he saw the blaze. According to dispatch, it was only a brush fire, no buildings involved yet. But a brush fire in these woods could be a major disaster if it got out of control.

His cell phone beeped in his pocket, and he fished it out and answered without looking to see who it was. "Brennan."

"Pete, it's Susan. I don't know if you're on duty tonight, but I've got a fire on my property and—"

"I'm on my way there now. I wondered if it was your place."

"Oh! I can hear the trucks now."

"We're bringing the tanker in case the pond's too low to pump. Dispatch said it was a ways to the water."

"Yes, it is. Okay, good. But . . ." She sounded out of breath, and near tears. "I'm not as worried about the fire as I am about Davy."

"Why's that?"

"I don't know where he is. His car's here, but . . . I haven't seen him since I got home. And he's not answering his phone."

He fought the steering wheel as his truck bounced over the rutted county road. "Is that unusual?"

"He usually answers on the first couple of rings. But his voice mail won't even pick up now."

"You don't think he's down there in the fire, do you?"

"I'm a little worried he . . . set it."

"What? Why would he do that?"

"Maybe it's nothing, but I'll feel better when you're here."

"So you don't know how the fire started? You weren't burning or anything?"

"Of course not."

"No . . . I didn't figure. Where are you now?"

"I'm on my way down to the woods. The fire's still on the ground, but it's spreading awfully fast!" She was breathing hard now, and her voice wavered. "Oh! Thank God . . . The trucks are pulling in the yard now."

"I'm right behind them. Talk to you in a minute."

He closed his phone and pulled into her winding driveway behind the tanker and the brush truck. He radioed to be sure they'd dispatched an ambulance, too, in case Davy was out there.

As he reached the house, a Hanover Falls police cruiser appeared in his rearview mirror. The vehicles drove straight across the meadow. Pete was glad they didn't have to cut any fences to get to the blaze. And he hoped the vehicles didn't inadvertently start any fires driving on the dry meadow grasses.

He pulled ahead of the fire engine, the pickup bouncing across the rough terrain. He spotted Susan standing off to one side, her hands over her mouth. From across the meadow he couldn't tell whether she was trying to keep from inhaling the smoke, or if it was a gesture of fear. Or worse.

Pulling up beside her, he motioned for her to get in.

She climbed up and slumped into the passenger seat. "Thank God you're here." Tears and soot streaked her face.

"Still no sign of Davy?"

"No, and"—she held up the cell phone—"he's still not answering."

He edged his truck closer to the tree line. If it had been his kid, he probably wouldn't have been worried. Davy was in his twenties. He was a big boy. But he quickly checked that thought. He'd never had a kid. What did he know? Still, Susan seemed overly concerned, and that was exactly what worried him. He'd seen her cool and composed under pressure at the shelter. He trusted her judgment when it came to her kid, and if she was this worried about her son, there was probably a reason.

Braking at the edge of the meadow, he opened the pickup door and prepared for the worst. He reached across the console to touch Susan's arm. "You stay here until I see what's up."

A tall cedar at the center of the conflagration crackled, shooting flames above the brush. The tanker truck only held three thousand gallons of water. If the wind got behind this thing, it would be like spitting on hell.

$\mathcal{F}$rom the cab of Pete's truck, Susan watched in terror as the fire spread low along the ground, slithering like a snake to the southwest. Memories came rushing back. The shelter roaring with flames, that grim row of stretchers lined up in the parking lot. Pete walking across Grove Street, his eyes holding horror—and news that would change her life. They were memories nightmares were made of.

She shook them off and searched for Pete's silhouette among the team working at the edge of the wood. The crews had put out the biggest fire in the cedars, but they seemed to be losing ground with the brush fire. It crept ever farther along the edge of the wood.

Where *was* Davy? She tried his cell again, with the same frustrating results. If he was in town with friends, they'd surely heard about the fire by now. News traveled fast in the Falls, especially when sirens and emergency crews were involved.

It was all she could do to sit tight in this truck and watch from afar, but she knew the worst thing she could do was get in the way of the crews trying to do their job. David had come home from many a fire wanting to punch out a few bystanders' lights because they'd hindered the crew with their rubbernecking.

A knock on the passenger window made her start. An EMT stood there waiting. His name badge said *Harker* and she wondered if he was related to her neighbor.

She rolled the window down. "Is there anything I can do to help?"

"No ma'am. Chief Brennan asked me to check on you. Said you might need to be treated for smoke inhalation."

"No, I'm fine. Do I need to move the pickup, though?"

The young man looked toward the tree line, then back again, as if gauging the distance. "I think you're okay right here. I'll let you know if it looks like you need to move."

"Did Pete—Chief Brennan—tell you my son is missing?"

"Yes, ma'am. We're keeping an eye out. It doesn't look like there's anybody in those woods. But don't worry, we're on standby if they need us."

Had Pete told the crew what she'd said about Davy setting the fire? She wasn't even sure why she'd blurted that out. Surely he was past that now. But that didn't alter the horrific image that persisted: Davy, hanging from a tree, burning. She shook it off and shot up another prayer.

"Thank you," she told the EMT. "I think I'm going to walk back up to the house"—she hooked a thumb behind her—"see if he's showed up there yet."

"I'll let Chief Brennan know," he said. "I'm sure he'd appreciate a call if your boy's there. Let me give you a number—"

She held up her phone. "I have Chief Brennan's cell number."

She didn't miss the slight arc of his brow.

"Thanks again," she said. "If anyone needs water or anything, give me a call. Chief Brennan has my number. I can bring drinks down. I'll put the coffee pot on, too."

He touched the brim of his helmet. "'Preciate it, ma'am, but we're good to go."

She picked her way back up the hill in the dark, stopping every few feet to turn back and check on the fire. It seemed smaller now, though whether from the distance or because they were actually gaining on it, she couldn't be sure. A chorus of howling dogs from neighboring farms had started up and she shivered, thinking about the other wildlife that lived in these woods.

God, keep Davy safe. Wherever he is, please be with him.

She went around the house to see that Davy's car still sat in the driveway in front of the garage and only the kitchen light shone through the window, just as she'd left it.

Inside, she tried calling Davy's cell phone again. Nothing.

She threw some water bottles in the Deepfreeze in the utility room and put a pot of coffee on to brew, even though she was pretty sure none of the responders would come to the house. Except maybe Pete. And she hoped he would. She needed to talk to him. Explain to him why she was so worried about Davy. She was not looking forward to that conversation.

She went out to the back porch to clean up the grill and toss out the half-baked potatoes. She looked down toward the fire again and saw Pete's truck headed up from the meadow and across her property. Her heart stopped. He was driving fast.

Her hands trembled.
"Did you find something?"

21

Susan held her breath, watching Pete climb from behind the wheel of his pickup. He walked up the drive, his expression stoic. "I think we've got the fire under control," he said, his tone even. "Hard to say what started it."

A trickle of relief went through her. At least Davy wasn't there. They would have found him by now. Feeling drained and weak, she stepped off the deck and started toward Pete, biting back the tears that flooded her throat.

He looked alarmed. "Is everything okay? Have you heard from Davy?"

"No. Nothing." Swallowing her tears, she fanned her face with one hand. "I'm sorry. I'm just worried sick."

"Of course you are. Who wouldn't be?" He closed the distance between them and enveloped her in a bear hug. His clothes smelled of soot and sweat, exactly the way David used to smell when he came home from a fire.

She let herself rest in Pete's embrace, not caring that it didn't mean to him what it meant to her. She knew he would have offered the same comfort to anyone in her circumstances. And he was good at his job.

After a few seconds he gently let her go. "When's the last time you tried to call him?"

She looked at her watch, trying to compose herself. "About fifteen minutes ago."

"Have you called any of his friends?"

"Most of them are off at college. And he hasn't really gone out much since he's been home. But I guess I should do that. Check with his friends, I mean." She was embarrassed to admit she didn't even know who Davy had seen since he moved back. She'd been so caught up in things at the shelter—and the whole mess with Andrea Morley.

"I'd offer to drive into town and search for him, but if he's not in his car, I don't know what I'd be looking for."

"I understand. And thanks, Pete. I appreciate it."

"I'm going to run back down and see how the crew's doing, check out the scene. Maybe they've found some clues by now. But—" He looked at her as if gauging her receptiveness to what he was about to say.

"What?"

"I'd like to call Andrea Morley in to do an inspection first thing in the morning."

She stiffened. "A fire inspector? Why? You think it's suspicious?" She heard the hard edge in her own voice and tried to soften it. "And why Andrea? Isn't there somebody else who could come?"

"She's the only one around here using dogs. I'd really like to get dogs in there before the site is contaminated. But there's no use going down there now. It'll be pitch black by the time she could get here."

Susan closed her eyes. "If you think that's best."

"I really do."

"What makes you think the fire was set? Is it just because of what I said about Davy? Now that we know he wasn't even here, couldn't it have just been . . . I don't know . . ." She shrugged. Why had she ever said anything?

"Susan," he said gently, "it may have just been kids playing with matches, or a careless cigarette tossed out, but until we know for sure Davy wasn't involved—"

"I smelled cigarettes! Earlier." She'd completely forgotten until now.

"You did?"

She nodded. "Earlier. When I went around back, looking for Davy."

"But you didn't see smoke then?"

"I . . . I thought I did. In the distance. But it wasn't until later that I saw the fire. That's when I called."

He looked thoughtful. "If you smelled cigarette smoke, it wasn't from the scene of the fire. No way you would have smelled that way down here."

"What do you mean?"

"If you smelled cigarette smoke, someone was smoking near your house."

"But there was no one here. You think someone was sneaking around the property?"

"We'll hope the cause of the fire will prove to be accidental. But I'll be honest with you, that's not what I'm expecting to find."

She studied him, waiting for him to expound, but he shook his head, took off his cap, and ran a hand through tousled hair before putting the cap back on.

"Pete? What are you not telling me?" Her hands trembled. "Did you find something?"

"Let's find Davy, okay? Then we'll figure out what we're dealing with. Harker said you were putting coffee on. I could use a cup, if you don't mind. Can we go inside?"

"Sure. Of course." She reached for the back door.

Pete held it open for her, then followed her into the kitchen. He looked around the large kitchen–great room combination. "Nice place. Always thought it would be nice to live in the country."

"It is. Most of the time. Gets a little . . . dark. At night."

He laughed. "Hate to tell you, but it gets dark at night in town, too."

"You know what I mean."

"Yeah. I do." His expression grew sober and she was sorry she hadn't let him make her laugh.

She grabbed the carafe from the coffeemaker. "You want sugar? Cream?"

"No thanks. Black."

She chose a tall mug from the cupboard and had it half full of steaming coffee before she realized it was David's favorite mug. Davy must have been using it. She'd pushed it to the back of the cupboard the first time she saw it after David's death—not ready to throw it away but not wanting to see it every time she opened the cupboard either.

She filled it to the brim and handed it to Pete.

"Thanks. Aren't you going to have some?"

The way he said it, she had to say yes. And if it would keep him there longer . . . She poured herself a smaller mug and nodded toward overstuffed chairs in the great room. "Have a seat."

He looked down at his clothes. "I'm covered with soot."

"Over there, then." She motioned at the round oak dining table and chairs at the end of the room. "You won't hurt those. I'll go make some calls."

"Maybe for a minute." He took his cap off again and placed it on one corner of the table. Pulling out a chair, he turned it backward and straddled it.

David used to sit at the table that way. Seeing Pete there, in her kitchen, something twisted inside her. She turned away. This whole night—the fire, Davy, Andrea Morley, and Pete being here now—was stirring up too many memories.

At the desk on the opposite side of the great room, she found the phone book and looked up the numbers of several families Davy had hung out with when he'd lived at home. She wasn't even sure which of her son's classmates were still in the Falls. Answering machines picked up at the first two numbers she called. She left a brief message saying she was trying to locate Davy. She dialed Janice Andrews's number, and the single mom answered on the second ring.

"Hi, Jan. It's Susan Marlowe. Is Jake around?" She glanced at Pete, who was watching her with an expression she couldn't read. "I'm looking for Davy. You haven't seen him tonight, have you?"

"Hang on. Let me ask Jake." She heard muffled voices as Janice hollered for her son. She came back on a few seconds later. "Sorry. Jake hasn't seen him since last weekend."

"Okay. Thanks."

"No luck?"

She shook her head.

Pete drained his coffee mug. "You said earlier that you were afraid Davy set the fire. What made you think that, Susan?"

She looked at the floor. "I shouldn't have said that," she said finally. She needed to tell Pete. She inhaled, then blew out a heavy breath. "When Davy was a kid, about eleven, he started some fires. Playing with matches, but he set some fires . . . purposely. We took him to a counselor. They thought it was just his way of trying to get his father's attention. The behavior stopped shortly after that. But Davy's been struggling recently. I think he has some depression. A mother's mind works overtime, I guess."

She motioned to the phone and dialed the next number on her list before he could respond. The phone was ringing on the other end when she heard the crunch of gravel on the driveway. With the phone still to her ear, she hurried to the foyer and peered out the front window.

Davy climbed out of a blue pickup and yelled something friendly—but profane—at the driver. Susan didn't recognize the driver or the vehicle. The young man laughed and revved the engine, then fishtailed down the drive going at least forty. Dust clouded behind him, heavy motes illuminated by the mercury-vapor yard light.

She breathed out a sigh. "It's Davy," she told Pete. She flipped on the porch light and opened the front door.

She smelled the alcohol the minute Davy reached the porch steps. "You're drunk."

He seemed to see her for the first time. "Mom! Hey now!" His words were slurred. "Why would ya think a thing like that? I—"

"I've been looking all over for you." She prayed Pete didn't come out here. "Where have you been? Why didn't you answer your phone?"

"I wazh . . . out." He looked around and sniffed the air. "What's with all the smoke?"

"We had a fire. Get in the house," she hissed. "And please . . . just go straight downstairs to your room. Chief Brennan is here, and I don't need for him to see you like this."

"What fire?"

He staggered up the porch steps and through the front door.

Pete was standing in the foyer. "Everything okay?"

Susan got the feeling he'd watched everything from the window.

She winced. "A little too much to drink, I think. Davy, you remember Chief Brennan?"

Davy gave him a drunken grin and extended a hand that missed Pete's by several inches.

Pete made up the difference and shook his hand. "Haven't seen you for a while."

Susan nudged Davy toward the basement stairwell behind the open staircase that led to the second story.

"I'm goin', I'm goin'." He shrugged out from under her touch and shot her a look, his eyes bloodshot and unfocused. He turned and started down the stairs but stumbled on the top step.

Pete lunged and caught him. "Let me give you a hand there, buddy." He draped one of Davy's arms around his neck. "Hang on."

Susan wished the floor would open up and swallow her.

She followed them down, then hurried ahead to open the door to Davy's room. She flipped on the light. His bedroom was a mess, but that was the least of her embarrassment.

She tried to straighten the rumpled blankets before Davy fell onto the bed, moaning. *Dear God, please don't let him be sick.*

Pete helped her get Davy's tennis shoes off and pulled the covers up around him. He straightened and winked at Susan. "Nothing a good night's sleep won't cure."

She dropped her gaze and shook her head, humiliated. "I'm so sorry."

"Hey, at least he didn't drive home drunk. You gotta give him credit for that."

"Oh!" She clapped a hand over her mouth. "But his friend probably did. I don't even know who it was, but I should have stopped—"

"It's okay." He tapped his cell phone on his belt. "I put in a call as soon as I saw Davy get out of the car. They'll stop the kid and make sure he's not DUI."

He went to the door.

"Thanks, Pete." She turned out the light, pulled the door shut behind them, and followed Pete up the stairs.

He stood in the middle of the great room, looking awkward. She wanted to break down and have a good cry. But she'd already embarrassed herself crying on Pete's shoulder earlier. She blew out a breath and slumped onto the sofa.

"Thanks for everything tonight, Pete. I . . . need to let you go home. The last thing you need tonight is to get involved in my little family drama."

He motioned in the direction of the basement stairs. "You think he'll be okay? Does this happen often?"

"I'm not so naive as to think he never goes out drinking anymore, but this is the first time he's come home drunk since high school. And it better be the last."

Pete grinned. He took a few steps backward and reached behind him where he'd left his cap on the table. He rubbed a hand over his sandy hair and placed the cap on his head. "You sure you can handle this? You don't have to work tonight, do you?"

She shook her head. "I'm going to let Charlie handle it tonight. Bryn and Garrett are doing the overnight shift so I'm not too worried."

"Good. Get a good night's rest. I'll give you a call before we bring the dogs out in the morning."

"Okay." She went to open the back door for him. "I—I don't want to have to talk to her, Pete."

He hesitated, looking confused. "Andi?"

She nodded.

"I don't know . . . She'll probably have some questions that only you can answer. You or Davy."

She blew out a breath. "I'm too tired to think about it tonight."

"Of course you are." He gave her a quick hug. "Go to bed. We'll worry about it tomorrow."

"Okay. Thanks again. It was good having you here . . . through all of this."

"Not a problem." He popped his cap off and dipped his head in one smooth motion. "Talk to you tomorrow, okay?"

The tenderness in his voice made her go soft inside. She nodded, near tears again, but not wanting him to know it lest he feel obligated to stay.

She closed the door behind him and went to watch through the curtains as he drove around the corner of the house to the front drive. She watched until his taillights disappeared at the end of the lane. Only then did she let herself break down and weep.

He would have been a
good dad if he'd ever
gotten the chance.

22

Wednesday, June 24

$\mathcal{P}$ete pulled into Susan's driveway just before eight the next morning. Good. Andi's car wasn't there yet. She'd planned to be there about eight fifteen and he'd made it a point to arrive earlier, so Susan wouldn't have to greet her.

He'd been surprised Susan was so adamant about not wanting Andi here. He'd sensed there was no love lost between the two, and last night, driving home from Susan's, he dared to flatter himself that it was because of him. This morning that seemed crazy.

Davy's car still sat in front of the garage where it had been last night. He'd be surprised if the kid was up before noon.

Susan's son hadn't impressed him, but, then, they hadn't met under the best of circumstances and given the burden the kid had been carrying, it was understandable. He only hoped Davy hadn't been involved in the fire. It didn't seem likely, given the time the fire had started, but he couldn't be sure. What Susan had told him about Davy starting fires as a kid would make him a primary suspect. He'd better have a good alibi.

When Pete let himself think about a relationship with Susan Marlowe, the whole thing with her sons gave him pause. It was bad enough to think about marrying a woman with children at home. Quite another thing to be saddled with a girlfriend who had troubled adult children. Susan's younger son lived out of state and, to hear her talk, Davy would probably move out soon, too. Good. He wasn't interested in being "Dad" to any kids of any age. The days of wishing for that were behind him.

And yet, something had happened inside him when he'd helped Susan get Davy down to his room last night. He was still examining what that meant. The truth was, something about the kid had touched a soft spot in him. He could remember the day when he'd *been* Davy Marlowe. Not that he'd lost his dad as a kid, or even struggled to know what to do in life the way Davy did. But he'd had his wild side back in the day. And his parents—God bless them—had been there for him. They'd never made too big a deal of it, but they hadn't tolerated it either.

The whole situation made him think that he would have been a good dad if he'd ever gotten the chance.

He parked behind Davy's car and went to knock on the front door. Andi had agreed to meet him with an accelerant detection dog. He'd called Susan half an hour ago to let her know the plans. She still didn't sound too thrilled about the prospect of Andi doing the inspection, but he knew they'd get better results with the dogs.

Susan answered the door wearing jeans and a rumpled sweatshirt that looked like it might have been slept in. She wore no makeup and her hair was tousled, curling slightly at the nape of her neck. Even with dark circles under her eyes, she still looked beautiful to him. "Come on in, Pete." She looked past him to the drive.

"Andi's not here yet. How's he doing . . . Davy?"

"He's not up yet. I probably ought to make him get up, but I'm not in the mood to deal with him right now."

"I hear you."

She led him through to the great room. He heard the coffeemaker sputtering, and the aroma of fresh coffee wafted under his nose. "Mmm . . . Smells good."

"Let me pour you a cup."

"Don't mind if I do." He pulled out a barstool and watched her as she got down two mugs from the cupboard and poured his coffee.

She set a steaming mug in front of him.

He took a sip and gave an appreciative sigh. "Thanks."

The doorbell rang and Susan turned to him, looking a little like a doe caught in the headlights.

He pushed his coffee away and slid off the stool, donning his cap. "That'll be Andi. I'll send her around back. You want to walk down with us?"

"I'd rather not." She looked at the floor. "Unless you need me."

He touched his cell phone. "I'll call you if I do."

"Thanks." The word spoke volumes.

Andi stood on the front porch wearing her khaki work uniform. Her curly hair hung loose to her shoulders and she'd taken care with her makeup. He remembered Lana telling him once that women dressed for other women, and he had a funny feeling that Andi's attire was meant to make Susan feel . . . inferior.

He'd had lunch with Andi Saturday, but he was starting to suspect she was merely on a fishing expedition, since she'd spent most of the time trying to lure him into talking about Susan. She'd gone a little wacko, accusing him of having a thing for Susan. Like a jealous schoolgirl.

But he hadn't told Andi anything. How could he when he didn't know the answers to her questions himself? And when she saw he wasn't biting, she suddenly had to rush off to see her sister.

He'd left their awkward lunch thankful he'd only wasted an hour of his Saturday off and thankful the fish *were* still biting by the time he got to Ferris Park.

Andi had to be the most perplexing woman he'd ever known. Smart and sexy, yes. But perplexing. He didn't know what her deal was with Susan. He only hoped he didn't get caught in the middle of them today.

Not that he could even imagine Susan getting involved in a catfight. She was far too gracious for that. But Andi did have a way of pushing just the right buttons . . .

"Morning." He tipped his cap and pulled the front door shut behind him.

There were two kennels in the bed of Andi's pickup. He hopped in the passenger side and directed her around to the back of the property. "You can get pretty close in the truck."

"The dogs need to run," she said. "Do you mind if we walk a ways?"

"No problem. Won't hurt me to run a little either."

She grinned, and he felt the pull of her charm.

She parked at the edge of the meadow. He followed her around to the back of the truck. She let the tailgate down and an Old Yeller look-alike jumped out of the first kennel.

"Is this that pup you had at the station the other day?" Pete said.

"Yep, it's Gulliver."

"He's grown already! You think he's ready for this?"

"Well, he's still in training, but he's coming along."

"Is he a Lab?"

"We're not sure."

"Oh? He from the pound or something?"

Andi gave him a look. "He came from the Humane Society."

"What? It's not politically correct to say 'pound' anymore?"

"The Humane Society would prefer not. You can call it an animal shelter."

"Yeah, but then the humans in the homeless shelter might be offended."

She glared at him, but her eyes held a smile. "Don't be difficult."

"Sorry. No offense intended."

"None taken."

"Um . . . I was talking to Gulliver here," he said, bending to pat the pup's flank.

Andi laughed and opened the other kennel. This time it was the black Lab he'd expected that emerged from the kennel.

"Sparky, right?"

"Yep. The one Lucas trained. My first."

"I remember."

At Andi's signal, the dogs took off across the meadow, stopping to sniff every ten feet. He and Andi headed after them, down the meadow path to where the charred evidence of yesterday's fire marked the earth. The sun was already warm on their backs and the humidity was climbing. It struck Pete that yesterday had been the first official day of summer. Time did fly.

When they were about a hundred feet from the fire, Andi called the dogs back to her and put them on leashes.

As they approached the burn site, the black dog's ears perked, and Andi's expression turned serious.

"Go get 'em, boy," she said, slipping the leash from the dog's collar and pulling a small sketch pad and pen from her breast pocket.

The yellow pup whined and strained at the leash, but Andi held firm. "Sorry, Gully, you have to stay with me this time."

For the next thirty minutes, they watched Sparky work. It never ceased to amaze Pete that a dog could be trained to perform like this. Especially a mutt. Andi handled the dog well, praising him and at intervals, taking notes.

She bagged several pieces of evidence, including cigarette butts found a short distance from where the fire had started. "This must be the son's smoking spot."

"According to Susan, he doesn't smoke."

Andi looked skeptical. She inspected the Baggie containing five or six cigarette butts and made a note on the pad where she'd sketched the scene. "Well, somebody does. And recently. Who else has access to the property? It looks to me like somebody was camping down here."

Pete pointed back toward the house. "There are farms on either side of her property, but according to her, nobody else comes out here."

"No teenagers having field parties, or kids camping overnight?"

"Susan didn't think so. She spotted this fire when it was small, so I think she would have noticed if somebody had been routinely camping down here."

"Unless they hadn't lit a fire till now."

"What makes you think someone's been camping here?"

She walked him over to a spot Sparky had alerted on earlier. What looked like the remains of several tin cans lay in the charred brush.

Walking farther into the woods, Andi pointed out broken limbs and footprints in the mash of leaves on the forest's floor. "Somebody's been out here long enough to cook a meal."

"You're just a regular Davy Crockett, aren't you?"

She gave him an enigmatic smile. "What do you mean by that?"

"King of the wild frontier . . ." His attempt to sing the old TV theme song fell flat. Literally.

Andi grinned. "If that was supposed to be a song, I don't think I'm familiar with it."

"Sorry. I forget how young you are. You do know of Davy Crockett?"

"Sure. The frontiersman."

"That's the one."

"Well, I guess I *am* a 'regular Davy Crockett,' like you say."

"Oh?"

She paused, scuffing the toe of her boot on the blackened undergrowth. He could tell she was trying to decide whether to say something or not. Finally she looked up at him, head tilted, looking uncharacteristically vulnerable. "I grew up in Shannon County. You know our claim to fame, don't you?"

"Shannon County? Poorest county in Missouri."

She nodded. "I think we moved up to second poorest. Let's just say we Morleys did our part in the race to be first. We had a house—if you could call it that—but 'wild frontier' isn't too far off." The shadows that darkened her face hinted at painful memories, but as quickly as they'd come, they lifted and she was all business again.

He didn't know what to say, so he kept quiet.

Finally she called for Sparky. The dog came running and they walked back up to the pickup and loaded the two animals back in the kennels.

"I'd like to talk to Susan. And her son." Andi pointed toward the house. "I saw a car in the driveway. I take it they're home?"

Pete nodded and looked back to where Susan's house sat. It struck him that she'd probably been watching them from her kitchen window. And while he could only guess her reasons, he knew she wasn't going to be too happy about him bringing Andrea Morley into her home.

She hadn't expected
being here at David's house
to affect her this way.

23

Andi looked around the tidy great room where they were standing. She hadn't expected being here in David's house to affect her this way. She hadn't felt his presence when she'd walked on the property. But here, inside the house, she imagined she smelled his scent.

"Andrea, you've met Susan." Pete stepped aside and closed the kitchen door behind him.

"Yes, of course." She nodded and worked to keep her breathing steady.

Susan seemed decidedly cool. The recent fire had no doubt shaken her. Andi felt a little light-headed herself looking around the room.

So this was the place Dave had called home. Morning sun streamed through clerestory windows high on the wall and turned the space into a jewel box of colors. Had that recliner in the corner been Dave's? She looked away. It still hurt to be reminded that David Marlowe had made his choice. And it wasn't her.

Dave never would let her see his house, even when Susan wasn't there. Although, once, he'd given in to Andi's pleading to at least see where he lived. They'd driven by the place in his pickup while they were out on one of their trysts.

Tryst. Her sister had used that word once when Andi referred to a "date" with Dave. Rebecca had never met Dave, but she had no use for him. Andi let her think that Dave intended to leave Susan once the boys were out of school. And Rebecca always said, "If he cheats *with* you, he'll cheat *on* you. Any man who'd mess around while he's married to his wife will mess around with someone else once *you're* his wife."

"We're *not* messing around," she'd always insisted. And, technically, that was true. Rebecca didn't see it that way, though. But her sister didn't know Dave. Not the way Andi did. He was a man, but he was a good guy. He'd proven it in many ways. Not the least of which was not pressuring her to sleep with him, even after she made it clear that she was willing.

But even though she understood his religion was important to him, the fact that Dave had never made love to her made her feel she was less in his eyes. Less than Susan. And that wasn't true.

"Susan," Pete was saying, "do you mind if we talk to Davy?"

Andi shook herself back to the moment.

"I'd really rather not get him involved," Susan said. "He wasn't even home when it happened."

"He may have noticed something we're missing." She spoke in her best calm-the-witness voice.

Pete put a hand on Susan's arm and Andi felt a stab of jealousy.

"What would it hurt, Susan?" he said, speaking as he would to a frightened child. "Any information we can get will help us narrow it down."

"I don't know what he could tell you that I haven't already." She looked past Pete and narrowed her eyes at Andi.

A noise at the doorway between the kitchen and the front of the house made them all turn.

Pete brightened. "Ah, speak of the devil." His chipper mood was obviously for the kid's benefit.

Davy stepped into the room and squinted against a ray of sunlight that breeched the curtains.

Dave's son. Her breath caught. Davy looked so much like his father it was eerie.

"This is my son Davy," Susan said, sounding reluctant.

Andi moved toward him, mindful that for now, at least, Pete had overruled Susan's wishes, and she needed to act quickly. "Hi, Davy." She held out her hand.

He shook it. "Hi."

Keeping one eye on Susan, Pete addressed Davy. "Your mom may have told you . . . We've had the accelerant detection dogs out this morning, inspecting the fire you guys had yesterday. The inspector would like to ask you a few questions."

"I don't know anything about the fire," Davy said, brushing tousled hair from his eyes. "I wasn't even here when it happened. Didn't Mom tell you that?" He flashed his mother an annoyed look.

"We just wondered if you could answer some questions about what the dogs found up at the fire scene," Andi said.

"I guess . . . But I haven't set foot out there since I was . . . I don't know . . . in eighth grade, maybe?"

"Any chance your friends might have been out there yesterday?"

"What do you mean?"

His innocence was genuine and she didn't want to push him too hard, but for the sake of her report, she would probe a little more. "We wondered if maybe your friends remember this place, came out here sometimes to hang out."

He shrugged. "If they do, it's news to me. And Mom would know it if they did." He shot a glance at Susan.

"So you haven't seen anything unusual around here recently? Strange vehicles on the road, or unusual activity on the property . . . ?"

"No. Nothing." He met her eye, and she knew he was telling the truth.

"Okay. Well, here's my card. If you think of anything, or—" Andi glanced pointedly at Susan. "If you'd like to talk to me privately about anything you remember later, don't hesitate to give me a call."

Davy took the card from her, glanced down at it, then back at her. "What . . . what'd you say your name was?"

She motioned toward the card. "Andrea Morley. You can call me Andi."

Davy looked at his mother, then back at Andi. His eyes narrowed. "You're the one—" His jaw clenched and his face grew beet red. He glared and spewed a foul name at her. Then without warning, he blew a wad of spit at her. Warm saliva sprayed onto the front of her uniform and beaded on her bare forearm.

"Davy!" Susan lunged and grabbed his arm.

Andi stood stock still. Held her breath, willing herself not to flinch. When she was sure he wasn't going to spit again, she wiped her arm on the front of her shirt, using every ounce of her reserve to remain calm, maintain her dignity.

But the room spun around her, and all she could see, all she could feel, was her father's saliva in her face. It was his voice she heard calling her that name.

Susan's son couldn't have known about that. Could he? She'd never told David. Never told anybody. Was that simply the word that sprang to people's minds when they looked at her?

As if in answer, Davy shrugged out of his mother's grasp and repeated the vulgar epithet.

Almost instantly, a steady arm came around her, held her up. *Pete.* Her resolve melted. She turned away, covering her face, afraid she would faint from the shame.

"Are you okay?" Pete whispered.

She leaned into his strength, sucked in a breath.

Davy stormed out of the room, apparently finished. She didn't know how, but the kid knew about her and David. And he hated her for it.

Susan started after him but whirled and came back to stand in front of her, close enough that Andi could smell her perfume.

But she didn't apologize for her son. Instead, she glared at her, as if Andi were to blame for Davy's outburst.

Andi tightened her arm around Pete's waist. "I just want to leave," she whispered.

"Yes. Please leave," Susan said. Susan wouldn't meet her eyes, as if doing so might taint her.

How dare she . . . after what her son had done? No.

But then Susan turned her glare on Pete. He stood silent, looking bewildered, and obviously unhappy with Susan. And Andi felt a strange satisfaction seeing the two of them at odds.

She didn't try to protest Susan's ultimatum either. She would leave. She had what she'd come for.

And she had Pete's arm around her. Mission accomplished.

*P*ete stood in the middle of Susan's great room praying—actually praying—he could get out of here without having to break up a fight between these two women.

Susan looked like a mother bear defending her cub. But what the cub needed was a good cuffing.

Right now it seemed to him that Andi was the one who needed defending. The humiliation on her face when Davy had spat on her . . . It made him cringe for her sake. He felt helpless, and strangely torn between these two women.

There was no doubt that something special was developing between him and Susan, especially after the other night with Davy. But he had feelings for Andi, too—and at the very least, a professional allegiance to her. Right now she looked like she needed a friend in the worst way.

And Susan was not going to be that friend. He looked from her to

Andi and back again. These two women could not be more different, and he was afraid if they stayed in the same room much longer, those differences would boil to a violent head.

He took a step toward the door. "I think we have everything we need, Susan," he said, hoping to hurry Andi out.

Instead, she turned on him and planted her feet on the hardwood floor. "I didn't realize you were heading up this investigation, Chief Brennan."

"I only meant . . ." He shrugged and looked to Susan as if she might tell him what to do.

Susan walked to the back door and opened it. "I'd like you to go now," she said again. She cut her eyes to Pete. "Both of you."

"Susan—" Pete had no clue what he meant to say next. He ought to just do what she asked and leave. He couldn't get a break from either of these woman.

Too late. Susan challenged him, eyes blazing. "I told you I didn't want her in my home." Tears threatened, but not before she turned her venom on Andi. "And you . . . you have the nerve to come in here and interrogate my son?"

Andi narrowed her eyes. "It's a little hard to interrogate someone when he's spitting on you!"

"Davy answered your questions. I'm sorry for my son's behavior, but you deserve—" Susan covered her mouth with her hands as if it were the only way she could keep herself from saying something she'd regret later.

"Susan . . . ?" Pete took a step toward her. Her fury was completely out of proportion to the situation. If anyone should be furious, it was Andi!

Not looking at either of them, Susan took a deep breath. "Please . . . just go." She spoke evenly, but firmly.

Andi stomped to the screened door and Susan opened and held it while Andi went through. Pete stood in his tracks, trying to decide if he should stay and try to talk to Susan, find out what on earth was going on with her. Or if he was better off following right behind Andi.

Susan seemed oddly calm now, but she still refused to meet his gaze. Grabbing his cap from the table as he went by, he stepped out onto the deck, his head reeling with questions.

He heard the door close behind them. Now what?

This was when she missed
David the most. When she
needed him the most.

24

"Are they gone?"

Susan whirled at the sound of Davy's voice on the stairway.

"Yes. They're gone." She locked the back door and leaned against it. She wasn't sure how long she'd been standing there, but long enough that the dust from Pete's and Andrea Morley's vehicles had settled. "Come here, Davy. I want to talk to you."

He came and stood in the doorway between the living room and great room, looking more like a petulant adolescent than the twenty-year-old he was. This was when she missed David the most. When she needed him the most. *God, give me the words to say to reach this boy . . . to help him.*

But that was just it. Davy wasn't a boy. He was a young man, and it was time he started acting like one. Time she started treating him like one.

"That was uncalled for! You spitting on her like that. Speaking to her that way . . ."

He narrowed his eyes at her. "Why didn't you tell me who she was? I can't believe you let her in this house."

She slid onto a stool at the bar, afraid her legs wouldn't hold her another minute. "Davy, I wasn't crazy about having her here either. Believe me. But Pete wanted her to do the inspection on this fire. Because she uses the dogs. He thought that would be best, and I trust his judgment."

"Does he know? About Dad—and her?"

"I don't know. I don't think so." She prayed he didn't. Prayed with all her heart. "But that's not what we need to talk about."

"Whatever." Davy took a step backward and she knew he was just waiting for an escape.

"Would you please sit down?" She pulled out the barstool beside her.

He draped a long leg over the stool but didn't quite sit. She didn't press the point.

"This . . . *fiasco* . . . isn't the only thing we need to talk about. Do you remember coming home last night?"

He hung his head, a hank of sandy hair hanging in front of his face. "I remember."

"What was that all about?"

"What?"

"You coming home drunk. Since when do you think that's acceptable?"

"I never said I thought it was *acceptable*." He mimicked her.

She let it ride. "But you did it anyway."

He shrugged.

"If you're trying to get my attention, David Michael, you've got it. Okay? But I'm not putting up with this. I was worried sick about you. You didn't answer your phone. I didn't have a clue where you were." She despised the feeling that Davy's future hung on the way she handled this incident.

"Mom . . . I'm almost twenty-one. I'm still supposed to give you a play-by-play of where I am every minute?"

"When you are a guest in someone else's home, it's just common courtesy to let them know when to expect you."

"Oh, now I'm a guest in my own home?"

She nodded. "That's what you are right now. It's sure what you're acting like—and not a very thoughtful one either. Listen, if you need a couple of months to sort things out and figure out what you want to do with your life, I don't have a problem with you staying here. But, Davy, we need to get some things ironed out. If you're staying, you need to find a job. And start helping out around here. And I need to know where I can reach you."

"Are you serious?"

"Dead serious. And once you start working, I'd appreciate some help with the bills."

He made a sound that she knew muffled a curse.

She chose to ignore it. No need to provoke him. But she was going to get to the bottom of this.

"Listen, Davy, I need the honest truth from you. Do you know anything about the fire—how it started?"

"Mom . . ." He spread his hands palms out. "I know why you think I did, but I swear to you, I had nothing to do with that fire. I told that woman the truth. I haven't been down there since I was a kid."

"Were you smoking?"

He looked at her like she'd lost her mind. "No. I haven't smoked anything since Danny and I tried to smoke one of Dad's cigars when we were kids. We both puked our guts out and had to hide out in the woods until we could walk straight again."

She gaped at him. "I never knew that."

His mouth quirked. "There's probably a lot you never knew. And I don't know about Danny, but I promise you I've never touched anything remotely tobacco related since."

She believed him and she didn't think she was being naive about it.

"So what about that woman?"

She opened her mouth to speak, then clamped it shut.

"Are you just going to let her get away with it?" he challenged.

His question caught her off guard. "First of all, don't think for a minute that I missed the fact that you just changed the subject." She shot him a grin she hoped would lighten the mood.

The corners of his mouth twitched upward.

"We'll get back to the subject at hand, but I'll answer your question first. I honestly don't know what to do about—Andrea Morley." She could barely bring herself to say the woman's name. "I know I need to . . . forgive her, but—"

"Forgive her? Are you crazy, Mom?"

She wished she hadn't spoken the words aloud. Forgiveness was a cornerstone of her faith, but she wasn't sure she could ever honestly forgive what had happened. "What would you do if you were me?"

He made a gun of his hand and pulled the "trigger."

"Davy."

"Well, I would."

"No, you would not. Don't even talk that way." She was pretty sure he was just letting off steam, but she wouldn't encourage him.

"Well, I sure wouldn't let her in my house," he said.

"Look, I'm not saying I want to be best friends with her, but even if she did what . . . what we suspect she did, there's not one thing I can do that will make it all okay."

"What we *suspect*? Mom, wake up! Get your head out of the sand."

She closed her eyes. She had to stop pretending. With Davy. And with herself. "I don't have my head in the sand, son. Believe me, I'm aware of . . . what happened. But we can't go back in time and change it. Or fix it. And we have to live in the same world as . . . that woman. All your dad's friends were with the station, so if I keep in touch with them, chances are good I might run into her now and then."

"Don't forget Chief Brennan's friends."

She looked at him, questioning. "Pete's friends?"

"Admit it, Mom. It's Chief Brennan that keeps you connected to the station now. That's why you'd run into her. You don't really have any reason to be down there otherwise."

"I . . . I'm not—" She sputtered and started again. "No, Davy, I deal with the station because of the shelter. Your dad's buddies have helped a lot getting the shelter back up and running."

"I hate to say it, Mom, but you sound like me when I was trying to convince you I didn't have the hots for Jennifer Froeme." The look he gave her was so like his father that it stole her breath.

She gave a nervous laugh. "*Did* you have the hots for Jenny?"

"Don't change the subject, Mom. The question is, do *you* have the hots for Chief Brennan?"

"Davy! Cut it out!" He'd totally flustered her. "And how did we get from there to here? Talk about changing the subject!"

"I saw you guys making googly eyes at each other."

"When? I don't know what you're talking about." She clammed up before he accused her of protesting too much. His comment made her decidedly uncomfortable, and yet she wanted to stay in this place where they were right now, joking and teasing each other the way they used to when they were just an ordinary family. Before tragedy had taken David from them. And before the truth about David had torn them to shreds.

Mom and Dad, Davy and Danny. She'd missed that so much, she ached. She hadn't realized how much until this moment.

As Charlie had once reminded her, she'd gone through the tragedy of losing her husband at the same time as she'd dealt with the empty nest. Sometimes, like now, she felt as if she were waking up from a long sleep to finally join the real world again.

Of course, if Davy came home drunk again tomorrow night, she might wish she could hide away again in that never-never land where she dwelled too often recently.

She punched her son in the arm playfully, willing the old Davy to stick around. "You're talking crazy."

"Oh, look who's talking. You're not pulling the wool over anybody's eyes but your own."

His teasing grin was the best gift she could ask for, and she didn't even try to argue with him. Nor did she broach the subject she knew couldn't wait much longer. Two subjects, actually. Davy needed to make some decisions about his life. If he wanted to stay here in the Falls, fine, but he needed gainful employment immediately. And if he was going back to Indiana, he needed a job lined up there and a date on the calendar.

But more important, they needed to talk about David and what had happened with Andrea Morley. She didn't want bitterness toward his father eating Davy alive, and she didn't want to risk that he'd run into Andrea somewhere and say or do something foolish.

What exactly she would say, she had no clue. And she needed to give herself the same lecture she intended to give Davy, because she had enough bitterness brewing for both of them.

She also needed to tell Danny. But not over the phone. Maybe she could talk him into coming home for a visit while Davy was still here.

She prayed she might someday be able to forgive David for what had happened. And she supposed if her faith was what she claimed it to be, she needed to somehow find forgiveness for Andrea, too. But that day hadn't come yet, and until then, heaven help the woman if she set foot anywhere near this house again.

An involuntary chill snaked down her spine . . .

25

Thursday, June 25

Susan grabbed her purse off the counter and pulled the garage door shut behind her. The shelter doors opened in less than an hour, but with all the excitement over the fire, she'd never made it to the grocery store, and if she didn't buy some food, Davy would be eating stale Cheerios for supper. Dry.

She headed out the driveway and slid her phone open to call Charlie and let him know she was running late. But before she could enter his number, her phone rang.

"Susan? It's Pete."

She hesitated. They hadn't talked since she'd "kicked him out" of her house yesterday morning. She'd lain awake for hours last night thinking about what she would tell him about Andi and David. And then it had struck her that, despite what she'd told Davy, maybe Pete had known all along that Andrea Morley and David had been . . . involved. If that were true, she had a few choice words for him. Either way, they needed to talk. "Hello, Pete," she said finally. "Do I owe you an apology?"

He gave a low chuckle. "No more than I owe you one. I should have taken you more seriously when you said you'd rather not talk to Andi."

"True, but I could have been a little more . . . diplomatic. And Davy—" She sighed into the phone and pulled over to the side of the driveway. She turned off the ignition. "I'm embarrassed for the way he acted, Pete. I guess I owe her an apology, too."

"Andi? Listen, that's why I'm calling. I just talked to her and she said your fire appears to have been started from a campfire that was left smoldering."

"What?" She didn't like him calling it "her" fire. "That doesn't make sense."

"Or possibly from a cigarette. She found both at the point of ignition."

"That makes no sense," she said again. "No one camps down there. No one even goes near the meadow now that the boys are grown. The property is posted all the way to the highway."

"Well, according to Andi, those cigarette butts she found near the burn site are recent. And there's no way someone could have thrown a cigarette that far from the road. I don't mean to doubt you, but are you positive they're not Davy's?"

"Ninety-nine percent sure. He's always had an aversion to cigarette smoke. Any kind of smoke. He hates it when I come home from the shelter smelling like cigarette smoke. And I'm pretty sure I'd smell it on him if he was lighting up."

"Is it possible some of his friends are smoking out there?"

"What are you saying?" Her stomach plummeted. "Was it only cigarettes or . . . something worse?"

"Oh, no, no . . . I didn't mean to imply that. What I'm getting at is that somebody was camping out on your property. And with Zeke Downing showing up and trying to get in contact with you, I just want to make sure it's not him."

"Why would he be setting up camp at my place? If he wants to talk to me, he can just knock on my door. In fact, he did." She told him about the note she'd found on her front porch. "After seeing the other note, I'm pretty sure it's his handwriting."

"Do you still have it?"

"No, I threw it away."

His sigh came over the phone. "I wish you'd be more careful."

"I'm truly not worried about the guy, Pete."

"Yeah, and that's exactly what scares me, Susan. Knowing you, you'd invite him in and cook him dinner."

"But why would he come all the way out here to camp? That doesn't make any sense."

"I'm not saying it is him, but it's somebody, and if it's not your son or his friends, and you haven't given anyone else permission to be on your property, then I don't like it."

"You and me both." She really didn't think Zeke Downing was a threat, but the idea that while she was in the house, or sleeping in her bed, someone was up in the woods watching the house gave her the creeps. An involuntary chill snaked down her spine and made her glad she hadn't gotten the call while she was home by herself.

"Just be careful, Susan. I've asked the sheriff to keep an eye on your place for a few days just in case Zeke—"

"What? Good grief, Pete. The guy is harmless. I don't need—"

"No, he's not harmless!"

Susan drew the phone away from her ear, surprised by the vehemence in his voice. "What do you mean?" she said finally.

"I'm sorry. I didn't mean to shout."

She could tell he was making an effort to lower his voice.

He hesitated, then blew out a breath. "I didn't want to scare you, but I did some checking into this guy. He's got a record as long as your arm."

She furrowed her brow. "I hate to break it to you, but a lot of our clients have criminal records. And we knew that when Zeke checked into the shelter—before the fire. It's not like he's a serial killer."

"This is not a nice guy, Susan. His last conviction was less than a year ago. Aggravated assault and battery in Kansas. He served a few months and is out on parole. I don't know how he's getting away with hanging out in Missouri, but he must have a good reason to risk his parole."

Susan digested this new information. What would Zeke Downing need to talk to her about?

"I want someone to keep an eye out," he said. "Just to be sure."

She wasn't crazy about that idea, but she appreciated Pete's concern. And it did make her feel safer to know the authorities were keeping an eye on her place. "Okay. If you really think it's necessary." She made a mental note to let Davy know that the sheriff might be prowling around.

"I'll let you know if I hear anything, and you do the same."

"Okay . . . I will. And thanks, Pete."

"No problem."

She hung up, feeling incongruously better for having had a civil conversation with Pete. At least he hadn't washed his hands of her after yesterday. Although it occurred to her that technically he was just doing his job.

She put the car in gear and started to turn out of the driveway toward town, but looking the other direction for oncoming cars, an idea struck her. She called Charlie and told him she wouldn't be in till later. He sounded proud that she trusted him to open the shelter. She was glad Pete had encouraged her to let Charlie take more responsibility.

She stuffed her phone back in her purse and drove the quarter mile to the Harkers'. As she wound her way up the drive, Bill's coon dogs trotted out from behind the farmhouse barking up a storm. Within seconds, he and Betty were standing on their wide front porch, waving.

"Shut up!" Bill barked at the dogs. They instantly obeyed.

He took off his cap and slapped it on the leg of his denim overalls, sending a cloud of dust into the air. "Hey there, Miss Susan."

"Hi, Bill." She waved at Betty on the porch.

Bill's wife was as much a hermit as Bill was gregarious. Bill had told Susan once that Betty left the house only to get her hair cut, and that only a few times a year. But the woman had always been friendly enough whenever Susan stopped by, even inviting her in for coffee a few times. The Harkers had been good neighbors over the years.

Bill came off the porch, clearing her way through a herd of droopy-eared hounds. "For bein' neighbors we haven't seen much of you this spring. Everything going okay?"

"Things are fine, thanks."

"Wife said you had some excitement at your place the other day. I was headed to Springfield when she called, but by the time I got home, the fire trucks were already leaving."

"That's why I'm here, Bill. The fire investigator"—she swallowed the bitter taste that rose in her throat—"came out the next morning. They think someone's been camping down there."

"Camping? You don't think it's me, do you?" Bill laughed his hearty laugh. "So, they think it was a campfire that started the fire?"

"They're not sure. But yes, probably. I just wondered if you'd given anyone permission to be on your property. I know sometimes your grandsons hunt around here. They haven't been out recently, have they?"

"Not for a coon's age."

"They also found cigarette butts out there."

"Bill quit smoking twenty-five years ago." Betty put her hands on her hips, sounding defensive. "I wouldn't be standin' on this here porch with him if he hadn't."

"I wasn't accusing anybody. Just trying to figure out what's going on out there."

"Heard one of your boys is back." Betty was still in defensive mode. "Could it be him?"

Bill and Betty no doubt still remembered the fires Davy had set as a kid. "Yes, Davy is back for a visit. But it wasn't him, and he swears none of his friends have been down there either."

Bill looked skeptical. "Well, we'll keep a lookout, but I don't know anything about it."

"Thanks, I appreciate it."

"You wanna come in for a cup of coffee? I can put some on." But Betty's offer didn't sound like she was too keen on the idea.

"Thanks, Betty, but I'd better get going."

On the way back from the Harkers', Susan stopped off at home to see if Davy was there. The phone was ringing when she walked into the kitchen. It was Bill Harker.

"You didn't tell me the whole story," he said without preamble. "That don't sit right with me."

"What are you talking about, Bill?"

"The *Courier*. According to them, that fire was retaliation for the whole mess with your homeless shelter. Me and Betty never was too keen on that whole idea, but we didn't say nothin' on account of being neighbors and all. We try to mind our own business, and beings the shelter's in town, we figured it doesn't affect us none. But this hits just a little too close to home."

What was he talking about? "Um . . . I haven't seen the paper. I'm not sure what you're referring to."

"Like I said, the *Courier* said the fire was set by some homeless guy who was out to get you."

Her heart dropped into the pit of her stomach. "That was in the *Courier*? Tonight? Do you still have your copy? I don't take the paper anymore."

"You can come over and borrow it if you like. Wife might have clipped some coupons out of there, but I think the front page is still intact."

"It was on the front page?" This was not good.

"Front and center."

Who would have talked to the news about the fire? And how was it already front-page news when she'd just gotten the fire inspector's report herself moments ago? Besides, a routine brush fire barely made the Runs and Calls column. It wasn't front-page news unless somebody made it so. And Pete was the only one who would have said anything. Unless . . .

She paced the length of the kitchen. Surely Andrea Morley wouldn't have contacted the *Courier*. This wasn't Morley's town, and she had nothing to gain from the story. It had to have been Pete.

She grabbed her purse off the hook by the garage door. "Thanks for the offer, Bill, but I need to run into town anyway. I'll pick up a copy at the newsstand."

"Suit yourself."

She hung up the phone and went to the stairs. "Davy?"

No answer. He must have his headphones on. She banged on the wall.

A few seconds later she heard his bedroom door open. He appeared at the bottom of the stairwell, his iPod clipped to the waist of below-the-knee athletic shorts, telltale wires leading to his ears. He held what looked like a sandwich in one hand and popped out an earbud. "What's up?"

"What are you eating?"

"Peanut butter. There's nothing to eat in this house."

"Yes. I know. I'm going for groceries."

"Knock yourself out."

The sarcasm she usually found humorous didn't sit well with her since his blowup with Andrea Morley. But she wasn't going to pick a fight right now. "Do you need anything from Hanson's?"

"We're out of milk."

"Yes, because you drink a gallon a day all by yourself. I've got it on the list. We're out of everything. Anything else you want?"

"No." Davy turned back toward his room.

"Hey, hang on . . ."

He whirled back around, looking impatient.

"I just wanted to warn you that the sheriff might be on our road more than usual for a few days."

"Huh?" He yanked out his other earbud.

"Pete asked them to keep an eye out."

Davy's jaw dropped. "Because of the . . . *drunk* thing?"

She rolled her eyes. "No, son, because of the *fire* thing. They still think somebody set the fire and Pete just wants to be sure it wasn't Zeke Downing. I'm locking the doors, too, so keep them locked."

Davy shrugged but didn't reply, and she saw that he'd already stopped up his ears with those stupid earbuds again. At least she didn't have to listen to his music. She was too consumed with other issues and too weary to tackle the Davy situation right now.

But things needed to change around here—and soon.

She had the odd feeling everyone was staring at her . . .

26

*W*hy was Hanson's so crowded tonight? It was Thursday. Weren't people supposed to wait for the weekend to do their grocery shopping?

Susan grabbed a cart with a wobbly wheel, which didn't help her foul mood. She'd driven by two newspaper kiosks on the way into town, but they were both empty. Inside the store she located the *Courier* rack. It was empty, too. That didn't bode well.

Maybe the kiosk at Rhode's on the other end of town still had papers. She'd check after she got groceries.

Pushing her cart through the narrow aisles, she had the odd feeling people were staring at her. She remembered a time when it had been a pleasure to move about Hanover Falls. She'd loved living in a small town, and loved the fact that everywhere she went, she ran into a friend or neighbor. But she'd become slightly paranoid in recent months.

Things had changed after she lost Dave in the fire. And even more so now, with the ongoing controversy over the shelter. The fire at her house, however it had started, was not going to make things easier.

It didn't help that Davy was back living at home. And after his escapades the other night, she was afraid to guess what kind of reputation he'd made for himself since coming back to the Falls. He hadn't gone out partying since that night—hadn't gone out at all. And that wasn't good either. All his friends from the Falls were off at college. He hadn't found a group of friends in Indiana like the close-knit group he'd been part of here. She suspected that was one of the reasons he'd dropped out of school. And if the other night was any indication, the few so-called friends who'd stuck around the Falls weren't the best influence on her son.

She quickly gathered the groceries from her list, sought out the shortest checkout line, and emptied her cart onto the conveyor. The checker, a high school girl, chattered the whole time she was ringing up Susan's groceries.

When Susan handed over her debit card, the girl looked at her, then did a double take. "You look familiar. Do I know you?"

Susan smiled, feeling on the spot, especially since there were three people in line behind her. "I don't think so."

Thankfully the girl finished the transaction in silence.

After loading her groceries in the car, Susan drove to Rhode's and parked in front of the convenience store. Good, there were still papers in this rack. From what she could see through the display window, the story about the fire wasn't visible. At least if it was on the front page, it was below the fold.

She put three quarters in the slot, opened the rack, and pulled out a paper. She tossed the advertising tabloids in a nearby trash can and took the paper to the car.

Unfolding the paper, her breath caught. It was worse than she thought. The bold headline strung across four columns: AUTHORITIES SUSPECT SHELTER DIRECTOR WAS TARGET. Her picture accompanied the article. It was the photo from the original shelter's grand opening, which was the one they'd run after the tragic fire, and the one Bee Quinton had run occasionally with her articles or with a letter to the editor about the shelter controversy.

No wonder the checker at Hanson's thought she looked familiar.

Susan skimmed the story, which carried Quinton's byline, and as far as she could tell from her quick read, all the quotes were attributed simply to "authorities," or "an employee of the department," referring, she thought, to the Clemens County Fire District, although it was unclear from the way the article was worded.

She read it again, word for word.

A brush fire one mile west of Hanover Falls brought Clemens County fire trucks and medical personnel out in force Sunday evening, according to an employee of the department. What was first thought to be a routine brush fire now appears to have a possible sinister cause.

The fire occurred on the private property of Susan Marlowe, director of the Grove Street Homeless Shelter. In recent months, the shelter has been mired in controversy that began eighteen months ago when a fatal fire at the shelter killed five firefighters from Hanover Falls.

Authorities suspect the director of the shelter was a target and that the fire may have been set in an effort to frighten Marlowe into shutting the shelter down. There appears to have been a campfire on the property and cigarette butts were found at the scene, but authorities believe the fire was intentionally set.

Susan sat, stunned. Surely Pete wouldn't have given the newspaper any details, and neither would he have allowed anyone from the station to talk to reporters without his okay.

The rest of the article looked like Quinton had pulled paragraphs from past articles about the controversy.

Except for the zinger at the end: "According to someone with knowledge of the investigation, the future of the homeless shelter is in question after this latest incident."

Where was Bee Quinton getting this stuff? Fuming, Susan turned the key in the ignition. That did it. She was going to get to the bottom of this. Starting with Pete.

And for his sake, she prayed he wasn't at the station tonight because if he did turn out to be the "someone with knowledge" she was going to kill him.

*S*usan fully intended to go to the fire station and confront Pete, but when she crossed Main Street, she changed her mind. She went around the block and parked in front of the office of the *Hanover Falls Courier*.

She waited for ten minutes in the stuffy reception room before Bee Quinton appeared behind the counter wearing the same scowl she'd sported the last time Susan had talked to her. "You wanted to see me?"

"I'm Susan Marlowe and—"

"Yes, I remember."

"Is . . . there someplace we could speak privately?"

Without so much as a "follow me" the reporter turned and started through the maze of cubicles in the newsroom. Not sure if the queen bee—as Pete had started calling her—intended her to follow or if she was trying to ditch her, Susan followed anyway.

Quinton ducked into a cubicle near the back. When Susan stepped into the doorway behind her, the reporter hoisted herself onto her desk and sat there swinging her legs. She finally indicated the only chair occupying the space. Susan took the chair, not liking how it felt to have the reporter hulking over her.

"Now, what can I do for you?"

"I have a few questions about the article in the paper this week."

"What article would that be?"

The woman wasn't going to make this easy. But Susan let her get away with playing dumb. "The article about the fire on my property. You wrote that 'authorities believe—'" She slipped her copy of the newspaper from her purse and read the quote.

Looking up from the paper, she met Bee Quinton's stare as she sat on her desk with her arms crossed like an Indian princess.

Her intimidation tactics were working, but Susan wasn't about to let on. "I'm wondering just *which* authorities you spoke with, because none of the authorities I've talked to mentioned one word about"—she chalked quotations marks in the air—"the future of the homeless shelter being in question."

"I'm not sure I'm at liberty to say. I'll have to . . . get back to you on that."

"Well, it doesn't seem right to quote a so-called authority and not reveal to the public on *what* authority that source is speaking." Her face felt hot and her palms were clammy. She forced herself to count to ten. It would do no one any good if she lost her temper with the reporter, despite how annoying she was. Besides, she felt sure that Pete was the source. Or maybe he and Andrea Morley had both talked to Quinton.

"I'm sorry you're unhappy with the story, Mrs. Marlowe. We only reported what we—"

"It would have been nice if someone had at least contacted me. If you wanted an authority on the shelter, why didn't you call me first?"

"I think you know the answer to that."

Okay, the woman had a point there. After their last exchange, Bee Quinton had to know that Susan wouldn't have taken her call, much less given her any information.

Susan stood, hiking her purse strap higher on her shoulder. "I intend to talk to 'the authorities' myself, and I would appreciate it greatly if you would print a retraction on that comment about the shelter."

The reporter remained cool as a hunk of ice. "We would print a retraction if one was warranted."

Susan started to leave, but turned back. "And for your information—on *my* authority as the director of the Grove Street Homeless Shelter—the future of the shelter is just fine. If you want a story, why don't you come and talk to Charlie Branson, who went from being homeless to helping other people who are in his shoes? Or talk to any one of the dozens of people the shelter has helped to get back on their feet after a tough time. That might be a story worth writing."

She stormed from the newsroom not caring in the least about the low buzz of voices that followed her out the door. They were going to believe what they wanted to anyway. Let them talk.

*How long could he
backpedal before he admitted
he'd heard rumors . . . ?*

27

$\mathcal{P}$ete's cell phone vibrated. Weary to the bone, he pushed his chair away from his desk. He was tempted not to answer. His shift was over in half an hour, he had his fishing gear in the truck, and he didn't care if the whole town was on fire, he was escaping to Ferris Park first chance he got.

But his better judgment won out. He fished the phone from his pocket and flipped it open. "Brennan."

"Pete, it's Susan . . . Marlowe."

Marlowe? Four hours since he'd talked to her and suddenly they were on a last-name basis? This wasn't good. "Hi, Susan. What's up?"

"We need to talk. Have you seen the *Courier?*"

"Yeah . . . I saw the paper."

"Did *you* talk to them?"

"No. I thought you must have."

"Why in the world would I tell them the future of the shelter was in question?"

"That's what I wondered. So if it wasn't you and it wasn't me, who did they talk to?"

"She wouldn't say."

"She? You talked to the reporter? Quinton?"

Susan sighed into the phone. "I tried to talk to her. She wouldn't tell me anything. But if it wasn't you, it had to be Andrea Morley."

"Andi? Did she say something to you?"

"No, but she's the only other person who knew the things in that article."

"Why would she tell the paper anything about the shelter? That has nothing to do with her investigation of the fire." If it wasn't Susan who'd talked to the paper, he was truly puzzled.

"Pete, I have a question for you, and I . . . I'm just going to be blunt."

"Okay . . ."

"Did you know David was having an affair?"

He leaned back in his desk chair, stunned. "Did you just say what I thought you said? Was *that* in the *Courier* story? How did we get from A to B from there?" He was talking and he couldn't seem to shut up.

There was a long silence before Susan blew out an audible breath. "I think you just answered my question."

"Wait now . . . Wait just a minute. Don't go jumping to conclusions. Why would you think that about Dave? And maybe the bigger question is, why are you asking *me*?"

"Because you were his boss. If one of your firefighters was messing around, you would know."

"Well, I can guarantee *that's* not true." How long could he backpedal before he admitted he'd heard rumors about Dave? Good grief! Did she have any idea what kind of spot she was putting him in? But where was this coming from all of a sudden?

"Pete, I know about David and Andrea. What I want to know is"—her voice climbed a pitch—"did everybody in town know about it *except* me?"

"Andrea? *Morley?* You think David and Andi were having an *affair?*"

"What did you think that whole thing with Davy was the day she came to the house? Are you that blind?"

"Apparently." The rumors . . . had they been true after all? But *Andi*? He'd never heard that one. It made his mind reel. It also made some puzzle pieces start to fit into place. "Where are you, Susan?"

"I'm at home." She sounded near tears.

"Can I come out there? I don't want to have this conversation on the phone."

Another silence. Finally she whispered, "Okay."

He checked in with the dispatcher and went to gather his things. So much for Ferris Park.

Ten minutes later his tires kicked up dust on the county road, and Pete slowed, watching for the entrance to Susan's driveway.

He rubbed his jaw, trying to think of words that would take away her pain. And his disappointment. Because if what Susan said was true, Andi was not anything he'd given her credit for. And she'd taken him for one whale of a ride.

He was determined to withhold judgment until he had all the facts, but things were not stacking up in her favor.

*T*he teakettle started its crescendo at the same instant Susan heard Pete's truck on the gravel drive. She left the kettle and went to the door, still not sure how much she wanted to reveal to Pete.

She'd always felt sorry when she heard a woman's husband had been unfaithful, but she'd never realized how truly humiliating it was, as if the fault were her own. And maybe it was. But she couldn't think about that now.

She checked her reflection in the mirror by the front door. Nothing she could do about her red-rimmed eyes and sallow complexion. Pete would just have to understand.

The minute he stepped into the living room, looking at her with those kind, fathomless gray eyes, she knew she could trust him with whatever she had to say.

"Come on in. I've got water on for tea." The kettle's whistle screamed from the kitchen. "Or would you prefer coffee?"

"Tea's fine. Are you okay?"

Tears threatened and she turned away. She hurried to the kitchen and busied herself with fixing mugs of tea until she got her emotions under control.

The water had boiled over and she took the kettle off the burner and filled his mug. She watched him stir sugar into his tea. And finally her words poured out, as if they'd been threatening to boil over, too.

"I'll start at the beginning I know." Trying to abbreviate the story as much as possible, she told him how she'd recognized Andrea Morley from David's funeral. "It seemed odd at the time that she would be at the Springfield service," she said. "I didn't even recognize her that day, but—"

"Andi's main office is in Springfield," he said. "Maybe it was more convenient for her to come to the service there. Or maybe she was worried no one else would show up to support your family after the service in the Falls."

He sounded determined to give Andrea the benefit of the doubt. Susan frowned. It was almost like he *wanted* her to be wrong. "No, Pete. Andi didn't speak to me, didn't even stand near the family. It was almost like she was trying to stay out of sight. I thought she was a reporter at first. Besides, wasn't she at the memorial service in the Falls, too?"

Even before he opened his mouth, Pete looked like she'd caught him in a lie. "She . . . she *was* there," he admitted. "I remember she marched with the firefighters. Maybe she's just one of those funeral hoppers." He shrugged, then blew across his mug and took a cautious sip.

Why was he making excuses for the woman? Of course, he and

Andrea were friends. If he truly didn't know about Andrea and David, she couldn't blame Pete for defending his friend.

"I'm sorry," she said. "I shouldn't have said anything."

He reached across the table and lightly touched her hand. "I don't mean to brush you off. I just don't think . . . I hope you're wrong." He rubbed a hand over his face. "I do think it's a bit of a stretch to draw a line between Andi being at the funeral and her having an affair with your husband."

Hearing him say it that way, it did sound far-fetched. But he didn't have all the facts yet.

"When Davy was home at Christmas, he found a card—Andrea's business card—in the pocket of David's jacket." Her throat constricted, but she forced herself to finish, told him about what was written on the back. "It may as well have been a love note," she said, her voice hoarse.

He took her hand and closed his eyes. "I'm sorry, Susan. I'm so sorry."

"Pete, shoot straight with me. I need to know. Did you know? Did everyone but me know?"

"I told you the truth, Susan. I didn't know."

But he couldn't quite look her in the eye. She pulled out of his grasp and buried her face in her hands. "I think I've always known something wasn't right. I was just too afraid to explore it. But *Davy* . . . He saw them together."

"Where?"

She told him about Davy seeing David and Andrea together in Springfield.

He shook his head. "No one ever said anything to me about Andi and Dave. If it's true, I'm sorry, Susan."

"*If* it's true? You don't think it is?"

"No. I'm not saying that. It's just . . . if it is true, what good can come of knowing all this now?"

"What? I'm just supposed to pretend it never happened? I can't do that, Pete."

"You may never know the truth, but whether anything happened or not, David can't defend himself now."

She looked at him, incredulous. "Yeah? And what am I supposed to tell my son? Davy saw them, Pete. He said—" She closed her eyes. "He said they were all over each other. That doesn't leave much room for David being innocent."

Pete blew out a breath. "Let me ask you something, Susan. Was Dave a good dad?"

She stared at him. She wasn't sure where he was going with this, but she didn't have a good feeling. Still, she gave him the benefit of the doubt—for now. "Yes," she said. "He was a good father."

"Then I think that's what you tell Davy, what you remind him of. If your suspicions were true, and Dave was still here, I would be answering you differently, but—" He chose his words carefully. "No matter what happened—or didn't happen—you can't change it now."

This was starting to sound like the speech she'd given Davy. After a brief silence, she gave a humorless laugh. "I have a feeling you're not directing those words at Davy."

His eyes held a challenge. "Was David a good husband?"

"No!" she spat the word at him. "Not if he was messing around on me, he wasn't!"

He held up his hands as if fending off blows. "I'm sorry. Of course you're right. But think about it, Susan. What good will it do anyone— you or your sons—to dwell on Dave's faults now? There's nothing you could do to fix them."

Tears sprang to her eyes, and in spite of her resolve to not break down in front of him, she began to weep.

She hid her face in her hands, but she heard his chair scrape against the floor, and then felt his weight against her as he knelt beside her chair. Strong arms enveloped her and she let herself rest against Pete's chest.

She felt like she'd tricked him somehow, manipulated him with her tears. And maybe she had. Right now she felt like a stranger in her own skin. She didn't know who she even was anymore.

But she knew one true thing. Peter Brennan's arms around her felt good and right and true.

*Had everything she'd done,
everything she'd sacrificed,
been for nothing?*

28

Tuesday, June 30

*A*ndi grabbed the laundry basket and headed down the hall. She hadn't washed uniforms for almost a week and she'd worn her last fresh shirt this morning.

She started sorting the darks from the whites, putting her khakis in the washer as she sorted. As she checked each item for stains, she came across the shirt the kid had spit on. *Dave's son.*

Almost a week ago now. But a knife of pain sliced through her and unexpected tears burned behind her eyelids. It hurt. Still. More than she wanted to admit. It didn't help that Davy Marlowe looked like a younger version of his handsome father.

She doused the stain with laundry detergent, and suddenly she was back in the tiny house she'd grown up in. Her father had come home in the middle of the day to find her making out with Jimmy Coggins on the sofa. She could still feel the weight of his contempt, still feel his spittle warm on her face, and the humiliation she'd endured in front of the first boy she'd ever loved.

There'd been no washing machine in the shack her father called a house, so she'd scrubbed her blouse in the filthy kitchen sink and with every stroke of the scrub brush, she'd plotted her revenge.

She rubbed her eyes, willing away memories she'd thought banished long ago. She tossed her uniform shirt into the washing machine and stared into the swishing drum, watching the clear liquid soak into the fabric of her shirt, washing away Davy Marlowe's spittle.

It was obvious the kid somehow knew about her and Dave. Susan must have known, too. But how? Had Dave's family known about her all along? Even before the fire? He never said anything. Never implied that he and Susan had fought about it.

Had everything she'd done, everything she'd sacrificed, been for nothing? Her knees buckled and she caught herself, leaning heavily against the washing machine, surprised that the tragedy still had the power to affect her this way.

Dave had rarely talked about his family when they were together. She'd tried to get him to share that part of his life with her—well, not Susan, of course. Susan she wanted to pretend didn't exist. But she'd encouraged Dave to share his feelings about being a father, his pride in his sons. She'd hoped to someday be a part of their lives.

But only rarely did he talk about them. She thought it made him feel guilty to be with her and talk about the sons he had with Susan.

Once, not long before the fire, she'd teased him, saying maybe sometime she would show up at one of the boys' ball games. She was only testing him. But Dave blew up. She'd never seen him so angry. "So help me, Andi," he'd said through clenched teeth, "if you ever try to insert yourself into my life outside of *this*"—he'd indicated the cab of his pickup where they were sitting at the time—"it's over. This friendship is over. I swear it."

She'd smoothed things over and assured him she would never do anything to jeopardize what they had together. But afterward she'd sunk into a deep depression. What *did* they have together? It killed her that he'd called it a mere "friendship." Had their world really been that small? Contained in the cab of a pickup truck? It had seemed so much more.

To her, it had been *everything*.

Things had been different between them after that. Dave had been aloof. More cautious than ever. And from that day on, she'd lived in constant fear that he would shut her out, refuse to see her again. She tried everything to find the closeness they'd shared in the beginning. But she didn't know how to get back what they'd had.

And she'd done desperate, awful things trying to hang on to something she now knew she'd never owned in the first place.

$\mathcal{P}$ete slumped into the embrace of the sagging sofa in the break room. He hadn't sat down once today and his aching back protested. It was only Tuesday and already they'd had a crazy busy week. But so far they hadn't been called out tonight.

He'd barely had time to think about his conversation with Susan the other night, let alone process it. He'd held her in his arms, longing for words that would bring her comfort. He'd come up empty, and that fact bothered him a lot.

"I'm sorry, Susan," he'd whispered against her ear. But the words felt sterile and cold. He'd never had the first clue how to comfort a woman. That had been half the problem with Lana. Month after month when she hadn't conceived, she'd cry on his shoulder. For a while it had seemed enough for him just to be there. But then something had changed and he didn't know how to comfort her anymore. Had no magic words to make it okay.

He shoved the thoughts aside. He ought to take his own advice and leave the past in the past. There was nothing to be done about it now.

But it scared him to death that he would fail Susan the way he'd failed his wife.

It had only been five days since he'd seen Susan. But he suddenly missed her. Had the oddest sensation . . . as if he was *homesick* for her.

He heard the guys in the station kitchen laughing, giving one of the rookies a hard time about his cooking skills, or lack thereof. It was nice to hear the good-natured razzing between them. It built unity. Made them even more of a family. He had a good team at the station right now. He really needed to bring in a couple of new firefighters, but new hires always messed with the chemistry, at least for a while. He would enjoy this lull while it lasted.

He turned up the volume on the TV, but even as the commercial ended and the cop show came back on, he felt himself drifting. He'd catch a few z's before dinner and maybe stay late and finish up the paperwork he'd let go last weekend.

He was just dozing off when he heard his name. He rubbed his eyes and sat up. "Huh?"

"Sorry, Chief. There's someone here to see you. Some kid."

"Kid?"

"Well, a guy . . . maybe twenty?" He shrugged. "I don't know . . . I'm not a good judge of age. He's out in the hall."

Pete peeled himself off the sofa, trying to get his bearings. "You don't know who it is?"

"He wouldn't say. But if you ask me, he's been drinking."

So much for that nap. He trudged out to the front. Davy Marlowe stood there, bleary-eyed.

"Hey . . . What's up?" Pete extended a hand and Davy shook it.

"I just want to know one thing." His speech was clear, but Pete smelled alcohol on his breath.

"Oh, yeah?" Pete eyed him cautiously. "What's that?"

"Why would you bring that . . . *woman* to my mom's house?"

Pete pursed his lips and ran a hand over the rough stubble on his chin. "Davy, I didn't know. Andrea is one of the best fire inspectors in the state. And one of the few who could bring the dogs in. I thought that was important in this case. Andrea did me a favor. I've worked with her before and I knew she'd do a good job."

"Yeah, well, my mom didn't appreciate it and I didn't appreciate it."

"I'm sorry. If I'd known then—" He stopped short. He couldn't honestly say he would have done anything differently. He started over. "Your mom explained . . . I understand now why that was hard for you—both of you—having her there."

"Sure you do." Davy swore and took a step forward. He wavered and grabbed at a planter to catch himself. Pete reached out to steady him.

"Get your hands off me!" Davy shoved him off.

The outburst took Pete by surprise. This was one angry kid. He wondered if Susan was aware.

As if thinking of her had summoned her, Susan walked through the door. "Susan?"

"Mom?" Davy spoke in unison with Pete.

"What are you doing here, Davy?" She turned and looked out the door she'd just come through. "I saw your car in the parking lot. What's going on?"

"I could ask you the same question." Davy's speech grew more slurred by the minute.

He must have tanked up just before he came, probably had to, to get up the courage to come here.

Susan walked over and got in Davy's face. "You're drunk. Please don't tell me you drove here."

"Okay, I won't tell you."

"Davy, what is going on?" She looked at Pete like he should know.

He shrugged. "He just got here." Had she followed Davy to the station? Pete asked her, "Is everything okay?"

She looked like a trout that knew it was hooked. "I . . . I saw Davy's car. I've been looking for him."

"What for?" Davy glared at his mother.

Susan glanced Pete's way and lowered her voice. "We'll talk later, Davy. Right now, you're coming home with me."

"No. I've got my car."

"You are not driving in your condition."

"What condition?"

"Listen, Davy . . ." Pete had visions of slamming Earl Eland against the lockers at the shelter. He did not want a repeat of that fiasco, but neither was he going to stand here and let the kid mouth off to his mother. "Why don't you let me take you home?" He looked at Susan, asking permission with his eyes.

She gave a brief nod.

Pete risked putting a hand on Davy's shoulder. "We can talk, and I'll get your car back to you tomorrow. First thing."

Davy shrugged out of his reach but looked like he might be softening. Pete hoped Susan would stay out of it. What was she doing here anyway?

"You want to grab a burger on the way?" Pete dug in his pocket for the keys to his pickup.

He nodded at Susan behind Davy's back and ushered him out to the parking lot.

He'd talk to Susan later. He *knew* what to say to her. What he'd say to Davy, he had no clue.

He shot up a quick prayer—
something he found
himself doing more
and more these days.

29

Pete looked across the cab of his pickup where Davy sat hunched in the passenger seat staring out the side window. "So, are you hungry? You want to drive through for a burger?"

"Not hungry," he grunted. But he sat up a little straighter and actually looked Pete in the eye. "Thanks, though."

"No problem. Why don't you tell me what you came to the station to talk about?"

"I told you." Davy resumed his brewing posture and glared out the windshield.

"You're mad about me bringing Andrea Morley out to your house?"

"That and . . . that you're even friends with her."

"I work with her. Can't really avoid that."

"You could fire her. You're still the chief, right?"

Pete let up on the accelerator as they came to the small business district downtown. "She's not my employee. She has her own company. But she does the inspections on a lot of the fires we handle."

"Why did my dad do it?"

Pete heaved a sigh. How could he field that one? He shot up a quick prayer—something he found himself doing more and more these days.

"Davy, I don't even know if your dad is guilty of the stuff you think he did. And neither do you."

"Mom told you about the note . . . the card?"

He nodded. "Yes. She did."

"I *saw* them together."

"You did?" Susan had told him that, but he wanted to hear it from Davy's perspective—and to buy himself a little time. He had no idea what he could tell this kid that would ease his pain. Had David Marlowe thought for one minute about how this would affect his sons?

"They were in Springfield at this coffee shop," Davy said. "They were—" He bowed his head, then buried his face in his hands. "It was sick. I wanted to *kill* him. How could he do something like that? How could he do that to Mom?" His voice broke.

Pete pulled the truck into an angled parking space on the empty Main Street, put it in Park and shut off the engine. He reached across the seat and put a hand on Davy's shoulder, felt him shaking. "Let me ask you something. Have you ever done anything you knew was wrong? Something you knew would hurt the people you love, but . . . you couldn't seem to help yourself? No matter how much you tried?"

Davy stilled and Pete had a feeling he was getting through.

"Son, it doesn't matter how good our intentions are. Sometimes we screw up. If your dad was stepping out on your mom, he was flat wrong. I'm not making excuses for him. But you've got to let it go. You can't go back and change anything, and it'll eat you alive if you don't move past it."

The words that were coming from his mouth were an answer to a prayer, pure and simple. He felt as if he were saying things he didn't know himself. And, oddly enough, they were things he needed to hear himself. Something was going on between him and the man upstairs, and it didn't scare him half as much as he'd always thought it would.

Davy shifted in his seat. "That's what my mom said. About not being able to go back and change it. About letting go."

"You have a very smart mom." Pete got the distinct impression that the best thing to do now was shut up and let the words soak in. He tried to let them soak into his own heart.

There were some things he needed to let go of, too. Bitterness he still harbored toward Lana for giving up on their marriage. And, if he was honest, bitterness toward heaven, because God had let another man give his wife the babies she so desperately wanted.

He'd wanted kids, too. Maybe not as much as Lana, but it still hurt a little when the guys at the station came in handing out cigars to celebrate a new kid, or talking about the great play their son or daughter made in Friday night's game. Sometimes it scared him to think of growing old, retiring from firefighting, without a family to share his days with. A guy could only do so much fishing before he needed someone besides the crawdads to talk to.

"Chief Brennan?"

"Yeah, Davy?"

"Do you think my dad knew . . . that what he was doing was wrong?"

"I guarantee he did. And maybe—" He hesitated to say what came to his mind, because he had no way of knowing if it was true. But somehow it seemed like he should say it. "You know, I'm pretty sure if your dad had lived long enough, he would have come around. Would have at least tried to make things right. God has a way of nagging us until we either have to do what we know is right or shut God out. I don't think your dad was a shut-God-out kind of guy. Not in the end."

Davy seemed to consider that. And again, Pete knew that the words coming from his mouth were meant for him as much as for Davy.

Davy looked up from the corner of his eye. "Yeah. I've kinda been getting that lately, too. God nagging me, I mean."

Pete laughed, having a sudden memory of that "nagging" in his own young life. He'd always thought of it as his conscience, but somehow he knew now that it had been something far greater. Some*one* far greater. And he needed to get sight of that again.

He backhanded Davy's knee. "Hey, do me a favor, would you?"

Davy's brow furrowed.

"Don't take it out on your mom, okay? She has enough trouble as it is. She's hurting, too. And this is not her fault."

Davy hung his head, a hank of hair flopping over his eyes. "Yeah . . . I know."

He had a feeling Susan wouldn't need to worry about Davy coming home drunk again. And the knowledge made him feel a little drunk himself. "I know your dad loved you very much. And he loved your mom, too. In spite of everything. He was awful proud of his family. Bragged on you guys all the time. Made me a little jealous, if you want to know the truth."

Davy looked at him, but Pete didn't offer an explanation. He'd said enough for one night. And this wasn't about him. "Now, how about that burger?" He turned the key in the ignition and the engine roared to life. "You in?"

"Yeah." Davy straightened in the seat, daring to grin. "I'm in."

She threw off the covers and
went to look out the window.

30

Wednesday, July 1

Susan stirred when she heard a car in the driveway. She sat up on one elbow, trying to read the alarm clock. After midnight.

She threw off the covers and went to look out the window. Davy was climbing from the driver's side of his car. He was alone, but he appeared to be sober. She knew Pete wouldn't have let Davy drive home if he was impaired. What on earth had he and Pete been talking about all this time?

She started down the stairs, then decided against it. If she was going to expect her son to act like an adult, she needed to start treating him like one.

She tiptoed back into her room and crawled into bed, listening for him to come in. She heard him rummaging in the cupboards and opening and closing the refrigerator. She could picture him drinking straight from the milk carton the way he did when he thought she wasn't looking.

Her heart filled with love for her son. And pain for everything he was going through. Friends had said it was a blessing that at least the boys had been grown and gone from home at the time of David's death. They meant to comfort her . . . didn't mean to be insensitive. But Susan knew now that her boys needed their father as much as ever.

She needed him, too. David would have known exactly how to handle these choppy waters with Davy. The instant the thought formed, her stomach clenched. How much smoother this journey through grief would have been for Davy if not for David's indiscretion. Anger boiled inside her and she repeated a prayer like a mantra. *Help me forgive him, Lord. Help me forgive—*

"Mom?"

A tap on her door made her start and sit up in bed.

"Just wanted to let you know I was home." Davy's voice was clear and steady.

"Everything okay?" She tried to sound nonchalant.

"Yeah," he whispered. "And . . . I'm sorry. We'll talk in the morning. Sorry to wake you up. Go back to sleep."

She switched on the reading lamp on her nightstand. "It's okay. I'm awake. You want to talk now?"

He came and plopped on the end of the bed like he used to when he was in high school.

"I'm sorry for taking it out on you, Mom. I don't know why I did that. I know you don't need all the crap I've been giving you."

"Where's my Davy?" she deadpanned. "What have you done with my son?"

That earned her a grin.

"So," she said, "you and Pete had a good talk?"

He looked suspicious. "Why? Did he call you?"

"No. I was just asking."

The tension went out of his body. "Yeah. We had a good talk." He got up and started for the door.

Now she was dying of curiosity. But she clamped her mouth shut. It really was none of her business.

But before the door had closed behind him, Davy stepped back into the room and leaned his back against the doorjamb. "I've been worried that Dad—" he hung his head. "That he was in hell."

Susan stifled a gasp. "Oh, Davy . . ." She wasn't sure how to respond.

"But Chief Brennan—Pete. He said I could call him Pete."

Susan smiled, adoring Peter Brennan even more in that moment.

"Anyway," Davy said, "Pete asked me if I thought I would have gone to hell if I'd gotten in a crash on the way to the firehouse, drunk behind the wheel." Davy looked at her from under hooded eyes. "And I'm sorry about that, Mom. I know it was wrong. I'm not making excuses or anything."

She was too choked up to reply.

"The point is, the chief said he didn't think heaven or hell depended on what sin you were committing when you died. Only what you *believed* when you died. Do you think Dad still really believed in Jesus like he always said he did?"

Susan blinked, amazed at Pete's insight, and amazed at the answer she'd known all along. Yet she'd never contemplated how much her sons needed to know it, too. "I know he did, Davy. As much as one person can ever know another person's heart."

"Pete said what Dad did wasn't . . . unforgivable."

She nodded. Bless Pete's heart, it was true. "Davy, your dad, with all his faults, loved the Lord. If what we suspect is true, he obviously wasn't living out his faith very well, but I know in my heart that your dad loved God. I have a feeling—" She stopped, swallowing hard.

She wouldn't tell Davy how often over the last few weeks she'd blamed herself—at least partially—for David straying. If only she hadn't gotten so wrapped up in getting the shelter off the ground. If only she'd let David know how much she appreciated him. She'd begun to see that his flirting, even his posing for that stupid calendar, had been cries for attention—*her* attention. But the more he begged for admiration in what seemed unacceptable, immature ways—to her, anyway—the more she'd withheld it. They'd played a stupid game . . . and maybe it drove him straight into another woman's arms.

She swallowed the lump in her throat and willed her voice to steady. "I have a feeling Dad was carrying a lot of guilt. And I'd like to think he would have come around, would have—" She couldn't go on without weeping and she didn't want to fall apart in front of her son.

"I think he would have, too, Mom. Pete says Dad loved you. Really loved you."

She bit her lip to keep it from trembling. "Thanks, honey," she whispered.

Thanks, Pete.

*. . . within ten minutes
she wasn't even sure which
direction they were headed.*

31

Saturday, July 4

Not exactly ideal fishing conditions, huh?" Gazing out the passenger window of Pete's truck, Susan watched weekend picnickers setting up grills and staking out their corners of the park with blankets and umbrellas. The big fireworks show wouldn't start until after dark, of course, but everyone had come early for the best seat. "You think it will be this crowded at the pond?"

"Doesn't matter," Pete grumbled. "This crowd has already scared away every catfish within a ten-mile radius."

"Is that what we're fishing for? Catfish?"

"Catfish, bluegill, crappie, anything that'll take a bite out of my—"

A machine-gun volley of firecrackers went off.

Without a word, Pete turned the pickup around and headed out of the park.

"Now what?" Susan frowned. She'd looked forward to this day all week.

"If you don't have your heart set on Ferris Park and massive crowds of noisy people, I know someplace we can fish in peace and quiet and see the fireworks from afar."

Her spirits lifted. "Sure. I'm game."

He headed south and traversed a maze of country roads that Susan didn't think she'd ever been on. The morning fog had burned off, but the sky was still overcast, and within ten minutes she wasn't even sure which direction they were headed.

"I thought you were on call." How many outings had David had to leave early because of a fire?

Pete grinned over at her and patted the radio on his belt. "I am. Don't worry, we're almost there."

A minute later he pulled into a field and followed a grassy path back toward the woods. He parked the truck, jumped out, and came around to open Susan's door.

"Well, aren't you a gentleman."

He eyed the picnic cooler on the console. "I figure since you made supper, the least I can do is be a gentleman."

"You might want to wait until you've tasted the supper."

"I thought you'd never ask." He reached for the cooler and lifted it off the seat. "What's in here? Cement blocks?"

"Oh . . . that's my biscuits."

He chuckled, then stopped abruptly, studying her straight face. "You're kidding, right?"

She broke into a grin. "Kidding."

"Whew!" He made a show of wiping his brow.

"Are you wanting to eat already?"

"No, but let's take the food with us so we don't have to come back to the truck for it."

She took the cooler from him, and he started gathering fishing gear from the back of the pickup.

He held up two poles. "Star drag or lever? You have a preference?"

She laughed. "I hear words coming out of your mouth, but I don't know what they mean."

He poked out one cheek with his tongue and selected a pole. "Lever."

Susan followed him down a faded trail. He lifted strands of a barbed wire fence for her to crawl between, then handed the fishing rods over to her while he stepped over the fence.

They tramped through the woods for a few minutes before she heard the trickle of water. "It's a stream. Is this the Gasconade?"

"It's a tributary of it. The guy who trained me as a rookie owns this acreage. When he retired, he gave me a lifetime pass to fish on his place."

"Don't you usually fish at Ferris Park? I'm surprised you don't come out here instead."

"Ferris is usually quiet, and it's easier to get to. Gets awful dark out here once the sun goes down."

"Hate to tell you, but it gets dark at Ferris Park, too, once the sun goes down."

The look he shot her said he remembered when he'd spouted a similar line to her. "Touché," he said, gracing her with that winsome grin of his.

S he noticed he carried a big lantern along with the fishing gear. They came upon the river, and the scents of mud and fish and water hung in the heavy summer air. It was a good smell. Reminded her of her childhood. How long had it been since she'd been on the river?

Pete pointed upstream. "Let's head down that way a piece. There's a nice bank and a clearing where we might be able to see the fireworks better."

"From down here?"

"Maybe. If we can't, we'll drive back into town. I won't let you miss the show."

She shrugged. "Oh, it's not that big of a deal. It's just nice to be outside."

Pete unzipped a tattered sleeping bag and spread it on the loamy slope of the bank. Susan set the picnic cooler on one corner of the blanket and followed Pete down to the water's edge.

They found a shady spot, and he showed her how to work the reel on her fishing rod. "I suppose I'm going to have to bait your hook for you."

"I don't know the first thing about tying lures."

He opened a coffee can and plunged his hand in. "I've never been a lure kind of guy." He held up a handful of slimy worms. "Night crawlers. Bait the way God intended it."

She wrinkled her nose and took a step back. "Yes. I think I'll let you bait the hook for me . . . if you don't mind."

He grinned. "Bring your rod over here."

Before long, they stood in companionable silence watching their lines float like gossamer over the black water. The red-and-white bobbers rolled with the gentle current. The sound of the water lapping at the rocks was the most soothing thing Susan could imagine.

Pete pulled a grape Tootsie Pop from his breast pocket and offered it to her.

She eyed his pocket. "You don't have a raspberry one in there, do you?"

He clutched the stash of suckers dramatically. "Maybe, but I kind of like to hang on to those."

"The raspberry ones?"

He grinned. "Yep. They're my favorite." He poked around in his pocket and produced a cherry one. "Will this do?"

"I never took you for the selfish sort." She took the sucker from him, feigning disgust, but not very successfully, judging by his grin.

"Well then, you were sorely mistaken."

"I see that now. And I am sorely disappointed."

"Okay, okay . . ." He produced a raspberry pop from his pocket. "Take my last one. I'll eventually get over it."

She unwrapped the cherry pop, tucking the wrapper in her front pocket like he always did. "I wouldn't do that to you."

He chuckled and cast his line out again.

"Is this the part where I need to be quiet so I don't scare the fish?"

"Depends. How big a racket were you planning to make?"

She wrinkled her nose at him. "I just wanted to say thanks—for talking to Davy. I don't know what you said, but he's like a different kid." She corrected herself. "A different *man*. I have to keep reminding myself that he's not a teenager anymore."

"Well, he'll always be *your* kid. And he's a good kid, Susan. He's had a real blow. Nobody should be surprised that he's going through a rough patch. But he's asking the right questions." He reeled in his line and cast it again. The hook landed halfway across the river. "He'll get things figured out. Just give him a little time."

Susan slowly reeled her own line in, but it snagged in the brush near the shore.

Pete laid his rod down. "Hang on." He untangled her line and handed the pole back to her. "Try to get it way out there this time. Use your wrist."

"Like this?" Susan gave the pole a fling. Her line sailed out over the river, then plopped into the water six feet in front of her, the bobber ping-ponging against the rocks.

"Well . . . not exactly like that." He grinned. "Here . . . let me show you." He came around behind her and matched his forearms to hers. His arms were tan and muscled, and in spite of the afternoon heat, she relished their warmth against her skin.

"Am I holding it right?" she whispered, afraid her voice would betray her emotions.

He leaned over her shoulder until they were almost cheek to cheek.

His voice was a low murmur in her ear. "You don't have to whisper." Strong arms tightened around her.

Everything in her wanted to lean back into his embrace. Let him hold her, kiss her . . . But it was too soon.

Using every ounce of restraint she owned, she shrank from his embrace. "I'm sure you're a wonderful teacher, Pete, but"—nervous laughter escaped her lips—"I think I'm hopeless as a fisherman."

He blinked and reached for her. She recognized the hungry look in his gray eyes.

She took two steps backward but stumbled on a tree root.

He grabbed her arm and caught her. "Careful there . . . You going swimming?"

"Thanks." Brushing off the knees of her jeans needlessly, she grinned up at him and pointed to his fishing rod. "I think you need to fish over on your side and let me fish on mine."

He chuckled under his breath like a man who'd lost a skirmish but knew he was winning the war.

She knew better than to try to convince him otherwise.

They fished without success for a few more minutes until he said, "What have you got in that cooler?"

"Why? You think there might be better fish food in there?"

"I think there better be some man food in there."

She laughed. "Let me see what I can rustle up." She perched her fishing rod on a rock.

He followed suit. "I'll help. I'm sure not having any luck here."

She narrowed her eyes at him, wondering if he meant more than the fishing.

His expression gave away nothing. He opened the cooler and peered inside. "You want something to drink?"

"I could use some water. Thanks."

He handed her an icy cold bottle and twisted the top off of a second one. He raised it in a toast. "To all the fish who live another day, thanks to us."

Laughing, she raised her own bottle. "Here, here." She took a swig and relished the cool liquid spreading through her.

They ate the sandwiches and homemade potato salad she'd fixed. Pete finished his fifth chocolate chip cookie and gave a satisfied sigh.

"I think that calls for a nap." He stretched out on the sleeping bag, hands behind his head.

Eventually his soft breathing told Susan he was asleep. She watched him, amazed at the feelings that welled inside her. She hadn't felt this way since she'd fallen head over heels with David when they were in college.

Dear God, help me. I think I'm falling in love with this man. The idea filled her with equal portions of apprehension and joy.

Pete stirred as the sun slipped below the trees. He sat up and stretched, turning to her. "Did you sleep?"

She winked. "Somebody had to clean up."

"Oh, right. I suppose you washed dishes in the stream and gathered wood for a fire, too?"

"Yep. And caught a few fish for a midnight snack."

His jaw dropped and he looked past her to the fishing poles.

She laughed. "Gotcha! But no, I didn't sleep. It sure is pleasant out here, though."

"You're sworn to secrecy, of course. I don't want this place turning into Ferris Park next Fourth of July."

"Girl Scout's honor." She gave a little three-fingered salute.

He swatted a mosquito on his forearm. "We should be seeing fireworks before long." He unfolded himself from the blanket, gathered up the fishing gear, and lit the lantern. "Not sure why the fish weren't biting today, but I'll have to bring you back sometime and show you what all the hype is about."

She gave a noncommittal nod, but she liked the way he was thinking.

A muffled *boom* fractured the silence. A spray of colored sparkles lit the night sky and reflected in the black water of the tributary. Pete turned the lantern down and dragged the blanket closer to the water's edge. He sat cross-legged and patted the spot beside him.

She joined him, and for the next half hour they oohed and aahed at the spectacular fireworks display from what must surely be the best seats in the county. Pete put an arm around her shoulders and she let it stay, leaning against his strong body.

When Ferris Park's grand finale fizzled away, Pete's arm tightened around her and he reached up with his other hand to brush her hair away from her face.

She wanted him to kiss her. There was no denying that. But she put a hand on his smooth cheek and gently held him off. "It's been a wonderful evening. Let's just . . . go slow, okay?"

"You make that very difficult to do, lady." He ran a hand over her cheek, then sighed and scooted away.

He turned up the lantern and together, they gathered up their picnic and fishing gear and trudged back through the field in the lantern's golden haze.

Halfway to the pickup, Susan felt droplets on her arms. "Is it sprinkling?"

Pete looked up at the sky. "I thought I felt drops."

The words were barely out of his mouth when the sky opened.

"Follow me!" Pete gave a whoop and, fishing gear in tow, took off at a jog.

Laughing and squealing, Susan ran after him, scrambling to keep up. But no amount of rain could dampen her spirits. Tonight she felt like she was seventeen again.

*She touched his arm
and saw the effect in
his smoky gaze.*

32

Sunday, July 5

Andrea glanced each way before pulling into the intersection. She didn't think Pete had seen her, but if he had, she had an excuse ready about why she just happened to be at the grocery store at the same time he was.

After seeing Susan's car at the fire station again the other night, she'd decided it was time to quit being demure. If the man was so dense he couldn't see she had a thing for him, then she'd have to make sure he understood her intentions.

She waited in the parking lot until he was inside the store and watched which direction he went. She pulled into a parking spot in front of Hanson's Market, grabbed a grocery cart and tossed half a dozen items into it as she headed for the back of the store. She rounded the corner and looked down the cereal aisle, but he wasn't there. If he was like most of the men she knew, it was just a matter of time before he headed for the cornflakes.

She grabbed a box of healthy bran cereal and started reading the nutrition information on the side to kill time.

She didn't make it past the niacin and riboflavin paragraph before she saw him from the corner of her eye. She flipped her hair over one shoulder and continued her intent perusal of the box.

"If I didn't know better, I'd think you were stalking me."

"Pete! Good grief, who's talking? You're the one who keeps showing up every place I go."

"Well, hey, a man's gotta eat."

"Don't I know it."

His laughter caught her off guard. She studied the shiny white tile beneath her feet. "You know what I mean."

"Looks like you're feeding an army." He pointed into her cart.

"Oh. Not really. My sister is coming tomorrow night. We like to try out new recipes."

"Oh, well . . . have fun." He started to back his cart away.

She had to act fast. "You wouldn't want to come and be our guinea pig—er, I mean taste tester, would you?"

He laughed, but she could see he wasn't warming to her like usual.

"I . . . appreciate the invitation, but I've got a pretty busy week ahead. The holiday put us behind on paperwork."

"But you said it yourself—a man's gotta eat."

For once, he seemed unfazed by her flirtation. He looked past her down the aisle, then looked at his watch. "I'd better get going. Enjoy your time with your sister." He started to push his cart past her.

She moved her own cart to block him. "Hey . . . crazy idea: you wouldn't want to take advantage of that rain check on coffee tonight, would you?"

He looked confused. "Didn't know we had a rain check pending."

She sighed. "Could you pretend? Please? There's something I really need to talk to you about, Pete."

"Oh?" Concern washed across his face. "What's up?"

She scrambled to think of something. She hadn't figured on having to work this hard to get his attention. "I . . . I'd rather wait till you have time to talk. Could we meet for coffee in a little while—after you're done shopping?"

"Well . . ." He looked at his watch again. "I guess I could spare a few minutes."

"Wow." She narrowed her eyes at him and affected a pout. "Don't put yourself out or anything."

He had the decency to blush. "I didn't mean that the way it came out. Coffee sounds great. Java Joint?"

"Sure."

"I'll just meet you there, then?"

"Would you mind if I catch a ride with you? I'm running on fumes."

He shrugged. "Sure. Fifteen minutes give you enough time?"

"Make it twenty and you've got a deal." Always good to keep a man waiting. And guessing.

"I'm in my pickup." He pointed through the plate-glass windows at the front of the store. "I'll park right out front."

He was finally warming up a little. She touched his arm and saw the effect in his smoky gaze. "I'm so glad this worked out," she said. "Seems like I haven't talked to you in forever."

Twenty minutes later Pete wheeled his cart to the car and quickly loaded the groceries into the backseat of his pickup. He was curious about what Andi wanted. He didn't get the impression it was a business matter. In fact, he had a strange feeling she was going to confess about her relationship with David Marlowe.

He wasn't sure he wanted to hear it, and yet he couldn't continue to work with her and pretend that everything was as it had been. Especially now, with Susan becoming more a part of his life every day.

Within a few minutes Andi came out with one small grocery bag and a large sack of dog food lopped over one shoulder. He jumped out and helped her load them into the trunk of her car, which was parked a couple rows out.

Walking back to his truck, he clicked the button on his key chain, and the headlights flashed. She went around and climbed into the passenger seat. When she was settled, she pulled the visor down and wiped her forehead with a tissue from her purse. "It feels like August already. I hate this humidity."

He agreed. "It's messing up my fishing, too."

"Fishing?" She made a face. "Now there's a sport I've never understood."

"What? You don't like fish?"

"I like the kind you find in the frozen food aisle, not the kind you have to clean and fry—and smell."

He laughed, and they made small talk on the short drive to Java Joint. There were no parking spots in front of the coffee shop, so he let her out and went to park the pickup.

She was waiting inside the front entrance when he came across the lot. Her face lit when she spotted him. She grinned and pushed her sunglasses up on top of her head. Something about the simple motion got to him. He knew how this woman operated, and he was starting to suspect her reason for wanting to talk to him wasn't quite as urgent as she'd let on.

She slid into the booth across from him and flipped her curly mane over one shoulder.

He felt like a fish that'd swallowed the hook. "Do you want something to eat or just . . . coffee?" Maybe the line and sinker, too.

"Coffee's good," she said. "I already ate. I don't dare shop hungry."

"That wouldn't work for me. I'm never *not* hungry."

Her laughter lifted his spirits, and he remembered how he'd felt with Susan the other night. He felt a twinge of guilt that he was here with Andi. And he prayed they wouldn't run into Susan.

He'd loved hearing Susan's laughter as they ran through the rain and drove home dripping, but happy. And hopeful. At least he had been. He thought she felt the same. With the problems with Davy and at the shelter, it had been too long since he'd seen that carefree side of her. He checked his thoughts when he realized Andi was saying something.

It was hard not to admire the beautiful woman across the table from him, and he was curious about why she wanted to talk to him.

"Tell me what you want and I'll go order," he said.

Andi looked past him, studying the coffee menu on the board above the counter. "I'll try the peppermint mocha. Just a small, please." She dug in her purse and came up with a five-dollar bill. "Here."

"Nope. My treat. You can get it next time." He flushed, realizing his words assumed there would be a next time. He didn't want her to get the wrong idea, but it was too late to take back his words without opening a whole new can of worms.

Andi didn't seem to notice, but a few minutes later when he brought their coffee to the table, she cocked her head and eyed him, and without preamble said, "So what's the deal with you and Susan Marlowe?"

"What do you mean, 'What's the deal?'" He felt caught. Was *this* why she'd invited him for coffee? To grill him about Susan?

"Are you guys dating, or what exactly?" She shrugged, leaving the ball very obviously in his court.

"Not anything . . . *exactly*," he mumbled.

"Then what?" The gleam in her eye said she was going for broke.

Pushing his spine into the back of the seat, he put as much distance between them as the cramped booth allowed. "Not that it's any of your business, but Susan and I are friends."

"And is that how you see *us*? Friends?" She motioned between them.

He swirled the coffee in his cup, scrabbling for an answer that would leave him with his dignity. Why did he suddenly feel so guilty? He'd told her the truth. He *was* friends with Susan. And yet, after being with her on the Fourth, something had changed in their relationship. Something very good. Something that made being here with Andrea now feel more wrong by the minute.

He affected a wry grin, hedging. "I thought the whole 'going out' thing ended once you got out of high school."

She looked at him like he'd grown a third eye. "Who said anything about going out?"

"Then why does it matter what the relationship is between us?" He mimicked her, motioning between them the way Andi had.

She looked down at the table, smoothing her paper napkin over and over again. When she finally looked up, that glint was back in her eyes. Aimed at him. "Because, Pete. I'll be honest . . . it would not break my heart for you and me to be something more."

"Than friends?" The words stuck in his throat, and he suddenly had a little sympathy for David Marlowe. This woman knew how to make a man feel—

"Have you heard a word I've said?"

He blinked.

"Listen," she said, as if she were speaking to a child. "If there's something between you and Susan, I'd just as soon know it right now. Before I invest too much time in you."

"You have a biological clock ticking or something?" He'd aimed for humor, but the words sounded harsh and totally inappropriate once they left his mouth.

But Andi laughed. "Nothing like that. But I do like you, Peter Brennan. Quite a bit. I hope you don't mind."

Oh, boy. He opened his mouth, then closed it to rethink. He might regret it later, but if she was going to be brash, so was he. "I guess it's fair to assume you didn't have this same conversation with Dave Marlowe?"

She straightened in her seat and leaned back as if he'd struck her. "Where did *that* come from?"

He shrugged. "I thought we were putting all our cards on the table."

"David Marlowe has nothing to do with you."

"But he had plenty to do with you . . . didn't he, Andi?"

She edged a spoon under her napkin. "Did he ever say anything to you?"

"It's an easy question, Andi. Yes or no?"

"Why is this coming up all of a sudden?" She burrowed into the corner of the booth, crossed her arms, and narrowed her eyes at him. "Did Susan say something?"

"Why would she say anything? She was only his wife." His terse comment surprised even him. He'd had no intention of broaching this subject with her when they sat down for coffee. But he wasn't taking it back. He was fighting for Susan now. Andrea Morley had lost all appeal.

Andi slid from the booth and, without another word, made for the door. He would have let her go, except her car was two miles away in Hanson's parking lot. Convenient.

He left their takeout cups on the booth table and went after her.

He found her standing in front of the antique store next door, her back to him, head down.

"I'll take you back to your car."

Without turning, she held her cell phone up for him to see. "I'll get a ride."

"You calling a cab?" The Falls had what passed for a taxi service, but it didn't run after six o'clock or so, and it charged an exorbitant fee to go two blocks. "That's ridiculous. Let me take you. I'll keep my mouth shut if that makes you feel better."

Her shoulders slumped and she swiveled to face him.

Without meeting her eyes, he clicked his key chain. The lights on his pickup flashed and he went to open the passenger door.

She waited until he'd gone around to the driver's side before getting in.

They rode in silence for a long five minutes. As he pulled into Hanson's, he heaved a sigh. "Listen . . . I'm sorry. I was probably out of line."

"Probably?"

"Well, when you said you thought there could be something be-tween us, I just want you to know where I stand on stuff like that."

"Like what?"

"You and David Marlowe."

"What happened with me and Dave has nothing to do with you!"

"It has *everything* to do with me." He worked to keep his voice steady. "I like you a lot, Andi, but I have zero respect for someone who sees nothing wrong with—being with a married man."

"It wasn't like that." She looked at her hands in her lap.

"Really? Try telling that to Susan."

Her head shot up. "You told her? About me and Dave?"

"Actually, it was her son who brought it up first. And if you don't think that hurt, think again."

She closed her eyes. "Dear God . . ." When she looked up, she looked genuinely sorry. "Pete, I swear, Dave did not want to hurt his family. Neither one of us did. It just . . . happened."

"So you admit it."

"No, that's not what I meant. Nothing *happened*."

"You just got through saying, 'It just happened.'"

"Don't put words in my mouth. What I meant is, we didn't *do* any-thing. We were waiting—"

He harrumphed. "Yeah, right. I've heard that one before."

"No, Pete. I swear to you. Nothing like that happened." She spoke the words as if they were painful. "Dave was super religious and he thought it would be like—a mortal sin or something. He barely ever even kissed me."

"I'm thinking Susan would think 'barely ever' leaves a whole lot of room for questions."

Her expression turned hard. "Fine. Believe what you want. I'm tell-ing you the truth."

"I don't suppose you can tell me that you broke it off with Dave before the fire . . . before he died? Because I know that would be a great comfort for his widow to know that all you and Dave did was kiss, and then you broke it right off." Sarcasm didn't become him. He knew that. But right now he didn't care.

And her downcast eyes made him fear there would be no comforting Susan with the hope that Dave had ended things with Andi before he died.

He pulled up beside her car and threw the truck in Park.

She turned to look at him with an expression of pure misery. But for once, she had no effect on him.

She opened her mouth to say something, but she must have seen him shut down because she grabbed the handle and shoved the door open, slid from the truck, and slammed the door behind her without another word.

He gave her the courtesy of waiting to make sure her car started. Even though she didn't deserve it.

The knowledge made him smile to himself, even as it filled him with terror.

33

Friday, July 17

$\mathcal{P}$ete threw his line out again and settled back on the bank. He had at least four hours of daylight left and he intended to soak up every minute. The river had always been his place to *not* think, but today his brain roiled.

He unwrapped his third Tootsie Pop of the day and looked out over the muddy water, remembering the Fourth, when he'd brought Susan out here.

He hadn't given it much thought at the time, but the fact that he'd been willing to share his getaway spot with her made him realize that she'd already captured a special place in his heart.

The knowledge made him smile to himself, even as it filled him with terror. Was he ready to risk giving his heart to a woman once more? He'd gotten along just fine on his own for seven and a half years now. He'd always told himself he would never again complicate his life with a woman.

But that was like declaring you could live without Tootsie Pops without ever having tasted a raspberry one. Susan was pure raspberry. And once you'd tasted raspberry, you wouldn't be so foolish as to swear off all Tootsie Pops.

Susan probably wouldn't appreciate being compared to a Tootsie Pop. He chuckled out loud at the thought. The noise scattered the river's resident toads and insects. Pete shooed away a swarm of gnats.

But it was true. Now that Susan was in his life, he couldn't imagine life without her. He had a sneaking suspicion she felt the same about him.

And he wasn't sure which thought scared him the most.

*S*usan greeted the ragtag group in front of the shelter. Half a dozen men and two women smoked cigarettes and loitered in the narrow shadows cast by the building, seeking relief from temperatures that had climbed into the nineties today.

She would let them in early tonight to get out of the heat. But when she unlocked the door, a blast of hot air greeted her. The building had air-conditioning, but she turned it on only if the thermostat rose above eighty-five inside. Donations were down again this month and she was late paying several bills as it was.

She locked the door behind her and switched on the lights. Nothing. Must have blown a fuse.

She unlocked her office and tried the lights there. Again, nothing. Strange. The hall lights were on a different breaker from her office. The thermostat registered ninety-five degrees. It was cooler than that outside!

Making her way through the darkened building, she flipped several power switches with the same results. The electricity was out in the entire building. Charlie was still at work at the public library, but she thought his shift had started at one today, so the power must have gone off some time after he left or he would have let her know.

She looked up the number to report the outage and called from her cell phone but got only a recording saying that the office was closed. Of course. It was Friday. Seemed like every business in town hung up their Closed signs early on Friday afternoon.

The recording gave a number to dial for emergencies, but this wasn't exactly an emergency—at least not until it was time to serve supper. And given the fact that she was several weeks late paying the shelter's electric bill, she didn't want to make waves until she was sure it wasn't something simple like a breaker.

A sick feeling washed over her. Surely the power company hadn't shut off her lights. She'd gotten a second notice a few days ago, but they knew she always paid as soon as she could. They couldn't get blood out of a turnip, after all.

She dialed the real estate agency down the street. The receptionist answered on the first ring.

"This is Susan at the Grove Street shelter. Do you guys have electricity?" Susan asked.

"Electricity? Yes . . . Why, is yours out?"

Susan explained what was going on.

"We've got power here," the receptionist said. "They have an emergency number you can call."

"Yes, I have it. Thank you."

She hung up and went exploring. She'd learned how to check and change fuses, but that was the extent of her knowledge of electricity. She looked at the clock. It was almost five. Pete was off today and she hated to bother him on the few days off he actually took. But if she asked, she knew he'd come and check things out.

She punched in his number. No answer, so she left a message. "Hey, it's not an emergency, but would you give me a call if you get a chance?"

She continued checking switches throughout the building, but as she flipped the light switch in the windowless storage room, a shiver went through her. What if Pete was right? Could Zeke Downing be behind this? She hurried out of the pitch-black room trying to banish the thoughts. She was being foolish. What purpose would it serve for Downing to cut the power? She and Charlie carried cell phones with them at all times. With one call, they could have the police here in two minutes. And Downing had to know that. She was being ridiculous.

Still, being in the dark building alone gave her the creeps. She retraced her steps and went outside and explained the situation to the clients. "You can come on in, but there's no light and no AC, so you may rather stay out here until we get things fixed."

"I can take a look at it if you want me to," said Gil, a shaggy-haired man whose last name Susan couldn't pronounce. "I used to work for an electrician."

Susan hesitated. No doubt it broke forty different laws to let one of the clients do such work, but it couldn't hurt to let him at least take a look.

She unlocked the doors and a few of the residents followed her and Gil in, including Tracie, a young mother with two toddlers in tow. But within a few minutes, after discovering how stifling it was inside, they all went back out to the parking lot where at least they could catch a breeze.

Gil looked things over and shrugged. "I can't see anything wrong. Maybe they shut you off."

She wiped sweat from her brow. "I—we're a little late with the bill, but not *that* late."

He rolled his eyes. "I can tell you from experience, they don't have much mercy."

Her cell phone rang. Pete.

"Hey, beautiful. You rang?"

Her heart warmed. "Sorry to bother you. The electricity is off at the shelter."

"Really? How long has it been out?"

"I'm not sure. It was out when I got here around four thirty. It's ninety-five degrees inside, and I've got a mom with two little kids staying here."

"It's probably just a fuse."

"No, I already checked."

"Did you call the power company?"

"Yes . . . I got a recording."

"Let me give them a call. They've got an emergency number."

"I can call, Pete. I'm sorry. I know this is your day off. I just thought you might know what to do."

"I don't mind. I'm not doing anything important. Just fishing."

"Oh, Pete. I'm sorry." She knew how much he'd been looking forward to getting in some fishing. He'd probably even told her he was going tonight, though she didn't remember. "Seriously, just pretend I never called. We'll figure something out."

"Let me reel in this eighty-pounder I've got on my string first, and I'll be right there."

"Do you really—"

His laughter cut her off. "Sadly, a fish story. Haven't had so much as a nibble. Hang tight, I'm on my way."

~

*P*ete snapped his phone shut and dialed the power company's after-hours number. He explained the problem to Ray Hemphill, who, judging by the background noises—and what Pete knew about him—was enjoying a few beers on the golf course.

"I can tell you exactly what's wrong," Ray said. "She didn't pay her bill."

"What? And you shut the power off? Come on, Ray."

"We treated her like we treat any other delinquent customer. She had ten days to pay the bill after she got the second notice. And this is at least the second month in a row she's been late. We should have cut her off last month."

"*I'll* pay the stinkin' bill." He gritted his teeth. "Just get the power turned back on. She's got little kids staying there, Ray. Have a heart."

"We're not running a charity, Pete." Hemphill paused, then sighed. "Okay, you promise to pay the bill Monday morning and I'll have somebody get her back up and running."

"Tonight?"

"Yes, tonight, but I'll have to charge reinstatement fees."

"Fine. Do what you gotta do. Just get those lights back on." He spat in the dirt and hopped in the pickup.

So much for that fried catfish his mouth had been watering for.

He silenced her with two gentle fingers to her lips.

34

$\mathscr{G}$oodness, it's warm in here!" The heavyset woman who'd delivered the dinner prepared by First Baptist volunteers fanned her flushed cheeks. "I was feeling bad for not baking something for dessert, but I guess that ice cream will hit the spot, huh?"

"It sure will," Susan said, praying it wasn't melting in the freezer even as they spoke. "Thanks so much for bringing dinner. Everything looks delicious."

The woman looked around the room. "I thought this place was air-conditioned?"

"Oh, it is. Our power's been out. They should have it fixed shortly." Where was Pete? It had been over an hour since she'd talked to him.

"I thought it seemed awfully dark in here. I hope that ice cream will stay cold enough to—"

She stopped short as the lights flickered and came on. The box fan in the doorway sprang to life, and the refrigerator motor whirred and settled into a low hum. At the glorious sound of the air-conditioner kicking on, the clients sent up a cheer.

Susan flashed the volunteer a smile of relief. "Would you like to stay and eat with us? My early shift volunteers can't come in until seven, so there's plenty."

"Thanks, but I need to go home and get supper on for my husband."

Susan walked with her to the door, then came back and started dishing up plates of the unidentified casserole.

The room already felt cooler as air began to circulate, and the clients' relief was almost palpable. This group of clients had been here for several days with only a few admissions or dismissals, and they'd developed a rare camaraderie. Now they filed by the serving table, laughing and talking amongst themselves. They carried full plates over to the two long tables, and Susan watched with satisfaction as Gil helped the young mother with her toddlers.

With everyone settled in, Susan started to dish up her own plate. Suddenly it hit her that Pete was on his way for no reason. She put her plate down and dashed to her office for her cell phone.

She closed the door behind her and dialed Pete. It went immediately to voice mail. But Pete's recorded voice was interrupted by the buzz of another call coming in. She pressed Answer.

"Hey, you." Pete's real voice came through the phone. "It's me."

"Oh, good. I hope you haven't left yet. The lights came back on about twenty minutes ago, so no need to cut short your—"

He laughed. "Perfect timing actually."

A tap on the window that overlooked the central hallway made her glance up. Pete stood there, still in his fishing clothes, phone to his ear. He grinned at her through the half-closed blinds.

Cringing, she closed her phone and went out into the hall. "I am so sorry. The lights came back on not long after I called and then dinner arrived and I completely forgot to let you know. I don't know why our power was out, but—"

"Um . . ." He rubbed at the worn carpeting with the toe of his hiking boot. "Any chance you forgot to pay your electric bill?"

She tilted her head and stared at him. "Is that what it was? Did they shut me off?"

He nodded, looking like he was the one who hadn't paid the bill.

"Then how . . . ? *You* got them to turn it back on?"

"You can pay me back when you're able."

"You paid the bill? Oh, Pete. I didn't mean for you to have to—"

He silenced her with two gentle fingers to her lips. "It's all taken care of. Don't give it another thought. They never should have turned it off in the first place—not when you're providing beds and food for all these people."

She hung her head. "I am so embarrassed. I should have just paid it out of my own bank account. I . . . I honestly didn't realize I was so late. It's just that, with all the negative letters in the paper and now the stupid fire at my place, donations are way down . . . I don't even know how I'm going to keep the place staffed. I can barely get volunteers to commit as it is, and now with Bryn pregnant, I'll be losing her and maybe Garrett and—"

She looked up into Pete's face and the kindness there just made things worse. "I'm sorry. You don't need to hear all that." She turned on her heel and started into her office. "Let me write you a check right now before I forget."

Pete grabbed her arm and turned her to face him. "Don't you dare," he said. "I'm happy to do it. In fact, it's the least I can do, given all you've done for these people." He motioned toward the dining room, where pleasant sounds of dinnertime conversation wafted out.

"Still . . . it was thoughtless of me to even call you, Pete. Your one time to catch a break and—"

He reached both hands out and drew her into a hug. "Shhh. You selfless, thoughtful woman. Would you just stop? I don't mind. I was looking for an excuse to see you as it was."

"Liar." But that coaxed a smile to her lips. She found more to like about this man every time she was with him.

An outburst of laughter from the dining room reminded her they weren't alone in the building. The last thing she needed were rumors going around that she was making out with some man in the hallway.

Reluctantly, she extricated herself from Pete's arms. "Have you had supper?"

"No, and something smells awfully good."

She beckoned him to follow her. "You can dish up and bring it back to my office to eat."

"Thanks."

She gave him a knowing smile. He was becoming a bit more comfortable among the clients at the shelter, but she knew it still wasn't his favorite place to be. Especially not when it kept him from his favorite fishing spot.

She wouldn't have minded being at the river with him right now. Retrieving the plate she'd ditched earlier, she finished filling it and heated the food in the microwave.

Pete had filled his plate and stood waiting for her.

Susan offered seconds to the clients. When the others refused, Gil and one of the younger guys polished off the casserole.

"You guys are still planning on sweeping up outside, right?" she reminded Gil. A mountain of cigarette butts had piled up near the entry where the people waited to be admitted every night, and she'd asked the smokers to clean up the mess.

Kelly, the youngest of the guys, held up an overflowing paper plate. "Why do you think we're fueling up?"

She laughed. "Good point. And thanks, guys. I appreciate it. If you need to let your other chores slide till tomorrow night, that'd be okay."

"Already did 'em," Kelly said, puffing out his chest.

"Wow. You're good."

He beamed as if he'd done something Pulitzer worthy.

Susan put the perishables in the refrigerator, and she and Pete went back to her office.

They ate in silence for a few minutes, and she enjoyed Pete enjoying the meal. But then he looked up, pinning her with a slow smile.

"What?"

"You're really good at what you do."

She drew back. "What?"

He gestured toward the dining room. "The way you handled those guys just now. Not condescending, but yet you still got them to do what you wanted."

She smirked. "You might want to withhold your judgment until we see if they actually do the job."

"They will. I have no doubt. They have a lot of respect for you, Susan. That's obvious."

She knew he was just trying to make her feel better about not paying the electric bill. His praise embarrassed her, but it made her love him at the same time. "You're sweet. And before you get in so deep you can't get out, you need to know that the electric bill isn't the only one that's gone unpaid this month."

His jaw went slack. "Why didn't you say something?"

"If I had, would you have gone and paid *all* the late bills?"

He looked sheepish and slunk deeper into his chair.

"That's what I thought." She reached across the table and patted his hand. "It's not like we've never been late on bills before. When you totally rely on volunteers and charity, people know you're going to be late sometimes. I'm sure it'll all work out." She wasn't sure of that at all. It had never been as bad as it had these last few months. She feared the shelter had lost the favor of the community permanently. Between lost donations and dwindling volunteers, she didn't know how much longer they could keep going.

Pete pushed his plate aside and looked across the table at her. "I'm not a rich man, and I can't fix everything and make it all right, but I have a couple of propositions to make."

He propped his hands on his thighs, looking like a man who was about to dive off a cliff into unknown waters. "I wasn't going to say anything yet, but I've just made up my mind."

She waited in silence, curiosity eating her alive.

"I'll have to work around my schedule at the station, and I might not be the most dependable volunteer you ever had, but I'd like to fill one of the shifts a couple times a month. As long as you're on duty," he said quickly. "I'm not coming by myself . . . at least not yet."

"Pete." She knew what a sacrifice this was for him—and not just the time commitment, but the stepping out of his comfort zone. "Pete, you don't have to—"

He shushed her, but softened it with a grin. "Let me finish, okay?"

She nodded, trying not to let him see her elation.

"Thanks to you—watching you, and everything you do to give of your time and of yourself—I've been feeling a little bit like a slug recently."

"Oh, good grief. You are anything but a slug, Peter Brennan."

He held up his hands, palms out. "No. Believe me, I'm a slug. Everything I do is for me. And I think"—he pointed at the ceiling—"the man upstairs is trying to tell me something. And for once, I'm going to listen to him."

She opened her mouth, but he stopped her again.

"Let me say this before I change my mind."

She made her eyes wide. "There's more?"

His grin came and went. "I don't know if Davy has decided what he wants to do yet. But if he has any thoughts about finding work around here, we could use him at the station, just cleaning up and filing. It's nothing glamorous and it doesn't pay much, but if he wants to come on as a rookie when we start training for the next team, I'd love to have him. Maybe I can . . . I don't know . . . just be there for him, you know?"

"Oh, Pete," she whispered, tears springing to her eyes.

"Well, it won't be easy, and I can't play favorites. He'll have to pass the same tests the rest of the guys do. But I think he can do it." He shrugged. "I feel for the kid. And I know firefighters probably aren't too high on his list right now, but I think he's got what it takes. And I wouldn't mind helping him out . . . if I can."

She stared at him. She wasn't sure what she'd expected him to say, but never in a million years would she have guessed this. "I . . . I don't even know what to say."

"Well, 'Thank you, you wonderful man, you' would be a good start."

She dissolved into laughter. "Thank you, you wonderful, sexy man."

His eyebrows went up, making her laugh even harder. "I like your version even better," he said.

She'd told her sister it was
no big deal, but that was a lie.

35

Tuesday, July 21

$\mathcal{I}$t's no big deal, Becca. Forget about it. I'll talk to you next week."
Andi flipped her phone shut and dropped it in her purse. "Far be it from
me to stand between you and a man," she muttered.

She'd told her sister it was no big deal, but that was a lie. This was the
second weekend in a row that Rebecca had canceled their plans. Her sister was dating a new guy and supposedly he could only get together on
weekends. Well, what was *she* supposed to do? A fire inspector couldn't
exactly drop everything and go shopping on a weekday either.

Andi had been in a funk ever since the night Pete ambushed her at
the coffee shop. Rebecca knew that, but she didn't seem to care. All she
wanted to talk about was Ross. Ross this, Ross that. You'd have thought
the guy was a prince or something.

Andi tossed her purse into her desk drawer and kicked it shut. Just
watch. Rebecca would call her Monday morning and she'd be all bubbly
about her weekend with Mr. Flavor of the Week—or all heartbroken

because another relationship wasn't working out—and she wouldn't even ask Andi how she was doing.

And like a dutiful sister, Andi would listen and rejoice with Becca, or listen to her whine. But whose shoulder was *she* supposed to cry on?

Ever since Dave, her sister hadn't trusted her and hadn't cared for any man she'd gone out with. *Is he married?* was always the first question Becca asked. Even after Andi told her no, she still pushed. "No secret girlfriend either? You're sure?"

It hadn't helped when they'd run into Pete and Susan that night at T.G.I. Friday's in Springfield. "This is the guy you've been talking about? Who was that, his wife?"

She didn't appreciate Becca's sarcasm, but she wasn't about to tell her that it was Dave Marlowe's wife whom Pete was with that night.

She wondered if Pete and Susan were still together. Had he told Susan about having coffee with her that night after she'd followed him to the grocery store? She shuddered. If either of them knew the truth—

Stop it, Andi. Don't go there . . . Think about something else . . .

But the images came anyway. Memories she wanted buried . . . buried so they could never cause her pain again. She heard Dave's voice, so clear she had to look around her office to be sure he wasn't really there.

He was arguing with her. *It's only in your mind, Andi. He's gone. Remember? He's gone.* She rubbed her temples, trying to knead away the throbbing that had started there.

You'll never amount to anything. Don't even bother.

Wait . . . No, that wasn't Dave. That was her father. Why did she keep mixing them up? Even their voices had begun to sound the same. But that was because sometimes Dave said things like that.

She shook her head. She didn't want to remember. Didn't want to go there . . . but the memory was there before she could retract it.

They were watching TV in the corner of a department store in Springfield. She and Dave. He had his arm around her. She'd never felt so close to him. But then an interview had come on the TV. A national news show. There was a fire inspector. A woman . . . like her. But Dave's words had wounded her deeply. "You'll never get that kind of recognition working kitchen grease fires, Andi," he'd said. And he'd laughed, like he'd said something funny.

She lashed out at him. Right there in the store. And he apologized. Over and over. But after that, his words became more and more like her father's.

She cast about the room looking for something to distract her. Her eyes landed on the neatly penned to-do list on her desk. She read the items one by one, forcing her thoughts into submission.

She retrieved her purse from her desk drawer. Maybe she'd go to a movie tonight. She hated going to the theater by herself, but not as much as she hated sitting at home, letting her mind take her to the dark places when she had too much time to think.

She stepped out to the reception room where her secretary was working at the file cabinet. "Hey, Shelly, what are you doing tonight? You want to go to a movie?"

"Sorry, I've got a date."

Okay, fine. Nobody could say she didn't try. But it didn't look like she had a choice. She would sit home and let her mind take her where it would.

ou're awfully chipper tonight." Charlie eyed Susan across the supper table.

"Are you complaining?" She realized she'd been smiling for no reason. Well, no reason Charlie needed to know anyway.

He shrugged. "Fine by me. Just making an observation." He took another bite of the boxed macaroni and cheese she'd made at the last minute when the meal Falls Community Church had signed up to bring didn't materialize.

"This stuff isn't half bad." She stabbed a cheese-laden noodle and put it in her mouth, hoping to change the subject.

"I've had worse," Charlie said. "Had better, too."

She opened her mouth to say beggars couldn't be choosers, but thought better of it.

The forgotten supper had dampened her spirits a little, but Charlie was right. She *was* "chipper." Pete was working his first official shift tonight, and for the first time in ages she was excited to be at work. She'd dismissed two clients into low-income housing this morning, and two others hadn't shown up for the third day now, so the shelter was barely at half capacity tonight. She was grateful for the lower numbers. She didn't want to overwhelm Pete.

He'd called a few minutes ago and let her know he was running a little late. "I promise not to make a habit of it, but I think you'll be happy about my excuse."

"Oh?"

"Gotta go," he'd said, laughing, obviously aware that he'd left her dying of curiosity.

When Pete showed up fifteen minutes later, Susan was in the dayroom helping Tracie finish her assigned chores so she could take her toddlers to the park before it got dark.

Pete nodded a greeting at Tracie, then turned to Susan with his palms up. "Okay, put me to work."

She took a dustpan from the young mother and handed it to Pete. "Tracie, you go ahead. We'll finish up here." The toddlers were underfoot anyway. "Do you have sunscreen for the kids?"

"I still have a little from the bottle you gave me last week."

"Okay. Have fun."

Pete took the broom from Susan and swept up a pile of crumbs and dirt into the dustpan.

Susan smiled. "Ah, a self-starter. Good, I like that."

He smirked. "And what if I wasn't? Were you gonna fire me?"

"Don't think I wouldn't."

They tossed good-natured barbs back and forth until the dayroom had been swept and mopped. Two clients dusted halfheartedly behind them.

"Now what?" Pete asked.

"Now we're done for a while. Have you eaten?"

"I grabbed a burger on the way."

"Good. Dinner didn't show up tonight so we had mac and cheese from a box. Again."

"Hey, don't knock the stuff."

"Ha! Tell that to Charlie."

He laughed. "Not a fan, huh? Well, who can blame the man when he's used to church dinners every night?"

She patted her stomach. "Those church dinners are going to be the death of me. What is it with all these cheesey, gooey, calorie-laden dishes?"

"Maybe everybody is just making their very best recipes."

She flushed. "I didn't sound very grateful, did I?"

"I didn't say that."

"You didn't have to." She tried to look appropriately contrite.

Pete seemed not to notice. "For what it's worth, those church dinners aren't hurting your figure one bit." He gave her an appreciative once-over.

She turned away, blushing. "Okay, definitely time to change the subject. Follow me."

She crossed the room and led him down the back hall to the laundry room. With four clients gone, there were bed linens and towels to wash and fold.

"Oh, I get it—change the subject, change the sheets." He grinned.

"Something like that." She opened the dryer, pulled out clean sheets, and deposited them in Pete's arms. After moving a load of clean clothes into the dryer, she directed Pete to a high counter at one end of the room and motioned for him to deposit the clean laundry there.

She picked out a contour sheet and shook the wrinkles out. "So . . . you said I'd be happy about your reason for being late?"

"You may already know." Pete grabbed one end of the sheet and matched the corners.

"What's that?"

"Davy came in and filled out a job application today."

"He did? He never said anything."

"I told him he's got a job if he wants it. He could start next Monday."

"Oh! That's great!" She beamed, but her imagination quickly started filling in all the things that could go wrong. Davy not living up to Pete's expectations. Changing his mind and going back to Indiana about the time Pete got him trained. *Did she even want Davy in this line of work after the fire, after everything that had happened with Dav—*

"Hey . . . Cut that out right now." Pete's voice was gentle, but his words were firm.

"What?" She furrowed her brow at him.

"I see where your mind is going." Holding up his folded end of the sheet, he met her in the middle as if they were dancing. "You're thinking about all the things that could go wrong. All the ways Davy could screw up, or I could screw up, or you could—"

She winced. "Okay, okay. Busted."

He took the folded sheet from her and placed it on the counter behind her. Tucking one finger under her chin, he made her meet his gaze. "It'll be fine, Susan. Okay? We'll work things out."

She nodded reluctantly. "Okay."

He reached for her hand. "And we won't worry about anything *until* it happens, right?"

She hesitated, then grinned. "We'll try."

"Huh-uh . . . not good enough."

"That's all I can promise, Pete."

"Fair enough." He bobbed his head once, as though that sealed the deal, and grabbed the next sheet to begin the dance again.

It felt comfortable and safe having him here, and after a while she risked asking, "Can I ask what brought about this transformation?"

"The sheets? I'll have you know I've been folding my own sheets for years."

"That's not what I mean and you know it." But she did love the ornery gleam she so often saw in those gray eyes.

"You asked, so I'm going to tell you and trust you not to rub it in or say 'I told you so,' okay?"

"Cross my heart." She dropped one corner of the towel she was folding and drew an X on her chest.

"I think God's been trying to get my attention for a long time, and He finally got through to me. And this"—he panned the room—"is just part of that."

"And Davy?"

"That's another. Maybe . . ." He winked. "Or maybe I'm just using him as bait to catch you."

She rolled her eyes. "And, sadly, it's working."

"Sadly?"

"Just kidding."

He gave her a hangdog look.

"What?" she said. "You can dish it but you can't take it?"

His scowl bloomed into a grin. "Touché."

Why was she telling Pete all this?

36

*S*usan sat on the sofa in the volunteers' lounge beside Pete. They'd finished folding laundry and Susan had declared a break. But within minutes, the conversation had gone deeper than she'd ever intended. Did she really want to talk with Pete about David? Still, he'd asked. And sitting here with him now, she felt completely comfortable pouring out her heart.

She tried to explain how she'd felt after discovering David's infidelity. "As a widow—I hate that word, you know? *Widow*. It just seems like such a . . . stigma."

"I can imagine." His eyes said he truly could. "Kind of how I feel about the word *divorce*. Not that there's any comparison." He reached to place a hand on her arm. It seemed like recently he used any excuse to touch her. "Sorry, I didn't mean to hijack the conversation. What were you starting to say?"

"Oh, but I think you're right," she said. "I was just going to say that at least there was some . . . *dignity* in having belonged to someone. To

David. I was someone's wife. I'd been loved. But when I found out about *her*—" Her voice faltered. "I don't know how to explain it . . . It was humiliating. I had to face the fact that David hadn't loved me like I thought he did—"

"Susan, of course he did. Dave loved you. I would swear to that." He let his fingers linger on her sleeve.

The warmth comforted her in a way that was incongruous with the simple gesture. She placed her hand over his. "He sure had a funny way of showing it." Why was she telling Pete all this?

The answer came as a revelation: *because you love him.* And tonight she could believe that he might love her, too. And she wanted him to know these things about her.

"The man was an idiot." The minute the words were out, Pete closed his eyes, shaking his head. "I'm sorry. I shouldn't have said that."

She gave a little laugh. "No. It's nice to hear someone say what I've been thinking for all these weeks."

He smiled, but then his expression sobered. "He blew it, Susan. Dave made a huge mistake. And worse, he went and died before he could tell you how sorry he was—how wrong he was. But Dave was a good guy. He had a good heart. I truly think—if he'd had a chance—he would have come to his senses . . . come back to you."

"I wish I could be sure of that. But I don't know." She hung her head, feeling the humiliation all over again.

"Listen, Susan. Us guys can be jerks."

She peeked up at him from beneath damp lashes. "Takes one to know one?"

That made him laugh.

"Sorry."

"No. I had it coming. But I'm serious. We get to a certain age—" He stopped.

And she knew he was weighing his words, deciding if he really wanted to throw his thoughts out there for dissection. She loved that she was learning to read him like this. It was one of the things she missed most about marriage.

She waited, praying he would find the words.

After a minute he laced his fingers with hers. "I'm going to share something with you that the men of the world would not like me divulging. This is a male version of one of those divine secrets of ya-ya-hood, or whatever you call it."

She snickered at his butchering of the phrase, but she didn't speak, didn't want to break the spell.

Pete shifted on the sofa, angling his body toward her. "When a guy gets to a certain age, he starts to get scared. All these young bucks are coming up in his world and he suddenly doesn't wield the power he used to. A guy starts to—" A spark flashed in his eyes. "We're talking about hypothetical guys here, okay?"

She curbed a smile but remained silent, not wanting him to stop.

"So this hypothetical guy asks himself if he still has what it takes. And he lies awake at night feeling pretty sure the answer's no. That's not easy for a man who used to have control of his world. So when a sexy woman comes along and pays attention to him, he sees a way to make his world right again. To prove himself." He held up a hand. "I'm not saying it's right. In fact, I . . . er, this hypothetical guy knows it's dead wrong. But sometimes controlling our world is a lot more attractive than doing what's right."

Susan thought about his words. Wished David had lived to say those same words to her. Still, it eased the pain a tiny bit to hear it from Pete's point of view. To hear that it wasn't her. Not that she was blameless . . . she still had a lot to sort out, but Pete's words comforted her.

"Thank you, Pete. You'll never know how much it means for you to share that. I needed to hear it."

He put a hand on her cheek. "You need to hear this, too. You are a beautiful, amazing, sexy, fascinating woman."

She grinned up at him. "Is that a hypothetical man talking?"

But he didn't laugh. "No, Susan. That's me talking." He looked down, and she had the sense that he was gathering his courage.

"Pete—"

He looked up, captured her eyes with his. "I love you, Susan. And I want you in my life. I've made my choice. It's you I want. Always. Nobody else. Ever."

Her heart could scarcely hold everything his words meant. But she let their meaning soak in, let it begin to heal the wounded places inside her.

Pete had put his arm on the back of the sofa and now he reached up to thread his fingers through her hair. The simple gesture released a torrent of feelings. And when he leaned to kiss her, she wanted him to . . . more than she'd wanted anything in a very long time.

She gave herself to a kiss that began chaste and sweet. But when Pete moved closer and pulled her to himself, it was difficult to call the desire she sensed in him "chaste." A desire that matched her own yearnings, body and soul.

She placed her hands on either side of his face, wanting to slow things down but not wanting to let go of him either. Not wanting him to release her.

She clung to him, her eyes closed, her heart filled with a contentment it hadn't known for—

"Susan." His tone urgent, Pete slid his arms down hers, gently pushing her away.

She opened her eyes. His attention was on the office door behind her.

"Hey, Charlie," he said, his voice falsely cheerful. He rose slowly from the sofa.

Susan pressed into her end of the sofa, smoothing her clothes, feeling herself turn ten shades of crimson. "What do you need, Charlie? It's . . . awfully late."

A ghost of a smile touched the grizzled face. "Sorry if I'm interrupting something." He rolled his wheelchair backward a few feet. "I can come back later."

"No, not at all," she said, not daring to look Pete's way.

"I've been fightin' a headache all day. Wondered if I could get a couple of aspirin."

"Oh, sure. Of course. Let me get them." She jumped up, fumbling with the keys on the lanyard around her neck. She finally got the drawer open and counted out capsules.

"Thanks," Charlie said. He pocketed the pills and spun a one-eighty in his chair. But before he went through the doorway, he called over his shoulder, "Carry on, carry on."

The door eased shut and Susan stared at Pete, not believing what had just happened.

He stood there wearing a Cheshire grin.

"It's not funny," she huffed.

"It's a little funny." His grin got wider, if that was possible.

"No, Pete. It's *not* funny."

"Um . . ." He cleared his throat. "A tiny bit funny. Come on. You know it is, Susan."

She let a giggle escape, but her cheeks were burning. "That does it, Pete—you're fired."

He burst out laughing.

"I mean it, Pete. I can't believe I let that happen. That was completely unprofessional! I can't have clients walking in here to find me making out with my boyfriend."

"Oh, so you admit I'm your boyfriend?" He wiggled his eyebrows.

She put her hands on her hips. "You know what I mean."

"Well, if we can't make out here, I guess you leave me no choice but to ask you on a real date."

Now it was her turn to laugh. "Fine. I accept." There was a smug look plastered on his face.

She decided to wipe it off. "But none of this fishing at the river stuff. I'm talking a real date. Dinner, dancing, the whole nine yards."

"Oh, a football game, too?"

"Huh?"

"You said the whole nine yards."

She rolled her eyes. "Oh, brother. Besides, that doesn't mean football . . . does it?"

He laughed. "I don't know, but how about I'll concede football if you'll concede dancing?"

She pretended to consider his offer, let him worry for a minute, then extended her hand. "Deal."

He shook on it.

"Now get out of here before I make you kiss me again."

He pulled her to him and did just that. "I'll call you," he said, touching a finger to the tip of her nose. Then he grabbed his cap off the hook by the door and was gone.

. . . Pete could tell they were both pretty shook-up.

37

Thursday, July 23

The mood in the cab of the truck was grim. Pete, Randy Elsinger, and Lucas Vermontez were en route back to the station from a double fatality. It was the first fatality Elsinger had worked—a grisly car crash involving two teenage girls from Springfield. Vermontez was behind the wheel and doing a good job of debriefing the rookie, but Pete could tell they were both pretty shook-up.

He hoped he never got used to seeing death in all its ugliness. Because hard as these things were, they made you think about life. Made you evaluate whether you were living yours the way you wanted to be. The way you should be.

Pete leaned against the passenger door and glanced at his watch. Speaking of life the way it should be . . . here it was Thursday already and he still hadn't set a date with Susan.

He couldn't call her tonight, though. The guys needed him. His forty-eight hours were up three hours ago, but he'd stay over an extra twelve for Elsinger's sake.

How could he not, when he'd been asking his men to work extra shifts? The dry weather had spawned a series of brush fires and they'd had a string of emergencies to work. Even though he didn't have time to train a new guy, he hoped Davy Marlowe would take him up on the job offer. He could at least relieve some of the staff at the station until Pete got him working with a crew.

He pulled out his phone and tapped a text message to Susan. *Things are crazy here. Sorry I haven't called. Any way u r free Sat. nite?* He had no clue what modern etiquette said about texting a woman for a date, but it was his only option right now, and it seemed better than waiting to call her Saturday, or ignoring her altogether.

He hit Send and hoped he wasn't in the doghouse. Already.

*S*usan was up to her elbows in dishwater at the shelter kitchen when her phone trilled the text alert.

She gave an inward sigh of relief. Davy was the only one who ever texted her, and he'd been on her mind ever since she'd heard all the sirens a couple of hours ago. Davy . . . and Pete. She didn't know what had happened, but it must be pretty big. At least they weren't headed toward her place. Was every mother in the Falls convinced it was her child in trouble when she heard those sirens go off?

She'd stood outside the shelter with several clients watching police vehicles and trucks from both fire stations race by, headed east out of town. It brought back too many memories of what it had been like to be married to a firefighter. Did she really want to go through that again?

The text alert sounded again, and she dried her hands and slid open the cover. Not Davy. Pete. Another sigh of relief. *And about time!*

She read his text and smiled. Leave it to him to ask her out via a text message. She should probably play a little harder to get, but she didn't have the energy to play games. And Pete didn't strike her as a game-playing kind of guy. Well, except when it came to gin rummy.

She tapped out a quick message: *I'm free. Thot you'd NEVER call.* She added a smiley face and hit Send. If honesty didn't sit well with Peter Brennan, then he wasn't the guy for her.

Within a few seconds her phone trilled again. *Pulling Xtra shift. WILL call u tomorrow but save Sat. for me OK?*

She smiled and sent back a simple *OK*. She closed her phone. Everything suddenly seemed right with her world.

Friday, July 24

S o you were about to give up on me, huh?" Pete grinned into the phone, even happier than he'd expected to feel at hearing her voice.

"I actually forgot all about your solemn promise to call me."

That threw him.

"Hey," she said, laughing her musical laugh. "I'm *kidding*. But I have thought of nothing else since you told me you'd call the other night."

He laughed, feeling the tension drain from him. "I'm not going to be able to get a straight answer out of you tonight, am I?"

"'Yes' is a straight answer. I'd love to go out tomorrow."

"Ah, that's more like it. But . . . there is one problem. Would you mind too much if we stay in town? I promise I'll take you someplace nice in Springfield . . . soon. But we're so short staffed right now. I'm afraid to leave town as crazy as things have been."

"Oh, that's totally fine. In case you hadn't noticed, Pete, I'm not really a fancy restaurant kind of gal."

"I noticed. It's one of my favorite things about you."

"That, and I know how to eat, right?"

He laughed, remembering. And wondering where this woman had been all his life. It sobered him a little to realize the answer to that question. He was glad Susan couldn't read his mind. He didn't want to think about David Marlowe right now.

"You know what, Pete . . . how about if I bring dinner to the station Saturday night? For all the guys."

"You don't have to do that."

"I know. I want to, though. Seriously. How many will be on duty then?"

"Well, if they hear you're bringing dinner, probably every last one of them."

She laughed. "That'd be fine with me."

"You're sure you don't mind? There'll probably be ten or twelve of us."

"That's not bad. Just plan on it. Is six o'clock early enough? You think the guys can wait that long?"

"Don't worry, they'll wait. And, hey, bring Davy along."

He sensed her hesitation.

"I'll ask him," she said. "But . . . he really blew it and he knows it. I think he's still feeling a little uncomfortable about . . . your impression of him."

"Tell him not to be. Besides, if he's going to be working here, he's got to show his face sometime."

"Have you given him a start date? He hasn't said anything to me."

"Monday morning."

"That's wonderful. Pete . . . I just can't thank you enough. I really can't. You just don't know how much this means to—"

"Hey, save it. And I do know, Susan. Besides, Davy will be helping me out as much as I'm helping him."

"Well, I appreciate it."

"Oh, and hey . . . let me take care of dessert Saturday night, okay?"

"You sure?"

"Absolutely. You bring dinner. Dessert is on the house."

"Sounds like a deal."

"A good deal, I'd say. But don't expect anything fancy, okay? I'll probably just whip up a cake mix."

"I'm not expecting fancy." Truth was, she couldn't have been happier about the arrangement. What she'd told Pete was true. She wasn't a woman who cared about "fancy" anything. Especially since she'd started working with the homeless. Her country home and the simplicity of her life felt like luxury.

She hadn't realized it until now, talking to Pete, but ever so stealthily, the sense of contentment she'd lost when David died had crept back into her life.

No, that wasn't quite right. It had been hand delivered to her via Peter Brennan.

It wouldn't do to burn his
one contribution to this "date."

38

Saturday, July 25

 $\mathcal{P}$ ete closed the oven door and set an alarm on his phone so he wouldn't forget the cake. It wouldn't do to burn his one contribution to this "date."

It had seemed like a good idea when Susan proposed it—her bringing supper to the station—but now that she was due to arrive in less than an hour, he was having second thoughts. Major league second thoughts.

If the guys didn't know he and Susan were an item before, they would after tonight. He wasn't exactly giddy about the idea of fielding the razzing his men would give him once it became clear he had a woman in his life. Much less *this* woman.

He turned off the kitchen lights and headed back to the bay. He'd have time to change the oil in the brush truck and clean up before Susan got here. He'd already told the guys that dinner was being delivered, but he'd been purposely vague about who was doing the delivery. That was probably a mistake in itself.

He popped the hood and kicked a drain pan under the beast. The stupid thing had been going through oil by the case. But he shouldn't complain—at least he hadn't had to replace a head gasket in two or three months.

Half an hour later, Lucas Vermontez stood in the doorway between the dayroom and the bays. "Hey, Pete. Something smells awfully good in the kitchen, and there's a lady out there putting stuff in the oven."

Pete wiped his hands on a rag. "Susan?"

Vermontez shot him a knowing grin. "You didn't say the lady bringing dinner was someone we knew."

"That's right, I didn't." He tried to make his voice gruff and curb the smile that wanted to come, but he wasn't successful.

"Shall I tell her you're out here?"

"Tell her I'll be up in a few minutes." He checked his watch. "And take my cake out of the oven for me, would you? The timer should be going off any minute."

"You bet, chief."

Lucas disappeared, and Pete went back to the truck. A minute later he caught a whiff of Susan's perfume. He looked up to see her rolling up her sleeves.

"Need some help?"

Her bright smile was good medicine, but he waved her off. "Don't you get your hands dirty. I'm just about finished."

She gathered the empty oil containers at his feet and looked across the bay. "Is the recycle bin in the same place?"

"Yep. Thanks. Be careful or I might start trading out volunteer hours."

She grinned back over her shoulder at him. "That wouldn't be all bad."

He couldn't have agreed more.

He finished up and slammed the truck's hood, then went to wash up at the sink near the small bay door. Again, Susan appeared beside him.

She waited for him to finish with the soap dispenser, then pumped soap into her own hands.

"You smell mighty good," he said, working a lather up his forearms.

"I'll tell you what smells good." She diverted his comment. "That cake you've got baking out there." She nodded toward the kitchen. "I smelled it the minute I walked through the front doors."

"Yeah, the guys like that. Smells like home."

"Not my home. Seems like I hardly ever bake anymore. Even with Davy home."

"How's he doing?"

She rinsed her hands and pulled off a length of paper toweling. "Better, I think. He's got a lot of decisions in front of him, but at least he has a sense of purpose now." She looked up at him. "Thank you, Pete. I can't say it enough. I know you're taking a risk offering Davy a job."

He shrugged. "I need help. He needs a job. Seemed like a no-brainer."

"Yes, but you've seen Davy at his worst. And you still made the offer."

"Well, don't thank me too much till we see how it all turns out."

She sobered at that, and Pete wished he could take back his thoughtless words.

But she quickly found a smile. "That cake smelled like it was almost done. You're not burning it, are you?"

"Not if Vermontez followed orders. But maybe we'd better check. Be pretty embarrassing to have a fire *at* the fire station."

Her laughter lifted his spirits even higher.

*S*usan lifted crisp, steaming corn on the cob from a large stock pan on the fire station's industrial range and heaped them on a platter. She'd scored the last three dozen ears at the farmer's market this morning. With Pete's help, she laid out barbecued chicken, baked potatoes with all the fixings, and the corn on the buffet counter. A huge salad and store-bought wheat rolls rounded out the menu. Topped off with Pete's cake, of course. Susan knew every morsel would be eaten with gusto, and she vowed to bring dinner to the station more often, the way she had when David was alive.

Pete rang the dinner bell, and the crew instantly materialized around the tables in the break room, chattering and jockeying for position at the buffet counter.

The men carried overflowing plates to the two long tables, and when they'd all been seated, Susan looked around the room, memories flooding back. She felt as if she'd sat down with the ghosts of the five firefighters who'd been such a part of this station before the fire. The remembrances were not unpleasant, but bittersweet. Still, she shook them off, wanting only to savor the present.

Pete held up a hand. "Let's pray."

Silence fell over the room and then Pete's voice rose, spreading a blanket of blessing over them. "God, we ask you to bless this meal we're about to eat, and bless the hands that made it for us"—he gave Susan's shoulder a gentle pat—"and Lord, we ask you to keep the men of this station in your care, and that this town and all of Clemens County would be kept safe under your divine protection."

Susan's haunted feelings vanished and she was glad their heads were bowed. She wasn't sure she could have concealed her emotion, her *surprise*. Pete's heartfelt words filled her with pleasure, and more so when she realized that his firefighters hadn't been the least taken aback by their chief's prayer over the meal but had seemed to expect it. Pete sounded well-acquainted with the God he addressed. Another silver lining.

"Everything looks delicious." Lucas Vermontez began to excavate the mound of food on his plate. He eyed the counter where the freshly frosted cake sat. "And looks like it's fixin' to get even better."

"You can thank Pete for that."

"Don't get too excited," Pete said over a mouthful of chicken. "It's just a mix."

Randy Elsinger looked up over the ear of corn he was decimating. "Hey, cake is cake. If it's got frosting on it, it's a winner. It must be the same mix my mom used. It smells like home."

A general agreement rose from the table. Pete tried to brush off the compliments, but Susan could tell he was pleased.

To her delight, Pete gave the kitchen crew the night off and the two of them exchanged what Pete termed "snappy repartee" while they did dishes and cleaned up the kitchen. She had to fight off images of Pete in her own kitchen—as a permanent fixture. *Don't get ahead of yourself, Marlowe.* But, oh, it was tempting.

But first she had to be sure of something. She wiped an already spotless counter with the dishrag, trying to think how to begin. "I liked your blessing . . . at dinner."

He grinned. "You did, huh?"

"It kind of sounded like you're on pretty good terms with 'the man upstairs.'" She used the expression she'd heard him use before—one that sometimes seemed meant to distance himself from God.

Pete dipped his head. "Yeah, well . . . me and Him have had some talks lately. He likes to go fishing with me—the man upstairs."

"Really?"

"I didn't exactly invite Him the first time. He just showed up." He winked. "But I don't mind His company so much now. Kind of look forward to it, actually."

"I hope that doesn't mean you'll never invite me again. I kind of enjoyed that."

He dropped the dish towel he'd been using and pulled her to him in a side hug. "Matter of fact, He told me I ought to bring you next time."

She looked up at him, her heart soaring. "Is that a fact?"

He let his arm drop and picked up the dish towel again, worrying it between his hands like a rope. "I've learned something about myself. Sometimes my fishing hole is better than any shrink."

She smiled at that.

But a shadow crossed his face and he bowed his head. "Since Lana left me, I've—I've been afraid to trust anyone again. But I kind of figured out the problem wasn't Lana. It was me. I walked away from God, and since I decided not to trust Him"—he looked down at her with a sheepish grin—"well, if you can't trust God, who could you possibly trust?"

Susan smiled softly, afraid anything she said might keep him from sharing these precious words with her.

He went on. "So when I met someone like you—someone I thought maybe I *could* trust, I didn't want to put you to the test. Because if *you* failed . . ." His voice trailed off.

"And I *will* fail, Pete. We're none of us infallible. Only God." She reached for his hands and squeezed.

He squeezed back. "Yeah. I get that now."

"Oh, Pete . . . I'm so glad."

"Thank you."

"For what?"

"For not lecturing me. Not giving up on me. For giving me a chance to get my act together."

"I figured you'd come around. Eventually. You're a man. It takes a little longer to get through thicker skulls."

"Hey!"

"Just making snappy repartee."

He looked grateful for the diversion she offered. Grinning, he gave the dish towel a twirl and snapped it in her general direction. "I'll show you snappy."

She dodged his weapon. "Not funny." But she couldn't help returning his smile. Big-time.

He put down the dish towel and went to the door. He poked his head into the hallway and looked both ways before closing the door.

Susan knew what was coming even before he turned to give her that telling smile. He crossed the kitchen in three strides, and this time she let him take her in his arms, let him kiss her again and again until he drew away to look at her with an expression that melted her insides.

He brushed a wisp of hair back from her forehead and planted a tender kiss on the spot he'd cleared. "There's plenty more where that came from, but I don't trust myself to be a gentleman about it right now."

She laughed softly, and gave herself permission to finish falling in love with this man.

Pete's warning echoed
in her mind and
she held her breath.

39

Monday, July 27

 just need you to sign these forms and then we can get you settled."
Susan slid the papers across the desk to the elderly man.

She didn't like admitting new clients into the shelter after supper. It was better to have the whole evening to help a new client get acclimated, and to judge whether he or she posed any kind of threat to the others before the overnight volunteers came on. But it seemed as though a lot of people waited until the last minute to decide the shelter was their only option for the night.

The man's hands shook as he meticulously signed his name on the dotted line. Susan had already taken his photo and filled out the intake forms, and the seventy-year-old—according to a just-expired driver's license—didn't look like he would cause any trouble. But then she'd hoped that about Earl Eland and half a dozen other clients who'd ended up wreaking havoc on the shelter. But as David had told her once when she was discouraged, if she ever gave up hope that her clients could be rehabilitated, she may as well get out of this business. There was always hope. Always.

She smiled to herself, remembering how hope had soared after she'd talked with Pete at the station Saturday night, after she'd heard him pray, heard the intimacy in his simple blessing. And, yes, after the kisses they'd shared.

She pushed the thoughts aside. She couldn't mope around like a lovesick schoolgirl. She had work to do. Fortunately Garrett and Bryn Edmonds were on the schedule tonight. They were old pros at this by now, and she had no qualms about leaving them in charge. Knowing them, they'd come in a few minutes early. They'd been doing that recently, and while they always had an excuse why they decided to arrive early, she knew they were doing it to give her a break. She didn't dare to hope that they would keep coming after the baby was born, but she appreciated every minute they gave her now.

With the forms filed temporarily in her top desk drawer, she locked the office and led the man to the linen closet down the hall. She rummaged through the stacks of donated linens and selected a set of sheets and blankets for the cot. "Do you like a fluffy pillow or a thinner one?"

"What's that?" He held a hand up to his ear. "I don't hear too well."

She repeated the question louder.

"Don't make no difference to me," he said.

She pulled a plump new pillow from a shelf heaped with them—a gift from of one of the local churches—and placed it in his arms. "How does that look?"

He hugged the pillow to his chest as if it were a teddy bear. Tears wet his rheumy eyes.

"Oh! You're not allergic are you?" She checked the tag. "I don't think these are feather pillows . . ."

He swiped at his damp cheeks and glared at her. "I don't have allergies. It's just—" He looked at the floor, shaking his head. "You don't want to hear it . . ."

Susan put an arm around his shoulders. "Try me. I've been told I'm a pretty good listener, Milton."

No response.

"I'm sorry . . . would you prefer I call you Mr. Garfield?"

He shrugged out from under her touch. "I'd prefer you don't call me anything." His countenance changed from vulnerable to made-of-steel.

She should have been accustomed to the emotional seesaw by now. Not to mention the rejection. And she was halfway relieved she wouldn't have to spend the next hour playing counselor. Guilt flooded her the minute the thought was formed.

What had happened to the abundance of compassion she'd had when she first opened the shelter? There'd been a time when listening to the homeless pour out their sad stories had made her feel like she was accomplishing some good in her own small way. Made her feel needed. How had she become so jaded?

She showed Milton Garfield to a bed, keeping her voice low lest she wake several nightshift workers who were already sleeping there. "I'll be in the office for a few more minutes if you need anything. You can watch TV in the dayroom once you get settled in."

"I can't hear a word you're saying." He shook his head, looking disgusted. "I'm turning in."

The young man in the closest cot stirred and sat up in bed. "Shut up!" He rolled over and pulled the blankets over his head, mumbling curses.

"Hey, hey! It's okay, William," she said. "Go back to sleep."

She didn't try to repeat herself to Mr. Garfield. He seemed not to notice and lay down on the cot sans sheets. He arranged the stack of bedding over himself, sank into the pillow, and closed his eyes.

"Good night," she told him. "Breakfast is at seven." She pulled the door halfway shut and turned out the hall lights.

When she was out of earshot of the sleeping men, she called Davy on her cell phone. "Hey, have you had dinner? You want me to pick up a pizza on my way home?"

"I'd eat it," he said. "How about pepperoni and mushrooms?"

"You got it."

"Did your guy show up there?"

She stilled. "Pete?" She hoped Davy wasn't telling people that Pete was "her guy."

Davy laughed. "Not that guy. No, that homeless guy."

"Zeke Downing? Why would you think he'd show up?"

"Because he was here looking for you. Except he said his name was *Herb* Downing. Not Zeke."

"What? He was at our house? When? What did he want?"

"To talk to you. He didn't say what about."

"Is he still there now? Are you okay?"

"I'm fine, but he did scare me half to death. I was out washing my car, trying to get finished before dark, and all of a sudden I look up and this guy is just standing there watching me."

"Davy!"

"No big deal, Mom. He actually seems like a pretty nice guy."

This is not a nice guy, Susan. Pete's warning echoed in her mind and she held her breath. "Is he still there?"

"No. He left probably half an hour ago. But he was walking."

"What? He was on foot?" He'd walked more than a mile to her place? What did he want with her? "Did you tell him I'm here at the shelter?"

"Mom. I'm not that stupid. I didn't tell him anything—except that I'd tell you he'd been here."

Her heart hammered in her chest. "Did you actually see him leave the property?"

"I guess so. I mean he was headed down the driveway while I finished washing my car. That's the last I saw—"

"Lock the doors, Davy. All of them. If he comes back, do not talk to him. Don't even answer the door. Do you understand?"

"What's going on, Mom? Are you okay?"

"I'll be home as soon as I can. I need to go now."

She hung up and called Pete's cell phone, praying it wasn't sitting in the cab of his pickup while he fished down at the river. But he answered on the second ring. She repeated everything Davy had told her.

"I'm hanging up and calling nine-one-one, Susan. I think you should do the same. Tell them you are being stalked because that's essentially what this is. Have them send someone to the shelter."

The anger in his voice scared her. "It's Davy I'm worried about, Pete. I'm headed home."

"No. You stay put. I'll be there in five minutes."

"I'm more worried about my son."

"It's not Davy he wants. Didn't Davy say Downing left your place?"

"Yes, but what if—"

"Susan the guy might be waiting for you outside right now. Don't leave that building. Are the doors locked for the night?"

"Yes. I locked them at eight like always."

"Okay. I'll have the sheriff send someone out to your place, but don't you unlock that door until I call to tell you I'm out front. Do you understand?"

"Okay . . . I understand."

The fear in Pete's voice shook her up. She'd always thought he was overreacting when he accused Zeke Downing of stalking her. But now she wondered. If all he wanted was to talk to her, it seemed like he'd missed plenty of opportunities. Was he just toying with her? Trying to scare her?

Well, if he was now using Davy to get to her, it was working.

She heard voices again and strained to make out the words.

40

"Dear God," she whispered. "Keep Davy safe."

Susan looked at her phone. Pete was sending the sheriff out to her house. She needed to let Davy know that. Pete wanted her to call the police, but she wasn't convinced this was a 911 situation. Not yet. And another police run-in for the shelter might be the kiss of death.

She'd call Davy first, and then decide. She started to dial him as she headed for her office to wait for Pete, but approaching the door, she heard voices. She slid her phone shut and listened.

The door was ajar about an inch, and a slice of light knifed the carpet in front of it. She started to go in, but something made her stop short. The hallway was almost dark, but the blinds in the window between the hall and her office let slats of light shine through. She was sure she'd turned the lights off and locked the door.

It was early, but Garrett and Bryn must have let themselves in.

Feeling cautious, she raised her hand to knock on the door. Movement behind the blinds made her pause. She heard voices again and strained to make out the words.

"It wasn't you," a man's voice said. "Why'd you say it was?"

"I . . . I don't know what you mean." Susan recognized Bryn's voice, but the man's gravelly bass wasn't Garrett Edmonds's. Her pulse notched up.

"You told the cops you started the fire," the man said again. "Why'd you lie?"

"I . . . I didn't lie," Bryn said. "But . . . it was an accident. I didn't mean to. I lit a candle, and—" Her voice changed to a near whisper, and Susan had to strain to hear.

She edged to the other side of the hall so she could see through the slits in the blinds.

"Did you lose someone in the fire?" Bryn said. "I'm so sorry—"

"Bryn . . . It's okay."

Garrett. Susan breathed a sigh of relief at hearing his voice.

"You don't owe any explanations." Garrett spoke to his wife in a calming tone, but his voice was taut when he turned back to the man. "Why are you here? My wife is serving community service. She's done everything possible to make restitu—"

"No," the voice barked. "It wasn't her! Didn't you hear what I said?" He turned to Bryn. "I remember you. You worked at the old place, right? Across the street?"

Bryn nodded.

"I remember you," he repeated. "And it wasn't you I saw up there."

Susan moved farther back to the shadowed corner of the hallway for a better angle through the blinds. A man in a long army-green coat stood with his back to the window—Zeke Downing. A wave of relief rolled over her. At least Davy was safe.

Garrett had his arm around Bryn. Susan noticed that her pregnancy was beginning to show. Garrett looked concerned, but not really frightened.

Zeke didn't appear to be a threat, and Garrett had things under control. If Pete had called 911, the police were no doubt already on their way, but she probably should call, too.

"I'm sorry . . . Herb, is it?" Garrett said.

"My name's Herb Downing."

"Okay. Well, the director is here someplace. Why don't you wait here and we'll go find her?"

"I don't need to talk to her. Not now." Zeke pointed to Bryn. "*You're* the one I want to talk to."

Bryn gave a pained smile and pointed to herself. "Me? I don't understand." She sounded on the verge of tears and Garrett tightened his arm around her.

Quietly, Susan crossed the hall, intending to announce herself. But she hesitated near the door, listening again and watching through the blinds. She debated whether she should go in now. Zeke wasn't making threats, but he wasn't making much sense either. If he was mentally unstable . . .

But Garrett was handling it well, speaking in a voice she knew was meant to calm Zeke. "What do you mean, sir? What did you see? Are you saying you saw how the fire started?"

Zeke moved closer to the door where Susan could no longer see him clearly.

"That other woman," he said. "The one in the news. That's who I saw."

Garrett looked down at Bryn, his brow furrowed. He took a step toward Zeke. "Sir, would you be willing to give a statement to the police about what you—"

"No police! If I'd wanted to tell the police, I would have gone to the police!"

"Okay, okay . . ." Concern shadowed Garrett's face, but his voice remained steady.

Susan caught a glimpse of Garrett through the slits of the window blind and she thought he caught her eye and knew she was in the hallway.

"Why don't you have a seat?" he told Zeke. "Let's see if we can sort this all out. I'm sure Susan will be here soon."

That was her cue. She took a deep breath and opened the door. "Hi there." She tried to act as if nothing was out of the ordinary.

Bryn's shoulders sagged with relief.

"Susan, I'm glad you're here." Garrett took her cue. "This is Herb Downing."

Susan went to shake his hand. "Yes, I remember. Zeke, right?"

"You . . . you knew me as Zeke. But my name's Herb. Zeke . . . that's my brother." He tugged at the frayed cuff of his shirt. "It's a long story."

"You've been trying to reach me?"

He nodded. "I want justice."

Susan pulled the chair from behind her desk and moved it to the volunteer lounge area. "Why don't we move over here? We'll all be more comfortable."

Bryn and Garrett took a seat on the sofa, Bryn clutching her husband's hand like a lifeline. Susan indicated the recliner in the corner for Zeke, and she took the desk chair.

"Mr. Downing says he saw who started the fire," Garrett explained.

Susan glanced at Bryn. This had to be difficult for her, to rehash such a traumatic experience. "Zeke—I'm sorry, should I call you Herb?"

"Yes. It's Herb." He shifted in the recliner, leaned forward, and rested his elbows on his knees. "I done some things that weren't right, but I didn't have anything to do with that fire and I want my name cleared. I don't know what's going on, but the TV said this here woman"—he pointed to Bryn—"started the fire, and that's not right."

"What makes you think that, Herb?" Susan made her voice smooth.

"Because I know what I saw. I went up to the office that night," Downing said. "I wanted to get my papers back." He looked over at Garrett. "The office was upstairs in the old shelter."

"I . . . I was there," Bryn said. "I remember." Her ashen face said she was remembering all too clearly.

"Yep, you were there," he said. "I remember you. But you didn't start that fire. Why did you lie about it?"

"Bryn didn't do it on purpose, Herb," Susan said. "She accidentally left a candle burning and—"

"There was a candle all right, but what I saw wasn't no accident. That woman set a fire. Took some papers and lit 'em on fire. I saw it with my own eyes." His voice rose and his face darkened. "I thought she was gonna put 'em in the trash can, but she didn't. She set 'em right there on the desk, still burning. And . . . well, I got out of there. I only heard what happened later—that people was killed."

Susan's mind reeled. "You're saying you saw someone—a woman— purposefully light the fire that night?"

"Yes. That woman on TV."

Susan watched a spark of hope that had shone in Bryn's eyes deflate. The man was delusional.

But Susan encouraged him to go on. "Did you recognize the woman?"

"I told you, it was that one on TV. She told those reporters they didn't know what had started that fire, but she was lying. *She* started it. But she denies it."

"Did you talk to her?" Could he possibly be telling the truth? "Did you tell anyone else about this, Herb?"

He tensed and she regretted the question immediately. She had no business interrogating this man. But they had to keep him here until the authorities could question him.

Where was Pete? He should be here by now. A furtive glance at the clock over her desk told her barely three minutes had gone by since she'd hung up from talking to him.

"Help me understand, Herb. Can you start at the beginning?"

That seemed to settle him again. "It was wrong—I'm not gonna say otherwise—but I ran off that night. I was up there and I figured they'd pin it on me. I already had a record, and who was gonna think that pretty lady did it?"

"Why were you up there?" Susan risked. Clients weren't supposed to be on the second floor at all.

"I figured if I gave you my real name my record would come up and—" He scratched his head. "Let's just say I wasn't exactly square with my parole, so I figured you'd boot me out and send me back. That's why I gave you my brother's ID."

"You were trying to get your intake forms back? That's why you were in the office?" So the long rap sheet Pete had found for "Zeke Downing" had actually belonged to this man's brother. She felt relieved that her judgment of Herb matched the man she knew, not the man Pete had investigated.

He shrugged. "I don't know what you call 'em but, yes, my papers. But I wasn't in the office. Never. I swear it. I saw her before I could get in."

He wasn't sounding so delusional now. "Go on," Susan said.

"Well, like I said, I ran. I hitched a ride to Kansas that night, and the next day I saw it on the news. Sure enough, they was lookin' for me." He rubbed a hand over his face. "I'm not proud of it, but I kept goin'. I hitched all the way back around to Ohio and hid out there for a while."

He looked around the room, appearing to lose his focus. But when he spoke again, he seemed lucid. "A while later my brother—Zeke— told me a woman had confessed to starting the fire."

Bryn nodded and Garrett tightened his arm around her, exchanging a look with Susan.

"From what I heard, the story wasn't right. They were saying it was an accident and that just flat wasn't true. But I wasn't about to get involved again. I figured if that woman lied about how the fire started, she'd lie and say it was me if I showed up again."

"But . . . I didn't lie," Bryn said.

"Like I said, it wasn't you. That's what I don't get."

Again, Garrett exchanged a look with Susan that asked, *Is he telling the truth?* But neither of them said anything.

Herb leaned back in the chair, seeming less on edge now that his story was unwinding. "I moved back to Springfield, stayed in a shelter there for a while. But a few weeks ago we was sittin' there watching the news and this report came on about the fire. Caught my attention 'cause I thought they were interviewing the woman who started it. And it was her, all right, but they were callin' her an inspector, and she was actin' like she was some hero or something."

Susan's blood turned to ice. "Andrea? Are you talking about Andrea Morley, the fire inspector?"

"Yes. I tried to find the story again, but I don't know much about computers and the one they had at the Springfield shelter was worse than worthless. I took a letter to the police in Springfield—"

"You mailed a letter?"

He shook his head. "No. Delivered it by hand. I didn't want 'em tracing my postmark or anything. But they never did anything about it."

Remembering the note he'd left her, Susan guessed they probably couldn't make out two words.

"Well, you did the right thing, Herb. I need to ask you one more time . . . Are you saying you actually witnessed Andrea Morley light a fire in the office that night?" These were incredible accusations, but how could he have made up something this wild?

"That's just what I'm saying." He turned to Bryn. "I still don't get why you said you did it. Why would you cover for her like that?"

"But I did leave that candle burning. I'm sure of that. And—"

"You may have left a candle burning, but that's not what started the fire."

Bryn put a hand to her mouth, and Susan could almost see the thoughts that were dancing through her mind. Again, she exchanged a look with Garrett. If what Downing said was true . . . Bryn had carried such heavy guilt all these months, and now this homeless man was offering the possibility that she was innocent after all. It broke Susan's heart to think of Bryn having that thread of hope dangled in front of her, only to be cut again if these were just the ramblings of a nutcase. But if what Zeke—she couldn't quit thinking of him as Zeke—if what *Herb* Downing said was true, she couldn't even imagine the implications.

Garrett sat forward on the sofa and leaned in closer to Downing. "Can you tell us what the woman you saw looked like?"

"I can tell you exactly what she looked like. I just saw her today. Told her I knew what she'd done." He said it as if they were a bunch of dimwits.

"You talked with Andrea today? Are you sure it was—"

Susan's cell phone trilled, making them all jump.

Pete must be here. She needed to talk to him, but she didn't want to scare Downing off either. If there was anything at all to what he was saying—and she was starting to suspect there was—they needed him to testify to the authorities.

She excused herself and stepped out in the hallway, fumbling to slide the phone open. "Hello?"

She hurried to the entry.

"Mom?"

Susan clutched the phone tighter, hearing a tremulous edge in Davy's voice.

"Mom, you need to come home."

"Davy? Why? What's wrong?"

"Hang on."

She heard him talking to someone, but his voice was muffled and she couldn't make out what he was saying.

"Where are you? Davy?" Then it hit her. Pete had called the sheriff. "Listen, Davy, is there an officer there?" She lowered her voice to a whisper. "Pete got worried about Zeke Downing and called the sheriff, but tell them he's here. Zeke Downing is here at the shelter."

"No, Mom. You don't understand. It's *her*."

"Who?"

"That . . . Andrea woman. She's here, Mom, and—something's wrong with her."

She jumped out and tore up
the steps to the front porch.

41

Susan clutched the phone, trying to assimilate everything she'd heard in the past twenty minutes. *Could things possibly get any crazier?* "What does Andrea want, Davy?"

"I don't know, but . . . something's wrong with her, Mom." He whispered into the phone. "I think she's sick or something."

"What do you mean, 'sick'? Is she there now, Davy? Let me talk to her."

Again, muffled voices, then Davy came back on the line. "Mom, please come home. She's really messed up."

"Davy, don't let her in the house. Do you hear me? Do not let her in! Pete called the sheriff. They're sending someone out there now."

"Yeah, I think so. Okay, thanks." Davy said, his words suddenly careful and cryptic.

The forced calm in her son's voice, his coded words, sent terror through her veins. "Davy? Davy!"

But the line was dead.

*P*ete's phone rang just as he was pulling up to the shelter. "Susan, I'm here. Have you talked to Davy again? Is everything okay?"

The door to the shelter burst open and Susan ran to his pickup, waving her cell phone. What was going on? He reached across and opened the passenger door. She practically dove into the cab.

"What's wrong? What is going on?"

Her face was bled of color. "It's Davy. He said Andrea Morley is at the house and—"

"At your house? With Zeke?"

"No, Zeke's inside." She motioned over her shoulder back at the shelter. "Oh, Pete, something's wrong. Zeke claims Andrea started the fire. The Grove Street fire." The frantic words poured out of her. "And Davy said something's wrong with Andrea. I've never heard him sound so scared."

"Whoa . . . What? Slow down . . . what are you talking about, Susan?"

"I'll explain on the way . . . Please, Pete, I've got to get home. Something's terribly wrong."

He put the truck in Drive, but confusion made him keep his foot on the brake. "But Zeke's inside the shelter? Is everybody okay?"

"Yes! Garrett's there. And Bryn. They're all okay. But we've got to get to Davy." She was on the edge of hysteria.

"Susan, calm down. Did you call the police?"

"No! Oh, dear God . . . no, I never called." Her eyes were wild. "Zeke was there and—"

"I already told the sheriff to send someone out to your place. But call nine-one-one right now and tell them to send someone to the shelter." He cast about the parking lot. "You're sure Bryn and Garrett are okay?"

She nodded, her jaw tense. "Yes, they're fine. Garrett's handling it."

He was reluctant to leave the shelter without waiting for the police to arrive. Zeke Downing concerned him far more than Andi—especially given Davy's last encounter with her. The kid was probably overreacting. Still, Susan wasn't one to freak out over nothing, and she obviously believed her son was in real danger.

"Please, Pete. Go!" She punched the emergency numbers into her phone and clutched it to her ear.

He gunned the engine and sped out of the parking lot. It was after eight thirty and the sun was sinking fast. He flipped on his headlights. It would be almost dark by the time they got to Susan's.

She filled him in on everything Downing had said, and five minutes later Susan unfastened her seat belt and hugged the passenger door as they pulled into her driveway. Andi's pickup was parked near Davy's car on the drive. He pulled up beside it.

Before he brought his truck to a full stop, Susan threw the door open. She jumped out and tore up the steps to the front porch.

Pete stopped to look in the cab of Andi's truck. Empty. What was she thinking, coming out here like this?

"Davy!" Susan pounded on the front door. "Let me in, Davy. It's Mom."

"Is the back door unlocked?"

"I told him to lock himself in the house." Her gaze darted from Andi's car to the house and back. "Where is she? Pete? Where is she?" Her voice was shrill.

"Let's go check in back."

He jogged around the side of the house with Susan close behind. But he stopped short at the corner. He held up a hand, motioning for Susan to be quiet.

Strident voices came from behind the house. "Stay here," he whispered. "I'll check it out."

She glanced behind her toward Andi's car and when she looked back at him, her eyes were fierce. "No. I'm coming with you."

He didn't even try to change her mind.

*W*hy are you doing this?"

At the sound of Davy's voice, Susan stifled a gasp and clutched Pete's arm.

"I think you know why." It was Andrea Morley's voice, but it sounded strained and . . . odd.

"Please. Just wait till my mom gets here. You can talk to her. She . . . she'll know how to help you."

"I'm afraid it's too late for that."

"No . . . no, it's never too late."

It sounded like Davy and Andrea were up on the deck. The back deck rose only about eight feet off the ground, but a wild rosebush—one David had planted the year Davy was born—rambled up the side, blocking their view. It was nearly dark now. Out beyond the lawn, the mercury-vapor yard light was just beginning to come on.

"You're a lot like him, you know. He could act all concerned one minute—like he really cared—and the next minute he'd stab you in the back."

"You're talking about my dad?"

Susan couldn't hear her reply, if there was one.

A few seconds later Davy's voice rose. "Don't. Don't do that. Please. Just . . . give me that, okay? Just hand it to me. You . . . you don't want to do that."

Susan's breath caught. She and Pete exchanged looks. Did Andi have a gun?

She started forward, but Pete held her back. He put a finger over his lips, motioning her to keep silent.

"I don't want to," Andrea said. "But . . . I have to."

Another silence, and then Susan heard weeping. Andrea's, she thought, but it was hard to tell against the thin wail of sirens that started in the distance. She didn't know whether to be relieved or alarmed. If this woman was as unstable as she sounded, it might put her over the edge to have the police swarm the place.

Pete must have thought the same thing. He stepped around the corner of the house and shouted Davy's name. "Are you okay?"

"Pete? Mom?" Davy's voice broke and Susan ran past Pete, toward the deck. The steps were on the opposite side but she caught sight of Davy through the rails. He was crouched near the railing, his hair tousled and his complexion ghostly pale in the canted evening shadows.

"Davy, are you okay?" she yelled again.

"Mom . . . don't come up here."

"Why? What's wrong?" She made her way around to the steps, but before she was halfway up, she saw them. Her heart stopped.

Dear God, please help us. Please, God!

Andrea sat on the floor of the deck, slumped against the railing adjacent to Davy. She held some kind of knife in her right hand. It looked like the knife Pete carried in his tackle box. Her left wrist was smeared with blood, and there was a pool of blood on the boards beneath her.

"Pete!" Susan screamed and charged up the steps. "Oh, dear God!"

Andrea's eyes went savage when she saw Susan. She raised her arm and held the knife against it.

"Mom, stop. She'll do it! Just stop."

The sirens grew louder and Davy froze, a look of desperation in his eyes.

She sensed Pete on the step behind her, then felt his hand lightly on her back.

"Andrea . . . Andi . . ." Susan forced a calm she didn't feel into her voice and eased to the floor of the deck, inching forward as she spoke. "What do you want? Why are you here?"

"It doesn't matter anymore." She pressed the knife into her wrist and fresh blood oozed from the wound.

A crescendo of sirens on the road drew her attention, and Pete saw his chance.

42

$\mathcal{P}$ete held his breath and crouched on the step as Andi stared, her eyes dull, at the ribbon of blood trailing down her wrist and pooling in her open palm.

"Andrea, put the knife down." Susan spoke in a soothing voice, edging closer.

But Andi only pressed the knife deeper. Pete calculated how long it would take him to reach her.

A crescendo of sirens on the road drew her attention, and Pete saw his chance. He pushed past Susan and scrambled, nearly on his hands and knees, up the narrow steps of the deck. In one fluid motion, he grabbed Andi's arm and shouldered his way behind her, restraining her with an arm around her torso.

The knife slipped from her fingers and he kicked it out of reach. Andi slumped against him, whimpering.

Susan ran to Davy, breathing hard. "Are you okay?"

"I'm fine, Mom. I'm okay. We need to get help." He stumbled to his feet, looking a little unsteady.

"Get me some towels," Pete yelled, inspecting Andrea's wounds. A couple of the cuts were deep and she was bleeding badly, but it didn't appear she'd severed an artery.

Susan ran through the back door and returned a moment later with a stack of folded dish towels.

Andi was cooperative now, her eyes vacant, her forehead furrowed in pain. Susan helped him hold the towels to her wounds and apply pressure.

"You're going to be okay," Susan said, her voice soothing. "Everything is going to be okay." She glanced up at Pete, her eyes pleading that she wasn't making promises in vain.

It sounded like the chorus of sirens was coming up the drive now.

Keeping pressure on Andi's wrist, he turned to Davy. "Run out front and show the police where we are. Tell them we need the ambulance back here."

Davy sprinted off the deck and around the side of the house.

Andrea mumbled something unintelligible.

"What did you say, Andi?" Susan brushed a tumble of curls away from Andi's ashen face.

She stared up at Susan, looking more vulnerable than Pete had ever seen her. "It was you Dave loved," she whispered, her voice slurred. "I always knew that . . . deep down . . . I knew he would never leave you. And I . . . I killed him." A low keening moan came from her throat and terror filled her eyes. "I killed them all. I didn't mean to! It wasn't supposed to happen—"

"Andi, shh . . . shh . . ." Susan put one hand behind Andi's neck, cradling her like a child. "Don't talk now. Help is coming. You're going to be okay. Just rest now."

Susan stroked tendrils of dark hair back from Andi's face and whispered soothing words. Pete saw nothing but compassion in her eyes, heard nothing but tenderness in her voice. And he loved her for it.

A shout came up from the yard and Pete looked over the deck railing to see two police officers running. A dim strobe of lights bounced off the roof and reflected from the other side of the house.

Pete waved the officers over. "We need the ambulance!" No sooner had he spoken than the lights of an ambulance pierced the darkness of the backyard.

Davy ran ahead of the vehicle, directing the driver across the lawn. Two EMTs came running with their jump bags and a cot in tow.

Pete helped them set up the cot, then watched as Susan stood at Andi's head while they stabilized her. Andi would be okay—physically. But she had a long road ahead to heal her mind. And her heart. And it struck Pete that her healing would likely take place behind bars.

As they carried Andi's cot off the deck, Susan went to watch at the railing, her hands over her mouth as if she couldn't believe what had just taken place.

He was having trouble believing it as well. He went to her and wrapped his arms around her from behind, resting his chin on her head. "You okay?"

She nodded, but he felt her tremble against him.

"Do you think she really did it?"

"I think we heard her confession. And—maybe an apology?"

"Oh, Pete," she whispered. He tightened his arms around her and they stood that way, drawing comfort from each other, until the pulsating lights of the emergency vehicles disappeared into the valley and the crickets took up their nighttime song.

Wednesday, July 29

Susan closed the door to her office, started a pot of decaf, and went to her desk. She spread a fresh-off-the-press copy of the *Hanover Falls Courier* out across her desktop and began reading.

HANOVER FALLS, MO—An amazing turn of events in this small Missouri town has given a new and surprising ending to a tragic story that began twenty-one months ago when five Clemens County firefighters perished in a fire at the Grove Street Homeless Shelter.

Yesterday, fire inspector Andrea Morley, who rose to prominence as the first female fire inspector in a tri-county area, confessed to setting the fire that destroyed the shelter and changed the lives of many Hanover Falls families forever.

In a statement to police, Morley said she never intended for anyone to be hurt, she only wished to create a situation where she could use her skills as a fire inspector. Morley also confessed to setting a second fire last month on rural property owned by the homeless shelter's director, Susan Marlowe. Police chief Rudy Perlson said there would be an investigation into other fires for which Morley served as investigator to determine whether foul play was involved.

Morley is currently undergoing psychiatric evaluation after an apparent suicide attempt on Monday night at Marlowe's home. Susan Marlowe's husband was one of the firefighters who died in the blaze almost two years ago.

Morley's revelation has profound implications for one Grove Street shelter volunteer. Bryn Hennesey Edmonds, also the widow of one of the fallen fire-fighters, took responsibility for the fire when she confessed, three months after the blaze, to having left a candle burning in the shelter's second-floor office. Edmonds is currently performing two hundred hours of community service on felony charges of involuntary manslaughter, but Perlson said he expected all charges against Edmonds to be dropped.

Bryn Edmonds declined to be interviewed, but said in a written statement to the *Courier*, "I am saddened to hear the news, and Ms. Morley and her family are in my prayers. This news does not, however, change the fact that I committed an act of negligence. Still, I'm grateful to know that it was not my actions that caused this tragedy. The things I have learned through this experience don't have a price tag. I am a different person—a better person, I hope—thanks to God's loving care for me and the support and encouragement of my family throughout this tragic journey. My husband and I continue to pray daily for the other families who lost loved ones in the fire."

Susan's heart swelled, thinking what a gift this was to Bryn and Garrett. A huge weight off their minds as they welcomed their baby into the world with a clean slate and so much hope.

She'd had a weight lifted as well. She still hadn't processed everything Andrea had said to her that awful day, still wasn't sure she could even believe the words of a woman her husband had been unfaithful with— even if it was only an emotional affair, as Pete said Andrea claimed. It still hurt—worse even than losing David to death. But if she knew her husband as she thought she had, she could believe that, in the end, he had chosen to come back to her. Or more important, he'd chosen to be obedient to the God he'd always claimed.

If she was a fool for believing something that wasn't true, so be it. She chose to believe the best of a man who had lost his chance to make things right. And if she was wrong about that, she'd leave it up to God to straighten her out.

She smoothed out the front page of the *Courier* and returned to the news story. The article went on to recount Herb Downing's role in bringing Andrea Morley to justice. According to Pete, Chief Perlson said that Downing had agreed to testify and that he'd likely not face any charges in relation to his failure to report the crime, especially since he believed the guilty party had confessed. If someone wanted to push things, he might be charged as an accessory, but in that unlikely event, Perlson felt it would be very difficult to prove, and even if he was convicted, the chief felt sure a judge would be lenient given the circumstances.

Susan had been relieved to hear that. She didn't wish to see "Zeke"— as she would always think of him—punished. She wasn't sure how she felt about the sentence Andrea Morley was likely to receive. But any jealousy she'd felt toward Andrea had vanished, to be replaced by pity.

It seemed hard to believe that it had all begun playing out right here in the shelter less than forty-eight hours ago. They'd used several shots of the Grove Street fire in the newspaper article, and Herb Downing had reluctantly posed for a photo as well. They'd run one of the publicity photos of Andrea, and Susan was glad they'd offered her that small dignity.

The article took up the entire front page of the *Courier*, and Susan knew it would be picked up by every news outlet in the country. It would be a defining moment in Bee Quinton's career. She smiled to herself. As she'd told Pete, she didn't begrudge the queen bee her coup for a minute.

She had to admit Quinton had done a pretty good job on the story. She'd have preferred that her own connection to Andrea's suicide attempt hadn't been mentioned, but she was grateful that at least they hadn't dragged Davy's name into it—and especially grateful that there had been no mention of Andrea's connection to David.

No doubt reporters would come snooping around the Falls again for a while, and perhaps that angle of the story would eventually come out.

But she couldn't worry about that—wouldn't borrow that trouble unless it came knocking at her door.

Friday, September 18

*S*eptember had been long and hot, but today the breeze was cool beneath the poplars and dogwoods on the river.

Pete cast his line and gave the reel a lazy wind. He kicked a small stone into the murky water and watched its ripples echo in concentric circles across the blue-black waters of the tributary. Every choice had consequences that touched the lives connected to yours. For good or for evil. And he was more determined than ever that from here on out, the ripples of his own life would be for good.

He glanced a few yards downstream where Davy Marlowe stood fishing and shot up a prayer that Susan's son would be one of the lives he could touch. He was learning to listen for God's response when he prayed, and it struck him that maybe this prayer had already been answered in some measure. Davy looked relaxed and fit. His skin was tan, and he sported a new buzz-cut bestowed on him last night by a fellow probie. The kid looked good, and Pete thought he was doing well—inside as well as out.

He thought about a conversation he and Susan had shared one evening last week when he'd come in to help at the shelter. He'd affirmed her for following God's leading in her life, for her selflessness in starting the shelter and keeping it running against almost insurmountable odds. Susan hadn't just lived life in a safe harbor, but instead she'd let the winds of God's Spirit blow her where He wanted to take her.

He wanted to live that way.

When he'd said as much, she winked up at him. "Yeah, well, I think taking Davy under your wing will be a good start—the blowing every which way part, I mean."

"That's for sure. Seriously, though, Susan, he's doing great. The guys all like him, and he's a hard worker. It looks like he might even have a knack for mechanical stuff. I put him to work on the brush truck this afternoon and he had a new battery installed almost before I could get the old one out."

"You'd do anything to pass that mechanic's job off on some poor unsuspecting soul, wouldn't you?"

She was teasing, but it was partly true. If he could turn Davy into a halfway decent mechanic, it would be worth any amount of grief the kid had ever given him, or might give him in the future.

He looked down the shoreline and saw Davy's bobber go down.

"Pete! I've got something. I think it's—"

A catfish the size of a small dog broke the surface and thrashed against Davy's line.

Pete dropped his own pole and jogged over to watch the conquest.

Right now, it looked as if the only grief Davy Marlowe was going to give him involved bragging rights to the catch of the day. And he was only too happy to concede that title to Susan's son.

Pete grinned and slapped his knee, feeling Davy's elation.

"You reel that monster in, and then you'd better call your mom and tell her to heat up the biggest frying pan she's got."

Pete reached over
and took her hand.

43

Sunday, November 1

Susan thanked the usher and glanced at the bulletin. Today marked the second anniversary of the Grove Street fire and the entire church service was to be a memorial to the fallen firefighters.

She chose a pew near the back of the sanctuary. If she got too emotional, she wanted to be able to slip out. Part of her wished Davy was sitting here beside her, but she couldn't begrudge the reason he wasn't. He was working his first ride out as a probie. She hadn't seen him so excited in . . . well, in two years.

When he'd left the house Friday for his shift, he'd swaggered and preened and joked, "Bet you're pretty proud of me, huh, Ma?"

She'd teared up, not caring that he saw. She tried to lighten the moment, though. "My little boy, a real firefighter."

He'd sobered and pulled her into a hug. "Yep, a real firefighter. Just like Dad."

She managed to hold it together until he was out the door, but she doubted he had any idea how much those three simple words meant to her. *Just like Dad.*

Or maybe he did. Davy and Pete had become fishing buddies, heading for the river every chance they got. She would have been jealous if not for the fact that she saw Davy thrive and mature almost before her eyes.

The music swelled and the congregation rose. Susan sang the words as a prayer.

You will seek me and find me when you seek me with all your heart . . .

When the worship songs ended, Susan took her seat and bowed her head while the pastor prayed. She felt someone slide into the pew beside her and peeked through her lashes to see a tanned arm, sun-bleached hairs peppering the leathery skin beneath a rolled-up white shirtsleeve.

Pete reached over and took her hand. Her heart swelled. She knew it was still somewhat of a sacrifice for him to darken the door of a church. Especially today, when so many difficult memories would be dredged up.

But, oh, how wonderful it was to have him beside her, to feel her hand safely tucked in his. And to have a feeling that Peter Brennan just might be a part of the hope and the future they'd just sung about.

His thumb rubbed slow circles on the back of her hand, and she drew strength from his presence. They had marked one more anniversary of the blackest day in their lives. But God had given her new eyes to see—really see—the ways God had redeemed that day. And she suspected that if she kept her focus in the right direction, the best was yet to come.

Pete held her hand throughout the service. The memorial ended with the congregation being asked to file silently from the sanctuary. It was a fitting tribute to the fallen firefighters. The ushers handed out tissues at the door, and it was a good thing. There wasn't a dry eye in the house, including Pete's, and it only made Susan love him more that he could express his emotion that way.

Still not speaking, they walked across the gravel parking lot to Pete's truck. He opened her door for her before going around to climb behind the wheel. They sat together in silence for a few moments, wiping tears, lost in their separate thoughts.

Pete reached for her hand again. "It was a nice service."

"Yes. It was." *But I'm ready to move on, Lord. You've brought us all so far since that day. Thank you. But thank you more that you've given us a future.* She stole a glance at Pete and dared—as she had so often these past few weeks—to let herself dream that her future might include him.

Pete sighed. "It was a nice service, but . . . I don't know about you, but I'm ready to move on."

Her breath caught. It was as if he'd heard her prayer. "Amen," she whispered.

"Now, before we go to lunch . . ." Pete's voice brightened, and he let loose of her hand and popped open the glove compartment. He rummaged in the overflowing cavern and withdrew a small brown paper bag. He slammed the door shut and peeked in the bag as if he couldn't remember what was in it.

When he appeared satisfied, Susan eyed him, her curiosity piqued.

"I got something for you."

"For me?" Now she was really curious—despite the fact that the bag looked as if it had come from Myers True Value downtown.

She reached for it, but he held it away from her, transferring it to his left hand. "First I have to explain something."

"Okay . . ." She folded her arms and waited.

"There's something I did a while back that I've regretted deeply since the day it happened. And I guess . . . What I'm trying to say is that I want to try to make it up to you."

She and Pete had spent hours talking in the weeks and months since

Andrea Morley's confession. She'd learned so much about this man she already loved. And though they'd both confessed to mistakes in their lives, he'd never mentioned regrets where *she* was concerned. A pall of fear crept over her and she braced herself for what might be coming.

Her face must have betrayed her thoughts, because Pete laughed softly and cupped a work-roughened hand to her cheek. "It's not as serious as all that."

"What is it?" She eyed the bag, already feeling the lift Pete's laughter always brought.

"Patience." Again, he moved the bag out of her reach. "Do you remember the first time I took you fishing with me?"

"Sure. The Fourth of July."

He looked impressed that she remembered. "You asked me for something that day and I denied you."

"I did? What?" She didn't remember anything about that.

Finally he held the bag out to her. "This is my meager attempt to make it up to you."

Susan took it from him. The bag was surprisingly lightweight. "Can I open it now?"

He gave a nod, waiting. And looking like Davy or Danny did when they were little and waiting for her to open the gift they'd made for her at craft time in Sunday school.

She unrolled the top of the bag and peered inside. "Oh! Tootsie Pops!" Dozens of them. She pulled out a handful and started laughing. *Raspberry.* Every last one was raspberry.

Pete gave a sheepish grin. "You wouldn't believe how long it took me to save all those up. And how hard it was not to get into *that* bag while I was saving."

She put the bag to her face and breathed in.

"Well, now you don't need to go hyperventilating on me."

She laughed, but the truth was she was a little choked up over the whole thing. Pete didn't take his love for raspberry Tootsie Pops lightly.

It was the sweetest gift anyone had ever given her. "I'm just savoring that delicious smell—and trying to think where I'll hide these when I get home."

"Um . . . before I take you home—after lunch, of course—you wouldn't want to share a couple of those with an old friend, would you?"

She patted his cheek. "I'd be delighted." She thought of something and let her smile fade. "You know, Chief Brennan, as I remember that day at the river, it was you who asked me for something."

His half grin said he wasn't quite sure whether she was serious or not.

Oh, she was serious all right. "You don't remember?"

He shook his head. "I guess not."

"Well, like you, I've always felt kind of bad that I turned you down. So maybe I can make it up to you, too."

His face remained a puzzle.

Scooting to the center of the truck, she leaned across the console and kissed him good.

He came up for air chuckling. "Ahhh . . . It's coming back to me. I asked you for a kiss, didn't I?"

"Well, not in so many words, but I knew you wanted one."

"And you denied me," he accused.

"Well, you started it, hogging all the raspberry."

The bag rustled between them, and she realized Pete was trying to pilfer the gift he'd just presented her.

She clenched the bag shut, leaned away from him, and twisted her expression to look appropriately shocked. "Peter Brennan!" She gave his hand a sharp slap. "Are we going to be fighting over raspberry Tootsie Pops for the rest of our lives?"

"I can only hope so." His gaze turned smoky and he tipped her chin up with one finger. "Tell you what, I'll trade you a kiss for a Tootsie Pop."

"Wait a minute." She tilted her head. "Who's giving the kisses? You or me?"

He grinned. "Does it matter?"

"You sweet man . . ." She reached into the bag and held out a handful of suckers like a miniature bouquet. "There aren't enough Tootsie Pops in the world."

And then she proceeded to collect on her end of the bargain.

$\mathcal{D}$ear Reader,

I feel rather silly saying so, but it's always a little sad to write *The End* on the final book in a series. I know my characters are not real people (really, I do!) but it feels as if I'm saying good-bye to dear friends, and "moving away" from a town I've come to love.

Each book in the Hanover Falls series taught me something a little different, made me go just a little deeper into God's Word, and seek just a little harder after His truth. I love that about writing—and reading. How it causes me to see the world with fresh eyes, and makes me examine my own heart.

It still amazes me how much truth can be contained in a work of fiction. I hope you've enjoyed another visit to Hanover Falls and that you, too, have dug in just a little deeper into God's truth through the wonder of story.

Deborah Raney
August 1, 2011

349

Discussion Questions

1. In *After All*, Susan Marlowe discovers that her late husband was being unfaithful to her at the time of his death. Have you ever had to forgive someone who is no longer living or who is unwilling to speak to you? How can you come to terms with unresolved conflict when the person you were at odds with is unavailable—whether because of death, distance, or disinterest?

2. Susan comes to blame herself, to some extent, for her husband's infidelity. What did she think she should have done differently? And do you think she's right in shouldering the blame?

3. Fire Chief Peter Brennan has suffered a disappointing and failed marriage, which has colored his attitude toward marriage and women. Is it possible to hold marriage in high esteem if you struggle or fail in your own marriage? How?

4. Susan experiences conflict with a grown son when he quits his job and moves home. Have you dealt with "boomerang" children—those

who left home but have now returned? Was that experience difficult? How did you handle it?

5.   Pete Brennan has faced tragedy and death head-on and has managed strong men as the fire chief, but when it comes to the homeless shelter, he feels very much out of his comfort zone. What is it about homeless people that makes some people uncomfortable?

6.   What situations have you been in that were outside your comfort zone? Have you attempted to conquer fears that make you uncomfortable in those situations, or have you chosen instead to avoid the situations when possible? Are you happy with your choice?

7.   Andrea Morley is a very complicated and difficult-to-analyze character. Sometimes she seems to contradict her own personality. And often she seems to be attempting to convince *herself* that her deceit is truth. Given what you know about her, why do you think Andrea is this way? How do you think she's managed to have such success in the business world, given her brokenness? Have you ever known anyone like her? What are the challenges in relating to a person like this? If you had to diagnose Andrea's psychological state, how would you label it?

8.   Andrea claims that "nothing really happened" between her and Susan's husband. Do you see it that way? Do you think it would be easier to forgive an extramarital relationship if it had been mostly emotional, and never physically intimate? Why or why not? Do you think men and women would answer this question differently? Why?

9.   Susan decided to accept Andrea's claim that her affair with David was only emotional. What do you think about these thoughts of Susan's: *If she was a fool for believing something that wasn't true, so be it. She chose to believe the best of a man who had lost his chance to make things*

right. And if she was wrong about that, she'd leave it up to God to straighten her out. Is it ever wise to believe the best of someone, even if you're not certain they have earned being regarded in that light?

10. For almost two years Bryn Hennesey Edmonds believed that she was responsible for the fire that killed five firefighters, including her own husband. Can you imagine how you would feel if you were relieved of such a burden? Do you think Bryn was right in stating that she still carried some of the blame for her negligence?

11. Do you think Herb Downing (Zeke) deserved to be let off so easy? What responsibility, if any, did he have the night of the fire when he saw Andrea Morely start the fire, and ran away because of his own fears about being blamed? Have you ever been in a situation where fear paralyzed you from doing the right thing? If not, could you forgive someone else who found themselves in such a situation?

12. How did you feel about Pete taking Davy under his wing? Have you ever beome a mentor to another person's child? How is that sort of connection different than a parent-child relationship? What sort of complications are inherent in the relationship between grown children and the spouses of their parents who remarry? Do you think Davy saw Pete as a father figure?

About the Author

DEBORAH RANEY dreamed of writing a book since the summer she read all of Laura Ingalls Wilder's Little House books and discovered that a little Kansas farm girl could, indeed, grow up to be a writer. After a happy twenty-year detour as a stay-at-home wife and mom, Deb began her writing career. Her first novel, *A Vow to Cherish*, was awarded a Silver Angel from Excellence in Media and inspired the acclaimed World Wide Pictures film of the same title. Since then, her books have won the RITA Award, Carol Award, HOLT Medallion, National Readers' Choice Award, as well as twice being Christy Award finalists. Deb serves on the advisory board of American Christian Fiction Writers and enjoys speaking and teaching at writers' conferences across the country. She and her husband, Ken Raney, make their home in their native Kansas and love the small-town life that is the setting for many of Deb's novels. The Raneys enjoy gardening, antiquing, art museums, movies, and traveling to visit four grown children and a growing brood of small grandchildren, all of whom live much too far away.

Deborah loves hearing from her readers. To e-mail her or to learn more about her books, please visit www.deborahraney.com or write to Deborah in care of Howard Books, 216 Centerview Dr., Suite 303, Brentwood, TN 37027.